IBAN DR

"This is exactly the book I've been waiting for — a ...
draws on the legends of our land. The author, who is of Iban and
Melanau descent, was inspired by the tales she heard as a child in
Sarawak and this exciting story draws on Iban mythology as well as
the old ways of life that have all but disappeared. I look forward to
more from Mowe and hope she will inspire other Malaysian writers
to mine our local mythology for stories."

The Star, Malaysia

Iban
Dream

Golda Mowe

monsoon

monsoonbooks

Published in 2013
by Monsoon Books Pte Ltd
71 Ayer Rajah Crescent #01-01
Mediapolis Phase Ø, Singapore 139951
www.monsoonbooks.com.sg

ISBN (paperback): 978-981-4423-12-0
ISBN (ebook): 978-981-4358-80-4

Cover design by www.lonchan.com.

National Library Board, Singapore Cataloguing-in-Publication Data
Mowe, Golda.
Iban dream / Golda Mowe. – Singapore : Monsoon Books, 2013.
p. cm.
ISBN : 978-981-4423-12-0 (pbk.)

1. Orphans – Fiction. 2. Iban (Bornean people) – Fiction. 3. Borneo – Fiction. I. Title.

PR9530.9
M823 -- dc23   OCN827911577

Printed in Singapore
15 14 13   1 2 3 4 5

1

The small, dark-haired pig kicked and squealed when a man in a loincloth grabbed it from behind and lifted it off the ground. Its cries grew frenzied as another man, similarly attired, bound its front and hind legs together in a tight grip before laying it on its side on a clay surface. The frantic eyes searched its surroundings for escape; all the while it was squealing for mercy from the trees, the sky, the ground and from the men who held it captive. A taller and darker man, whose long, red loincloth was soaked black with the blood of earlier sacrifices, squatted next to the pig's head and whispered a message, a plea to his god. The pig became still with terror. But when the man rose and touched the tip of a spear to its neck, it renewed its struggles. The spear pierced its throat, and the pain sent it into a flurry of convulsions.

A spreading numbness followed, and suddenly the pig was free. The animal bolted up a well-trodden limestone path. There was nothing to either side of the track: no stream, no grass, no bush and no rock, but terror snapped at its heels. A storm cloud enveloped it and drove it into a frenzy of squealing and running. Eventually the fog cleared, and its eyes fell on a sight more horrifying than sharpened spears and blinding dark.

A man as tall and as harsh as the black totem pole before a

headhunter's longhouse glared down at it. The white hair that streamed down his head reached his ankles and was as hard and as straight as spiked thorns. To either side of him were two men with snarling mouths and black teeth. The pig prostrated itself before the god-man and grovelled. A jaw-breaking kick slammed into its face, splattering blood onto the god's fiery red loincloth.

Words that the petitioner had whispered into the pig's ear gushed out of its mouth. "The scent of your blessing no longer permeates my home. My people are restless. This man is restless. Tell me where I shall fell your wrath so I may continue to worship your might."

Sengalang Burong, the eldest of seven gods from the world of Tansang Kenyalang, the "Hornbill's nest," the god who shook the Earth with his presence, the god of the warpath, spoke: "It shall be as your master requests. He shall taste blood again before the rice-planting season begins."

The god reached for a horn-scabbard sword housed in a sheath of carved bone and tied it to his waist. Then one manservant placed upon his crown a war cap lush with upright hornbill feathers, and the other wrapped around his shoulders a cloak of brown falcon feathers. Sengalang Burong turned his face east, sprinted forward with arms outstretched, and jumped into a black pool.

The dark sky stirred. A Brahminy kite, a falcon grown to the span of a man, cut through the air and flew down to the world. Thick clouds tore to shreds in his path. The wings flapped and blew a storm on the surface of a calm sea, and the tropical sky turned red.

A barnacle-covered junk boat waved three fanlike lugsails in defiance to the unexpected gust, and, aboard the rolling decks, Chinese sailors slipped and tumbled as they tried to grab hold of the halyard and reef the sails. A merchant captain swung his arm about wildly as though flinging instructions to the wind. Unmoved, the sacred bird continued eastward. As he neared the shore, the cries of hapless villagers and the shouts of pirates reached up to him in snatches, together with the scent of blood the wind brought him. Even so, he stayed his course, uncaring, like the lush rolling forest behind the village and the yellow serpentine river that wound its way into the turquoise sea.

The sun had barely reached its noon seat when he alighted on a honeybee tree that loomed over the jungle like a silver tower. The branch groaned, and the tree bowed under his divine weight. He knew the warrior who had sent him the spirit of the pig, for he had used this man's blood-lust to his advantage many times in the past. Patches of land along the tributaries of the great Lupar River were still dark with the blood of people who had ignored his omens. Now as he pondered where he should let his wrath fall, he peered into the distance, and his attention was drawn to a house where mosquitoes swarmed about like a cloud of thunderstorm. Year after year he had sent warnings to that house through the voices of his sons-in-law: Telling them to leave, telling them to let the land fallow. Yet each time they had only offered sacrifices to appease him. No more. He had grown weary of their bribes. He was no minor god who could be persuaded with eggs and fowls, and he would send a warrior to prove it.

* * *

Mist rose from the land, carrying a fragrance of fern from the forest floor up to the canopy. Pillars of white and black and gold stood in chaotic rows, some covered in lianas, others with curtain-like tendrils of the air-roots of epiphytes plants. Life was in their roots, and life was in their branches, scampering, skittering or perching and swinging.

The sun turned the sky gold, then grey, and soon waned into a soft glow that disappeared into the horizon beyond Mount Menuku. Behind leafy shadows insects hummed an endless symphony, and on nights such as this one, when the moon shone bright, a hawk owl would sing its mournful *lulululul* song on a high branch.

From a place where the jungle thinned and gave way to cultivated fields, an old woman's singing joined the voices of the night. The mournful wail drifted out of a lone building, a structure some hundred and thirty feet long and one that sat on fifteen-foot pillars. Running along the whole length of the front was an open veranda that faced a swollen river some forty yards away. Under the structure, brown and black feathered fowls wound their way between timber columns as they picked bits of leftover that rained down from the floor crevices above. Snorting in a handful of pens directly under the rooms of their owners were grey-haired pigs of small to medium sizes. All around, a musty aroma of human and animal refuse lingered over the clay surface like a warm blanket.

Against one end of the house, an access ladder leaned. Iron adzes had notched the single log to form steps, while wooden wedges affixed a crude handrail to one side for the benefits of the elderly and toddlers. Upwards it went to the core of the building, showing the way into a long gallery that stretched open all the way to the other end. In this gallery, columns grew upwards to suspend the thatched roof, and halved bamboos lay in rows to form a mesh-like floor. To one side, closed wide windows and doors built into a woven wall provided access to the veranda. Scattered against the same wall were plank-like wooden beds meant for young bachelors. To the opposite side of the whole length were nineteen evenly spaced doors that marked individual family quarters.

One of the bark doors opened, and an old woman stepped out. Proudly hunched from years of toil, she wore a dark skirt around her waist but left her chest exposed to the warm air. A porcupine quill held her grey, twisted hair back in a flat bun. She paused before a pile of scattered rattan and muttered under her breath as she re-tied the bale before returning it to a row of similar bundles that had been lined up against the wall.

Four young bachelors sauntered to the common entrance, reached down and pulled up the log ladder to lay it on its side by the wall. One man went into his family room, which was right next to the entrance, while his three friends opened a veranda door and sat down cross-legged in front of it. They started rolling shredded fresh tobacco in dry palm leaves that had been cut into squares. A smoky lamp of wood gum wrapped in palm leaf was brought out from the room and placed in their midst. Soon the rusty, sweet scent of lit cigarettes filled the air.

The man who had supplied the light fanned himself with the front flap of his loincloth with one hand and wiped the sweat off his forehead with the other before re-combing the straight bangs over his forehead again with his fingers. Realizing how pointless his effort to cool himself was, he reached back and began twisting the long mane trailing down his back into a knot behind his neck. His fine face was clear of all facial hair.

Outside, a piece of washed loincloth fluttered in the breeze as it hung on a horizontal, thin pole. The wind whistled into a gust, making a narrow bamboo ladder that had been propped against the wall outside drop with a clatter onto the deck. It brought little relief to the heat, yet it was a welcome breath, with tidings that smoke would soon rise over the land to mark the coming of the annual season for the sowing of rice.

One man said, "Ooi, Saung. You should help your mother change the bamboo floor on your veranda. Your neighbour Ukang almost fell to the ground this morning."

Saung replied, "Hah, he uses that part more than I do. Let him change it. Else he can always stay on his side."

The group chortled and was immediately hushed by the old woman with a *heh-heh-heh* timed to the soft stomps of her foot. "This is no time for mirth. The shaman is calling on the spirits to come and heal the sick. Be quiet. Else go down to the ground and keep the evil spirits company."

After giving the grinning youths a final scowl, she joined the small crowd that had congregated in the middle of the gallery around a sinewy old woman. That woman, a shaman, rocked from side to side like one in a deep trance. Her voice rose and fell as she pleaded gently or begged piteously on behalf of a fevered woman lying on the floor before her.

Over forty men in loincloths and women in skirts spoke in hushed tones among themselves as they watched the proceedings. Some sat cross-legged, while older folks leaned back against the wall, with their stiff legs stretched out in front of them. Two mothers nursed naked infants in their arms, and nearby, bare young children played quietly, trying as best as they could to keep their games out of the adults' way.

A room's distance from the crowd, a young man burned a piece of thin stick over a lamp and rubbed the melting resin onto the smooth surface of a clean blade, upon which ashes from the lamp were added. Then he passed the concoction to his sweetheart, who rubbed it onto her teeth as he watched with a proud black grin. She was beautiful, and now, with her teeth blackened, she was perfect.

In the next patch of gallery, an old man stoked a small fire burning on a clay hearth that was placed next to a timber column. The smoke rose to warm the longhouse's trophy heads in their individual loosely woven rattan holders. Keeping the spirits contented was a serious affair, for the well-being of the longhouse and the fertility of the fields depended on it. Mangy dogs circled the fire, waiting for that non-forthcoming morsel of food, for their last meal had been two days ago after a successful hunt with the men.

A door swung open, and a young woman came out bearing a handful of betel vine leaves that she had plucked from her back garden. As she wound her way towards the shaman, people shifted their buttocks to let her through, until finally she placed the leaves on the floor next to the head of the sick woman. Then she took her seat next to the shaman.

Abruptly, the shaman's chant turned into a scream of great distress. Pigs under the house squealed, and children bolted down the corridor to the opposite end of the house, making the bamboo planks clatter after them. Then the same fear that had driven them off made them return to the edge of the crowd. An old woman slapped the floor beside her and called out in a hushed, angry tone, telling them to behave, else they would be taken by the incubus in the loft.

A seven-year-old boy, the son of the sick woman, observed her trying to lift an arm off the floor. Menjat twisted the front flap of his dark loincloth to the back and tucked it into his waist. Maybe the mosquitoes were tormenting her, he thought, for they had been tormenting him the whole evening. He reached for a piece of smouldering bark of the custard-apple tree and waved it in the air. A strong, incense-like fragrance drove the pests away. He returned the bark to its stone slab and crept towards his mother on all fours.

The shaman rose on her knees from a prostrated position on the floor and growled. Soon her growls rose to an angry pitch, and she began to claw the air, her body hunched over like a sun bear. Her coiled hair fell loose and tumbled over her bare back, hiding the protruding ridges of her spine.

The boy stared with mounting dread as his sick mother tossed and turned like a person possessed. Fresh sweat broke through her already drenched skin. She started tugging feverishly at her own hair, making the tendrils form a messy halo about her face.

The shaman growled at a piece of unfolded woven cloth which was lying to one side of the patient. Menjat's father had presented it to the shaman, believing that it was the source of his wife's fever. Geometric swirls of red, black and ivory appeared to dance in the play of shadow and light. It was known throughout the house that Menjat had been the artist of that motif, although none realized that the completed design was not as he had envisioned it. The boy had meant for it to be a drawing of three dancing serpents, but his mother had woven it into a pattern of swirling waters because she did not feel that her spirit would be strong enough to tame the python-spirit. She might know the songs for the element of plants and water, but she had never learned a lullaby for an animal motif, least of all a python. So in her simple cleverness, she had imitated the dance but changed the element. When the nightmares began, she had realized that she was wrong, but it was too late because the cloth had been woven.

A second shout in the shaman's high pitch chant startled the boy, making him press himself against the floor, close to his mother. He shivered as he watched the shaman's face crease into angry wrinkles and her dark teeth snarl into the empty air above the cloth.

Menjat's mother, Sika, moaned louder and slapped the bamboo floor as though trying to frighten away wild animals that had come too close. She retched and choked. His father, Apong, strode past him. Squatting next to his wife, he turned her face to the side and rubbed her back. Then he dipped his callused hand into a clay bowl of water and wiped her face clean of vomit and blood before laying her back on the mat. The shaman stood up and stomped her feet in a trance-induced dance around the patient. Apong washed away the rest of the mess through gaps in the bamboo floor. Then he kneaded Sika's arm, as though willing for health to return. She opened her eyes and stared at Menjat. Immediately her feverish brow furrowed, and she screamed.

Apong tried to hold her down, but at that moment she shrieked, "*Antu, antu...*" Evil spirit, evil spirit.

Her husband said, "That is your own son. Don't you recognize your firstborn *Indai* Menjat?"

Again she screamed, "Evil spirit, evil spirit." The group of people in the common gallery stirred as a strange chill began to permeate the crowd. Menjat stared at his mother; then his eyes moved to the people before going back to his father. All the while the skin on his back stung hot and cold. He was confused and afraid, though he did not understand the reason for it.

A stout woman, *Indai* Anyi, spat out tobacco juice through a crevice in the floor and called out, "No wonder there is sickness in this longhouse. The boy is possessed by an evil spirit. He will not be satisfied until he has drunk all our blood."

In the midst of the chaos, the headman, *Tuai* Taka, called out with a shout above the din of raised voices and stood up in the middle of the crowd. He squared his shoulders, giving everyone a full view of the two rosette tattoos that proclaimed his headhunter status. Then he said, "I dreamed of a small monkey-like being this afternoon while I napped in the field hut. It had sharp teeth and a tongue that trailed down to its chest. It towered over me, demanding for blood, demanding for the life of every single person in this house."

A few women from the crowd rose and described the specifics they believed proved Menjat's guilt: "Menjat's mother said he drew the pattern of the last cloth she wove. He drew it on the ground, in the field where she worked."

"*Indai* Menjat promised to weave a cloth out of his design if he collected material for the dye. She promised to sew it into a *Baju Burong*, a jacket of the birds for him. Every day he came home with his basket full of the intoxicating *kepayang* fruit and ginger roots for his mother. He found red *engkudu* and blue *tarum* plants where we could not. Has any one of our children ever done such a thing at so young an age?"

"He told my son that the animals talk to him. He told my son that the birds showed him where to search."

"He must have given himself to the evil ones while looking for dye. That was why the cloth Sika wove for him is so vibrant. All her other works are not as good as this one."

The shaman's voice made even the stoutest person tremble as she said, "There is no cure. There is no cure for this sickness. Evil has entered our sanctuary through this boy. He is the vessel. He must be sent away and the evil spirit will go with him."

Menjat wanted to protest. He wanted to say that he had not made a pact with any demon, and he stood up. Misinterpreting his intent, the women sitting at the back of the group got up and grabbed firewood placed under the trophy heads, while those in front lunged for Menjat, but Apong pressed himself between the boy and the people. Hard blows rained on the father's back, and he bellowed. They fell back.

His face creased in anguish, Apong said, "I have done the rituals. I have fulfilled the demands of the spirit that appeared to me in my dream. I have sent my son down the stream when he was only five days old. Menjat was returned to me whole. He was saved from a crocodile. Have you all forgotten the teeth marks under his small boat? Have you forgotten the dark tooth lodged at the bow? I still keep it as proof. Many of you were there as witnesses. None of you have the right to kill my son."

Tuai Taka called out, "Hey, *Apai* Menjat. That boy is evil. He must not stay in this longhouse, else I myself will kill him and feed his flesh to the wild pigs."

Apong held the boy close to his chest, and Menjat wrapped his arms around his father with equal intensity, feeling comforted by the rise and fall of his hard, strong breathing. Apong said, "Let me prepare him for his journey to leave this place. Let me get food, knife and a blanket for his travel." Menjat looked up, startled.

The headman said, "He must not bring a patterned cloth with him. He will use it to receive messages from the gods in his dreams. He is evil, and anything he learns will be used for evil."

The people shouted chaotically. "No, the boy shall bring nothing with him. He must leave this very night." They pushed both father and son towards the entrance. Five men picked up the common ladder and slid it down to the ground as the people continued to pelt man and boy with firewood and bones.

When his feet touched the ground, Menjat looked back up with pleading eyes and, in response, a woman splashed a pot of dirty water onto him. He stumbled, as though dazed from the slap of a stick. He started to climb back, to beg her to forgive him for something he had not done, but she recoiled from him as she would from a poisonous serpent. His father dragged him away, and they ran down a well-trodden path towards a field of fern. Nobody came down the steps after them, as no one intended to leave the safe confines of the house after the sun had set. Only the light of the moon accompanied them.

The boy looked about fearfully, for it was strange to look at the familiar field in silver light. Even the bush he used to play around appeared menacing. The dark jungle loomed ahead, its silhouette blending into the night sky. He ran after his father's long strides, believing that anywhere was safe as long as he remained with Apong.

Patches of moonlight penetrated the jungle canopy, giving some relief to the darkness below. Menjat stubbed his toe against a gnarled root as he tried to keep up. His father had not brought a machete, so they could only move forward by parting the undergrowth with their arms. Again Menjat stumbled as his foot sunk into thick layers of rotting vegetation. Dragging himself breathlessly, he half ran and half crawled as he chased his father's receding form so that when he reached his side, he clung hard onto his father's arm as though it was the only lifeline out of a dark abyss.

Apong led him for about two miles, away from the river and deep into a part of the rainforest where his son had never visited. The thick canopy made the area pitch dark. Sparse undergrowth eased the journey, but large surface roots slowed them down. Finally Apong stopped and squatted on the ground. His son tried to speak, but he hushed the boy. When Menjat released his arm to rub an aching foot, Apong silently moved away and stood behind a large trunk, where the boy could not see him.

The boy reached out for his father, but found only empty air. He panicked and shouted, "*Apai*, Father ..." With both arms stretched out in front of him, he stumbled back the way he had come, knocked against a tree and turned, the whole time calling for his father. The darkness made him lose his sense of direction. Trying to grab onto anything he could in the dark, he let out a shout when his small hand grasped a thorny rattan vine. His calls grew forlorn, as sobs and terror began to wrack his body. He was terrified to be alone; he was terrified of the demons living in the jungle.

Aimlessly he stumbled about in the dark, wailing and calling for the one person he had never imagined would abandon him. The ground began to slope, and he was forced to proceed on his haunches. He slipped and grabbed a bamboo. Fine, stinging hairs pricked his palm, and he screamed in pain. He whimpered and rubbed his hands together, but it only made the sting worse.

High above his head, a troop of macaque monkeys screeched at him for invading their territory. Again he was pelted with twigs, seeds and faeces. Calling for his father between sobs, Menjat slid and tumbled blindly ahead. On reaching level ground, he rose and ran as fast as he could with both arms stretched out in front of him, all but blind in the darkness. A few minutes of this blind flight, and he tripped on a root and knocked his head against a log. Dazed and disoriented, he lay face down for a moment on the damp ground. But the ever approaching shrieks forced him to rise and drag himself on all fours through the undergrowth. Finally he crawled into a crevice formed out of intertwined liana roots.

* * *

Close by, in the high branches, a young macaque called out to his fellows, "Wait, wait! He is a human child, a boy from the longhouse of Taka."

An adult turned, his yellow-tinted brown fur bristling and long tail curled. He shook the branch violently and said, "What does it matter to our game, Kayu Batu?"

"Do you not remember, Siol? This is not just any boy. Seven harvestings ago, the old chief tried to kill a baby boy from that house, but the river floated the boy into a group of crocodiles. Three of our kin ended in the bellies of those reptiles when they tried to take him."

"That is because we do not have a pact with those creatures. Men, however, made a promise not to hunt them as long as they don't kill a human."

"Mother said that the baby slept in the mouth of an old crocodile. The reptile rocked him to sleep. He must be that boy. He is of the right age. Their other children are either too young or too old."

Siol cackled. Then he said, "You are so full of rubbish. The old beast had a bad tooth, and he used a crack in the small dugout boat to pull it out. Look at the boy. Even his own people don't want him. What harm can he do? Even if we should kill him, no one will avenge his death."

Not to be outdone, Kayu Batu said, "But he slept inside the breath of an old reptile. Surely the old one must have given him a gift, for the reptile is known to be generous to those who ..."

Siol screeched and said, "Return to your mother's breast, half-brother. How is it possible that the same loin which had begotten me had also spawned you?"

Just then a macaque called out and reported that they had lost the boy. Siol beat the branch, frustrated that his fun for the night had been ruined. He swung to the ground to join his playmates in their search.

* * *

Some distance away, Apong stared longingly into the blinding darkness, all the while willing for a spirit to appear and to tell him that *Tuai* Taka's dream was wrong. He prayed for a god, even a demon, to give him a reason to run after his son's voice and to again feel the small chest breathe as he lay next to his sleeping firstborn. He strained his ears long after Menjat's voice had faded in the distance. He could not understand why the spirits had allowed him to raise the boy if they had intended to take him away. If the child was not meant to live, why had they not killed the infant? Why had they let him love his son for seven harvestings and then wrested the boy away from him? Were the gods playing a cruel game to break his heart? Yet he knew he could not risk Menjat finding him, returning to his people. As Apong retraced his way back to the longhouse, he made sure not to leave a trail for his son to follow. Bitterly, he wept.

2

One long day led to another as Menjat moved ever deeper into the jungle. He could only scavenge on the forest floor, for the trees were too tall to climb and the lowest branches were farther from the ground than the roof of his home. He ate young fern and the shoot of saplings. He looked for the larvae of red ants between the buttress roots. Though the ants bit, the sting was well compensated by the larvae's fruity sweetness.

Each evening when the light began to dim he would search for a hole to sleep in, and, being polite, he always asked for permission from the spirits living within. The cold dampness and relentless mosquitoes tormented him, yet he slept when overcome by exhaustion. On the fifth night he woke to the feel of cold scales brushing against his spine, but the snake only curled next to him, and the boy felt strangely comforted by its company. It made him feel as though he was back in the longhouse, lying on the mat next to his father in the family room and listening to the cicadas sing their nightly symphony. Here, too, the cicadas sang.

On the evening of the sixth day, Menjat came upon a group of orang utans. He had never seen apes before, but he recognized them because visiting bards had sung songs about their fur which was as red as a warm sunrise. A few young apes raced down to the ground towards him. One touched his hair, and another nibbled his loincloth. Then the larger adults approached. The boy quaked with dismay, but he was desperate for help regardless of whatever form it took, for he was bruised and hungry.

Menjat prostrated himself before a male sub-adult and pleaded, "Please, man of the jungle, please let me follow you."

The ape rose to his full height and growled. Menjat heard him say, "Go away, boy. Go home."

The boy looked up, eyes fast filling with tears. "But I don't know the way home. The macaques would not leave me alone. They throw twigs and stones at me."

A loud crash made Menjat turn his head. His eyes widened and he trembled, for the male orang utan coming towards him on all fours was over five feet tall if he were to stand. His dark cheek pads were wide, like petals of the corpse flower, and his belly was huge, like a woman swollen with child. Covering his chest in folds was a large bag of sooty-grey skin that hung from his throat. Menjat saw that a log had crumbled under his great weight. Then he watched the animal move slowly towards him, testing the ground in front of him with the back of his hand.

The first ape moved away, and this one slumped down in front of Menjat. He touched the boy's bowed and shivering crown with his knuckles. A deep voice like the sound of sudden thunder said, "What is your name? Have you sprung up from the ground? Did a tree vomit you? Where is your mother, where is your father? You are too small to be a lone bear and too big to be a fowl."

Menjat's voice quivered as he answered with head bowed, "I am called Menjat. My mother is ill, and I lost my father in the jungle. I cannot find him. I cannot find my way home. Please, do you know how I can go home?"

A rumble issued from the animal, followed by a grunt. A young female, less than half the size of the male, crept forward and said, "Do you take *Tok* Anjak for a fool? He is a great teacher, feared by men for his strength and honoured by apes for his wisdom. Many of our kind follow him to learn his great ways. You cower like a spineless dog before him, and you dare ask him for a favour?"

Menjat looked up and met *Tok* Anjak's eyes. They were a soft brown and had the same gentleness as his mother's had, before she caught the fever-spirit. They stared at one another, unblinking. *Tok* Anjak finally broke the spell when he tapped the boy's head with his knuckles. "Where did you learn to understand our tongue?"

"I have always known what each animal says. That is how I find the best fruits and leaves to eat."

The male ape stared at him in wonder. Then he sniffed the boy's head and studied his face. Menjat reminded him of *Tok* Mangom, a crocodile who was so ancient he had all the knowledge of the world. He marvelled that the crocodile would have had a reason to give the gift of discernment to a mere boy. He asked, "Where is your home?"

"I am from the house of *Tuai* Taka. I live along the Layang River, away from the shadows of Mount Menuku, where fishes overflow to the banks and water reeds grew thick and green."

Tok Anjak turned to the female and said, "The spirits have led this boy to me for a purpose, Nuai. I will show him the way to the river, and he can then follow the trail made by Ribai, the river god, to find his way home. Maybe he will learn why he lost his father."

Grunts of fear rose from the apes around them. Their teacher could not possibly be considering going near a river. They would drown.

Tok Anjak continued, "We will not walk down the river with him. He shall go alone. If it is the gods' will that he should live, they will protect him."

Menjat prostrated himself once more before the ape. He realized that he had brought no gift and was humbled that a great spirit of the jungle would agree to help him.

The orang utan stood up to full height, and the long red fur that trailed to the ground doubled his great size. He said to the group, "This is Menjat. I welcome him into my company, just as I have welcomed the rest of you. He is my guest and will be as my own while with us."

With a shake of his mighty cheeks, he took a deep breath and inflated the bag of skin on his throat. A long call, as loud and as deep as the call of a sea giant, surged out of his mouth and shook the trees. The macaques that had been troubling the boy scattered into the dark recesses of the jungle.

* * *

With courage borrowed from the apes, Menjat now found the thick rainforest a place of wonder and awe. He was taught to climb high into the canopies where the adults moved slowly and laboriously as they tested the strength of each branch while the smaller ones swung and jumped with great agility. Orchids grew wherever the morning sun touched, some so dark they looked black, while others were as pale as the clouds; many were in whispers of green. Dew made the flowers sparkle like a thousand rainbows, and each time Menjat saw one, he would reach for the cup-like petals and carefully drink the fresh moisture within.

Nuai showed him where to collect wild fruits and where to dig for edible roots. She pointed out pitcher plants for water, and she also showed him how to chew on leaves and how to use the pulp to sponge for moisture in the barks. When it rained, *Tok* Anjak would call for him, and he would share the shelter of a large leaf with the ape. The ape's red fur was like shredded bark, and his body released a strong musk, but he was warm, and the boy looked forward to being called to his side.

After three weeks of moving without a trail, the sound of a small waterfall broke into their tranquillity. *Tok* Anjak signalled for the group to halt before swinging down to a tree lush with dark, elliptical leaves. The branches were bent under the weight of unripe green mangos, and in between these were bunches of tiny reddish flowers that waved and promised more fare to come. The apes grunted with delight, for in a few more days the air would fill with the sweet scent of ripe fruits.

The teacher plucked a green mango and indicated with a wave of his hand for Menjat to follow before he climbed down the tree. He made his way towards the stream. Roots gnarled forward, breaking through the soil and trapping small stones in their labyrinth. They abruptly stopped only yards away from the stream and an empty traveller's hut. Away from the shaded boughs, four feet high cogon grasses filled the sunny bank with silky strands of white flowering stalks that overflowed into the watercourse. *Tok* Anjak moved indifferently through the tall blades of abrasive grass as his weight made a clear path for Menjat to tread.

The large animal sat under a shady patch of roof outside the hut and took a deep breath. Then he exhaled with a wide yawn. Water, stained red with dead leaves and wood, sparkled as it tumbled down a low cliff and filled a pebble-covered stream bed as colourful as a woven cloth. *Tok* Anjak watched the sight for a moment. Then he crushed the green fruit in his hand and bit down on the large, flat seed to leave a clear imprint of his teeth on its ivory surface.

He gave the seed to Menjat and said, "Take this with you. If you find that your home is no longer in that house, come back to me. Show this seed to the spirits and animals you meet. They will tell you how to look for me. Those brown monkeys will also not tease you if they know you are mine."

Tok Anjak slipped his fingers in between the latticed wall, pulled out a halved bamboo from its base then twisted it free from the vine binding. He passed it to the boy, "This will help you walk when you are tired and dig for food when you are hungry."

Menjat jabbed one end of the pole into the ground a few times. It was as thick as his wrist, with a sharp point where it had been planted into the ground, and was as tall as he was. He was so intent on the pole that he did not notice the ape's departure. When he looked up, *Tok* Anjak was gone. An empty jungle returned his gaze. Unafraid for the moment, he parted the grass with his new walking stick and moved closer to the stream. Stooping on all fours, he gulped down the sweet water. He watched tiny fishes swim about like streaks of lightning beneath the surface.

But suddenly, unexpectedly, the frustration and fear he had felt before meeting the apes returned to overwhelm him. He trembled with every imagined screech, and his chest felt tight as he thought of his mother. Then tears welled up in his eyes as he recalled the accusations of his people. But soon he saw how clear and beautiful the water was, so he stepped into the stream and entreated it to clean him of all evil. He missed his parents, and he longed to tell them that he had never intended to make a pact with demons. He didn't even know how it happened. Maybe the demon was the old man he had met in the rice field – the bard who told such wonderful stories about growing things but one who never came to the longhouse. Or maybe it was one of the animals who had helped him.

The young river gurgled and swirled as he submerged himself. Like the gush of a thousand voices it said, "Come quickly, my son. This way, this way."

The boy climbed out and resumed his travel in the company of the watercourse. About him, the land sprouted young roots and soft leaves to nourish him. That evening he found sweet insect grubs inside a rotting log, and, not wanting to destroy the whole nest, he used a twig to scoop his dinner out. At night he slept in the branches, for *Tok* Anjak had told him to be wary of nocturnal hunters.

Day after day, the stream became wider, and on the fourth day it merged with another tributary and turned into a murky river. Menjat followed the watercourse downstream, watching out for crocodile tracks on the muddy bank. Just before nightfall of the fourth day, he stumbled into an abandoned camp. The residue of many campfires and countless human tracks made him run back into the shadows of the jungle.

The next day he continued, and the next, and on the seventh evening since parting from *Tok* Anjak, he found another camp with as many campfires. Again the mud was filled with human tracks and the bank scored by boats. This one, however, had a log stretched over two platforms, much like an open doorway without walls. The surface of the trunk had been scored with sharp iron, showing eighty slashes, a number beyond his skill to count. Menjat was familiar with the area, since he had followed his father fishing twice before, but the structure was strange to him. He moved away and climbed the highest tree he could find.

On the afternoon of the ninth day, he looked down a gentle slope leading to the open area of his longhouse. The boy rubbed his eyes a few times, unsure of his own sight.

It was gone. Only the pillars remained, and the ground was covered in ashes, with infrequent threads of smoke rising like anguished paeans to Petara, the Supreme Being. Hawks and crows peppered the ground and circled the air.

The people could not have moved, Menjat thought, for he had heard no such plans from the adults. The trophy heads had still been tied to the principal column when he was chased out of the house.

Frightened but not wanting to believe what he feared, the boy ran down a well-trodden path. As he got closer, he saw bodies without heads strewn on the trampled ground, some burned and others un-charred. He recognized the headman by the tattoos on his dark, bloated body. As he approached it, carrion birds screeched at him for eyeing their meal. He turned his head about frantically to search for his father but could see no sign of him. Running towards the field behind the house, he saw more bodies. His heart chilled as he watched crows and wild pigs scavenge. The sight and smell of ripe flesh nauseated him with terror and made him gag and weep at the same time.

Though the ground sent up a chill that made his feet cringe with each step, he forced himself to walk among the carnage. After a seemingly endless search, aggravated by mounting panic, he found the headless torsos of his father and younger sister. The crows feeding on the carcasses croaked and clawed at him, but the swing of his stick was more ardent, and he sent each bird on its way with a hard blow.

Stunned, the orphaned boy slumped onto the blood-crusted ground and wailed like an infant. He called out between howls, "Oh, Father, why have you not come with me? Why have you returned? Was it to get my sister and my mother?"

Between sobs Menjat looked to his left then to his right, but he could not see a single living adult to advise him. He cried and hollered until nightfall, until his voice became hoarse with incessant grief.

Then, in the light of the waning moon, he saw a large man walking through the field towards him. The hexagonal shield on his left arm and the tiered layers of long hornbill feathers on his head pronounced him a man of war. The man's shadow soon cast over Menjat's bowed form, making him cringe as he waited for the feel of sharp iron against his neck.

But it didn't come. The man, whose voice was beautiful and strong, called out, "Why are you crying, boy? Why are you howling like a dog and intruding into the peace of the spirits? If you are hungry, eat. Are you not crying over rotting meat?"

Menjat's voice quivered as he answered, "He was my father. She was my sister. I cry because I can no longer hear them call my name."

No sooner had he spoken, than there was a rushing sound. The air churned and flung debris into their faces. A man-sized Brahminy kite flew down and sunk its claws into dead Apong's chest. The bones cracked under his weight, making Menjat call out and fall back in terror.

The sacred bird turned fiery golden eyes to the warrior and said, "Why is this boy still alive? I have blessed my chosen one with the head of every man, woman and child from this longhouse."

"The boy had been disowned by his people. He is no longer one of them."

"He should die like every one of them."

The warrior scrutinized Menjat, his gaze fierce and piercing. He turned back to the bird and said, "He bore no affliction on his spirit. It is strong, like his body. His mother's hands had been gentle and his father had never struck him. His soul still clings to him."

"He should be broken over the land, like an egg that spills its goodness onto a hungry earth."

"Where now is the mercy of the great one? If a boy cannot place his faith on you, how can a man who seeks your counsel call himself wise?"

"You are a warrior-guardian. Where is his sword? Where is his shield? Where are the war feathers on his head? By what right do you claim to speak for him?"

"I was a boy once. I live because my enemy showed me mercy."

"He is weak, he is no warrior."

"His heart is yet as soft as the ground he once sketched upon, though his spirit is as strong as the pattern of many serpents."

The warpath god glowered for a long moment; then he said to the man, "My passion is not in his blood."

"Will a god crush a weak, insignificant boy to show his might?"

His challenge drew a screech of rage from the bird who then said, "I shall wait for him to grow to manhood. And then I will send him to meet death." With a loud flap, he released his grip on the body and jumped straight up into the air.

The warrior watched Sengalang Burong's flight until he disappeared high in the dark heavens. He turned back to Menjat and said, "Foolish boy. How quickly you forget *Tok* Anjak's care of you. You cry over a man who would no longer have you as his son. After he left you, he called himself *Apai* Pina. He forgot the name of his firstborn."

Menjat wiped the tears off his face and looked up. The man's skin shone like rich dark earth, and his straight black hair was as nothingness under the light of the moon. The whiteness of the hornbill tail feathers decorating his war cap shone like polished iron in the night, while the single black stripe on each of the hundred validated his courage, like the rosettes tattooed onto his shoulders and chest. Encircling his waist was a loincloth woven in copper red, with both ends decorated in bold strips of black and white bark-cloth then finished with tasselled ends that reached down to his shins. His five-foot-long and sixteen-inch-wide shield was carved from softwood and reinforced with a rattan lash. Strapped to its convex surface was the head of a terrifying monster. As the man lowered the shield and leaned it against his right hand, he revealed a sword handle and sheath brimming with human hair from the scalps of his trophies.

The boy's mouth gaped and his eyes widened as he studied him. Surely this must be Keling, the warrior-guardian who was said to live in Pangau Libau, a land between the heaven and the world. Menjat bowed to the ground and asked reverently, "Why has the great one come to pacify a boy? No bard has ever sung of such a thing."

The man's angry eyes crinkled, and he laughed. "Every warrior was once a boy; every great man came from a child. The spirits will test him and teach him strength. Once he is proven strong, the gods will grant him gifts to bless mankind."

Turning his back on the boy, the demigod trotted towards the jungle. Menjat rose to follow, for he hoped that Keling could tell him what to do, yet the warrior jogged straight ahead in wide strides. The boy tried his best to keep up, but after some hundred yards he fell down in exhaustion. He watched as darkness swallowed Keling's form.

Once again he was abandoned, and he sobbed with frustration. Then he recalled Keling's words, and he wiped the tears off his face as he resolved to be a man sooner.

Menjat picked himself up and with a start realized that his surroundings were fast disappearing into shadows. Remembering *Tok* Anjak's stories as to how the spirit of the wild pig and fierce dog roamed at night to search for food made him imagine darker shadows lurking in the night. He leaned his stick against a tree which did not feel too wide for him to hug. Then, wrapping his arms and legs around the smooth trunk, he inched his way up until he reached the lowest branch. Using the branches like steps, he climbed higher, to a windy height, until his hands fell upon a leafy bough, which he twisted into a simple nest. Above him the moon had hidden itself behind a thick cloud. He hoped it would not rain as he lay down and took out the mango seed he had kept tucked in the waistline of his loincloth, clasping it tight to his chest. Thoughts that *Tok* Anjak cared pacified his aching heart, for it meant that not everyone he knew had abandoned him. He still had a place to which he could return.

Keling sprinted through the rainforest, his pace ever swifter as the night grew older. He heard the boy fall and call out to him. He did not turn back, for the warpath god had agreed to let Menjat live to adulthood, and Keling knew full well that there was no spirit or god audacious enough to go against the will of Sengalang Burong.

Mist carrying the scent of apes formed a trail for him to follow. As the air began to send tidings of dawn, he saw an ape who looked as red as tongues of fire slouching against a white tree. *Tok* Anjak stood up to full height as Keling approached.

They embraced, and the ape said, "Fire and smoke had risen in the horizon eight times since we last met. It is a rare honour to meet with the great guardian even once in a lifetime, yet I have met him twice since my birth."

Keling said, "I have come because I caught your scent on an Iban boy."

A young orang utan placed before them bunches of ripe, blushing figs. *Tok* Anjak grunted, and the sub-adult scurried away. Both man and ape squatted on the ground and reached out for the treat. As they plucked fistfuls of the fruit, black ants spilled into their hands and scurried up their arms. Barely noticing the insects, they tossed the fruit into their mouths; the globes burst like pockets of nectar when they bit down.

Tok Anjak watched his visitor's face all the while. After consuming his third mouthful, he asked, "The boy is well?"

Keling grunted between bites; then he said, "He is well. I found him unharmed and crying lustily over his dead father. But I cannot say the same for his people. They are no longer of this world."

The ape rolled a fig between his fingers. "Then the boy is without family?"

"Yes, that appears to be so," the demigod replied.

They ate for a while. A long silence later, *Tok* Anjak said, "There are many taboos which separate men from beasts. Chief among these is the taboo on mating. Yet what do the gods say on adoption? Have not men brought dogs to live in their house, and do they not partner with these animals in the hunt?"

"There is danger of breaking the taboos when you raise one of a different species among your own. However, the dogs were never made to forget their nature. What of the boy? Can the apes bring him up as a human?"

Tok Anjak chewed slowly as he chose his words. "I can tell the season from the scent of rain or heat in the air. I know every fruit tree, and I can count the days from its next ripening. I can look into the eye of another and tell if he is brave or craven. But I cannot tell what manner of man a boy will become. I only know what manner of father I shall be."

Having heard and understood the purity of *Tok* Anjak's heart in his words, Keling smiled and stood up. "Look out for me tonight, my brother. I shall bring news from the gods."

One, two, three long strides, and the guardian disappeared into the dense jungle. *Tok* Anjak returned to the white tree and slouched on the ground between the buttress roots as he leaned his head against the trunk. He grunted good-naturedly as little apes grabbed for the leftover figs. Then he dozed off, apparently undisturbed by the scurrying of busy squirrels and the playing of mischievous youngsters.

Sometime later, a drop in the air temperature woke him. He stood up to full height and scanned the surroundings. Soon he sensed a movement in the overlapping leaves of vine and fern, and the movement gradually took on the form of a man.

Keling had returned in the dim light, carrying an eight-foot blowpipe in his hand and wearing only a plain, dark loincloth. A large, empty basket, woven with rattan in loose, curvy form, was strapped to his back. With his hair tied in a knot behind his head, he looked very much like a common hunter-gatherer.

He passed a red bundle to the ape and said, "We are brothers, *Tok* Anjak. I have provided for the boy that which you yourself cannot."

The great ape bowed as he received the package and asked, "You will send him back to me, then?"

"There is no one else. You know this. His people are no longer of this world. They did not seek to interpret the headman's dream properly and put all the blame of misfortune on the head of an innocent child. The dream was meant to warn them of an impending attack, yet the people had done nothing to prepare for a defence. When they abandoned the child, the spirits abandoned them. He is yours now to raise."

Tok Anjak opened the bundle, which enclosed a rattan cap and a sword. He handled the curved, three-foot naked blade. Its new, carved ivory handle was free of human hair. "This is not the way of my kind," he protested.

"This is the only way for you to raise the boy. The warpath god is adamant about his decision. The sword is a symbol of his claim on Menjat's life."

"I cannot give him this thing. The other apes will not tolerate the scent of blood on him."

"The sword will remain with you for as long as you live. Only after your death will Menjat have to walk the warpath. Live long my friend," he said and turned to go.

As the light grew faint, the dark form of the guardian faded into the mist. *Tok* Anjak frowned, slumped down and leaned back once more against the tree. The gods wanted to give the boy a nature of war. He pondered over the problem. His kind believed that if they harmed no one then no one would harm them. But he also understood that the smell of blood was good to Menjat's kind, and that the boy must avenge his family's death, else he would be considered a curse by other Ibans. The ape's heart was heavy when he finally decided that it was time for him to pass down the war knowledge he had gained from his solitary travels.

* * *

Tone by tone, the calls of chirping birds began to join the chorus of singing insects and grew ever shriller and louder as the rays of the sun lengthened. Menjat rubbed his eyes and stretched. He yawned, looked up and was startled by the stare of a large, pale python. The snake lowered itself until it came face to face with the trembling boy.

It hissed, "*Tok* Anjak is not a forgiving spirit. The ape can crush my head with his bare hands. You would do well to keep the mango seed in full view, lest one such as I swallow you without knowing who you are."

Frightened, the boy scrambled down the tree in frenzied haste and lost his grip on the trunk after reaching the lowest branch. He cried out as he plunged into a sparsely covered bush. Twigs scratched his skin, and a young bough slapped his arm as his body rolled down to the ground. He dragged himself up all the while wishing that he had never left the herd. He was alone again, afraid. Even the walking stick did not bring comfort as he picked it up. Terror seemed to have fallen down the tree with him, and was even now grabbing for him. He sprinted away and crashed through thick fern and crooked bushes. His foot caught in a root, and he fell down flat on his face. Immediately the panic left him as pain shot through his body. He pushed himself up and squinted at the angry bruises left by twisting surface roots on his chest and thigh. He sobbed, for it was the only cure he could think of for the throbbing pain.

Eventually his tears subsided – just in time for him to hear the sound of movement nearby. Another python? He felt for the mango seed, grasped it.

He breathed deeply, with relief, as a black porcupine, white-tipped bristles relaxed and close to its body, ambled past. Menjat jumped up to a squat and shouted a greeting as he held out the mango seed. "Brother Porcupine, have you seen *Tok* Anjak?"

The porcupine turned to face him and said, "No, I have not. But the ape usually goes north this time of year."

"Where is north?"

In response the porcupine looked up and made a few turns until he saw bits of sunrays. Then he pointed his nose to his left and said, "That way."

Menjat thanked him and hastened down the way pointed out to him.

In the days following, the boy showed the seed to every animal he met and asked if they had come across *Tok* Anjak. The mango seed made him brave—it seemed almost magical in the power it had to protect him and cause the animals to stop and answer. Many showed him where they had last seen the ape. In the evenings he would be welcomed by rose apple doves, brilliant in their pink crowns and green feathers, who led him to sweet fruits with their soft, shy cooing, for they know the old teacher well; *Tok* Anjak was gentle with their kind and often sang with them in his deep, guttural voice.

After two weeks of searching, Menjat heard a sentry call out his name. He ran towards the voice, which was soon joined by other hooting members of the herd. All his hurts were forgotten for a moment as he rejoined his young playmates with shouts of delight.

Then he saw *Tok* Anjak watching from the side, and a pang hit deep in his chest. Menjat prostrated himself before the ape and said,

"I am home, Father."

The orang utan smiled. Then he nudged the boy with his knuckles to make him look up. "Come, my son, come. Learn the ancient valour of my kind and grow to be strong, like my people."

* * *

As weeks turned to months, the joy of frolicking with his playmates soon made Menjat forget the pain he had suffered from the bruises and falls he had collected along the jungle floor. With the apes as friends and teachers, he swung between the branches with the gusto of youth.

As the years passed, Menjat's strength and speed began to surpass those of the apes. His thick, black hair grew wild and became as long as the fur of the most handsome ape. However, he had not forgotten all the ways of men, for he still wore a bark-cloth over his loins.

During the fruiting months, he played in the branches with high-spirited apes; but he travelled alone with *Tok* Anjak and Nuai for the rest of the year. Some nights the great ape would hold council with the elders of other species, and when he did, Menjat would sit next to him, all the while listening to and learning from the wise words of living spirits who roamed the jungle. On evenings when they had no company, the ape would regale the boy with stories of his younger days.

"It is always good to be curious, my son. Either you stay hidden and learn, or you show yourself and gain a new friend. That was how I met my blood brother, Semaga. It happened many harvestings ago, when I was still young and walked the land alone. That day, I heard the shouts of many men. I made my way towards the noise and saw six men pointing sharp spears at a young crocodile. Semaga had his front legs caught in a trap. He swished his tail at the men and knocked down one of their baskets. Do you know what was in there? Skins of snakes and lizards and crocodiles, but there was no meat. These men did not kill for food; they killed for skin. They were so hungry for skin they broke the human pact with crocodiles.

"In my rage, I broke a branch and threw it at one of them. I roared and jumped to the ground. They ran from me like cowardly dogs. Some of the men came too near Semaga's tail, and he whipped out and broke their legbones. You should have seen the way those men run, like crabs with mud in their eyes.

"I released Semaga from his bonds and returned with him to the river. He told me that he had gone into the jungle to find a cool and quiet place to meditate. His kind welcomed me, and his great-grandfather added the rank *Tok* to my name. He gave me a long life and rowdy followers for saving Semaga's life.

"You reminded me of *Tok* Mangom, for there is a hint of his stout spirit in you. Maybe you have met him and done a deed on his behalf. Your gift of speech with animals could only have come from him, for he was old and great and generous. He could meditate for days unnumbered, floating like a log in the river. Sometimes grass would grow on his back. Few living things realized just how close they came to his jaws."

The stories about *Tok* Mangom fascinated Menjat, for they reminded him of a crocodile tooth that his mother had kept wrapped in a piece of ritual cloth. He recalled evenings when his father had told any willing listener that Menjat would one day grow up to be a great man because of the tooth, and these memories filled him with pride. Yet on other nights, he would wish that he had never received it because he missed his family.

Many times *Tok* Anjak would take Menjat to a quiet place and instruct him on the strength of the crocodile, the bear and the hornbill. He taught the boy to watch out for the wily grace of the gibbon and macaque spirits. He reminded him that the iron is only as strong and as wise as the man who wields it. The old ape also taught him to seek wisdom from the land, for it was so great that it had sprung life and sustained it. He called the land "she" and compared her to a female ape that would only bear offspring for a male that pleased her, which meant that there was no continuity for a male who treated her with disdain.

Sometimes he learned from the other apes, too. Nuai, *Tok* Anjak's eldest granddaughter, shared her food with Menjat, and he helped her beat the under layer of barks into cloth. Beautiful Nuai was the last ape to know the art of sewing patterned bark-cloth. She was loved by Kumang, the wife of Keling, and was given dreams that guided her in the craft. The goddess of the weave showed her how to strip bark and how to soften it by beating. She helped Nuai notice the dance of spirits and taught her how to imitate the steps in her weave. Moonbeams, pitcher plants, palm trees and spirits sprung to life on her cloth. Her awl, a porcupine quill, was protected by the spirit of a carved monitor lizard. Jungle chiefs from the far lands of the north would travel south to seek her work because it was widely known among them that any one of her *pua* could present its owner to the gods in better light whenever he visited the heavens in dreams.

She taught Menjat how to carve patterns on bamboos with sharp rocks, as a record of all she had shown him. She also taught him patterns to carve on wood blocks and was pleased to see the fineness of his work.

Menjat grew up without meeting another human, for it was the nature of apes to avoid contact with human settlements and nomads. But on his twentieth year, Menjat left *Tok* Anjak's side and tried to approach a Penan group. On seeing him, they ran in terror. Rumour then spread among the tribes of a wild spirit living in the jungle, one of human form that acted and smelled like an ape. *Tok* Anjak laughed when he heard the tale from the birds, and he gave Menjat a new name – Bujang Maias – "Ape Man."

3

A late morning drizzle turned into a shower. The chaotic symphony of honks, barks and chirps bubbling out of the evergreen jungle canopy grew louder before settling into lone intermittent calls. In the understory, hidden behind the shade of multi-layered small leaves, Nuai spread a blanket over a shivering *Tok* Anjak.

A man who was a head and shoulder taller than the dying ape scrambled up the branches with stalks of wide yam leaves gripped tightly in his mouth. Seventeen harvestings had passed since Bujang Maias had made his home with them. His thick, matted hair now reached down to his ankles and was the envy of every male ape. The females would have considered him perfect except that his arms, though longer and stronger than a normal man's, were so stocky that they marred his comeliness.

Once he reached the nest, the man perched next to his father and held the leaves over his old face, tying the stems together, then spreading them out like a fan before lashing them onto a branch above.

A bark-cloth pattern of his own footprints draped *Tok* Anjak's legs and torso, while beneath his dying form geometric hawks flew, their magnificence standing out in stark contrast to the shrunken form of the old teacher whose tale they told. His breath wheezed, and dull fur clung limply to his body. The only comfort left to him now were the gentle songs that Nuai cooed and grunted as she sat by his side.

Realizing that the pouring rain was not falling on his face, he looked up and noticed Bujang. He tried to lift his feeble hand to touch his son, but the effort was beyond his strength, so he said, "You have been a good son." He pointed to a bundle of red cloth on his granddaughter's lap. "That is yours."

Bujang reached for the bundle Nuai passed him. He opened the cloth and gasped, for inside was a rattan war cap free of feathers and a rusty sword sealed in a broken sheath. He wondered how his ape-father had come to possess them.

Nuai caressed the cloth as she said, "A princess's hand has dyed these pineapple threads in a fiery trough and woven the cloth on her loom." She looked up and gazed at the cap in Bujang's hand. "The war cap was shaped out of rattan growing in a young world. But why is it bare?"

Tok Anjak said, "Bujang will have to earn the feathers himself."

As his human son stared into his face, the ape continued, "The birds are proud, and they think you are not good enough to wear their war insignia."

Bujang bowed his head, for he believed that the hornbills had not misjudged. Many times in the past, while he had played with apes in the canopy, the birds would honk loud to chase them off. Indeed, when he was fifteen harvestings, one hornbill had tried to break his skull with its hard beak, but *Tok* Anjak had thrown a stick from five yards away and knocked it off the branch where it perched. The hundred-foot fall broke its wing, and the bird died, flailing, as a wild cat pounced on it. Then the ape swung down to the ground and stomped on its tail feathers, ruining the beautiful plumage: no man-warrior would ever wear one of those on his valiant person. He crushed the glorious casque protruding out of its crown: no Kayan prince would carve the red and gold into canine teeth to ornament his ears.

The memory of his foster father's strength made Bujang reach out and rub *Tok* Anjak's arm, which had become as soft as the limb of a newborn ape.

Tok Anjak wheezed as he struggled to say, "These things came from the hands of the great warrior Keling. Be warned, my son. Not all will look kindly on you if you should tell them the truth. It is taboo to use the names of gods and guardians lightly. You will earn death in the hands of undiscerning men."

The ape let out a sigh and turned his eyes to his granddaughter, who repeated the words he had once told her years ago to tell to Bujang.

"Beware of the *ilang*, Uncle, for the nature of this sword is proud and cruel. Don't let its thirst for blood overwhelm your judgment. War is a great sadness. It is not the way of the people of the jungle. Our ancestors were once a race with many riches, but men came and took their lives because of these things. They ran into the jungle naked. Then the gods showed mercy and covered them with red fur, that they might not be mocked and shamed but stir fear in the hearts of their enemies. Promise your dying father. Swear that you will always remember the day when you wailed over your human father's body. Remember your own grief, and do not succumb to the bloodlust of the iron."

A lump of sorrow choked Bujang. He was not ready to let his foster father journey into the spirit world. There was still so much to learn and explore and see with him. Hot tears rolled down his cheeks as he watched the old one shut his eyes and release a breath that he would never again inhale.

Bujang bent down and laid his face against his father's, feeling warmth leave the shrunken cheek pad. Nuai wailed to announce the death of her grandfather, and her cries were echoed by bellows of lamenting that rose and rolled down the slopes like a wave, as the news of *Tok* Anjak's death spread through the jungle. The rain was forgotten.

* * *

Leaves rustled and branches snapped in a fast approaching line from a shallow valley in the southwest, then stopped. A long call, as the sound of wind echoing through a tunnel, resonated through the jungle. From the east came a distant reply from the Hill of Rocks.

Under the shadow of the canopy, three adult orang utans strained their ears and caught the reply above the din of jungle life. Eastward they turned. The trees in the old land were strong and bore them with ease as they swung and jumped on and over boughs and scaled trunks with more haste than apes were inclined to move. The higher up the slope they moved, the sparser and thinner the tree leaves became, and soon they found themselves swinging between the trunks of closely growing conifers and pines. At length they reached a break in the forest and climbed down to the ground, where they proceeded on all fours.

Here eucalyptus roots, whose seeds had been planted by generations past, greedily possessed the ground. Every now and then, the branches above them would snap or creak under the weight of playing young apes. The apparent leader made his way down the wide arches of boughs until he reached the edge of the forest, which opened to a wide patch of ground that had remained clear over the ages. This area was formed out of solid rock. The harshness of its hard surface was only mellowed by turfs growing in shallow bunches and leafy boughs reaching in from the outer edges. This day, a sweltering mist hung above the place like a soft veil between the heavens and the gathering below, of over a thousand apes. It was the largest collection of apes the rainforest had ever seen, for that morning students learned in the ways of the great teacher had come from far and wide to say their final farewells to *Tok* Anjak.

Though the forest was filled with the voices of youngsters at play, the air above the open ground was inundated with the wailing songs of female mourners. Around a curtained-off space that was assembled to shield the dead from the world of the living, the eldest apes sat in meditative grief. Panels of dancing spirits and a moon with her rays reaching across the sky guarded *Tok* Anjak from their grief.

A male ape separated from the group and sat by the edge of the forest, studying the line of trees. Soon he was joined by nineteen other apes. They wandered along the forest floor and down a low slope to the river in search of a tree wide enough to contain an ape. When they finally found a thick-bole gum tree, six apes took turns to shake it loose, and eight helped heave it out by the roots. The trunk was beaten with head-sized stones to a length of six feet. Next, sharp flints were used to split it open and to dig out the still soft core. Night fell, and they rested. Early the following morning, while the light was still grey, they returned to the mourning ground with the coffin. Three of their numbers entered the sanctuary of the dead and, by grasping the edges of the blanket beneath him, placed *Tok* Anjak into the hollowed-out log. Nuai cut a lock of her grandfather's fur and tied it into a knot before they sealed the opening of the casket with resin that had been collected from the crevices of bruised trees. The cloth panels were taken down and the curtained-off space exposed so the apes could pay their last homage to their teacher.

Between loud wailings, Nuai sang, "My grandfather is taken. He has left his children and grandchildren orphans. He has gone to follow the wind to the land of the dead. Oh, Grandfather, heed the song of birds and you shall find friendly hosts along your journey.

You shall have sweet fruits and leaves in all the resting huts. And you shall be served the fermented wines of the land."

The funeral rites continued for three more days, as befitted the passing of a great leader. Apes took turns keeping watch over the crude coffin at every hour of the day and night, lest any spirit or foolish animal should disturb him in his perpetual sleep. The most beautiful female voices continuously sang, one after another, as they wept over his passing.

On the morning of the sixth day, two young males lifted the casket onto their bent backs to head a procession down a slope and into the old jungle. On this steep slope, some of the buttress roots snaking the ground were as tall as saplings, and in many places the canopies were so thick no green plant could survive on the forest floor. Only the crackle of dead leaves and breaking twigs followed the silent mourners. Reaching down here and there from the high branches were the vines of stranglers, and though they would intermittently cross the path of a ripe bunch of figs, none of the apes stretched their hands for the fruits. As the slope gradually eased and became gentler, the scent of a corpse flower reached them. Soon the clay ground gave way to roots that overlapped and formed uneven mounds for the pallbearers to climb over.

Finally the procession entered a mournful, quiet valley. It was the heart of the rainforest, where breeze from the present-day world never visited and the air was as it had been in centuries past. They walked down a fading path between marked graves. Small pebbles circled one heap, a standing bamboo marked another, and leafy branches shaded a handful of mounds while tattered grey palm leaves covered two others.

Far in front of them stood four apes that had been there since dawn to dig a shallow grave. The two pallbearers carefully lowered the final abode of their teacher into the gaping hole, which was an exact fit to his coffin. Then the grave was covered.

Bujang planted four branches, one at each corner. He tied straight horizontal sticks in between them, about waist height from the ground. Then he arranged halved bamboos over the sticks to form a flat surface. He tied more twigs above the shelf and strapped on a thatched roof that the apes had woven. Nuai tied *Tok* Anjak's fur right under the roof and placed bark-cloths on the bamboos.

She hugged the last piece, which displayed the images of her grandfather's dancing footprints, and gave it to Bujang. "This is my gift to you, Uncle. I have nothing else for you to remember me by. May it help you follow in the footsteps of your father."

Bujang knew that it was time to part, for as an adult he was expected to travel the jungle on his own. In a tone as deep as the voice of an ape, he said, "I will treasure it, lovely niece. I will visit you often."

Nuai would not meet his gaze. Instead she teased the ground with the back of her hand. "Today I will lose another one I love. You used a sharp iron to split the bamboos. You were never meant to be an orang utan. Father was the last of our kind to remember the warring ways. That was why you were given to him. You were given to me because your spirit was young and tender."

Bujang squatted before her and said, "I don't understand. You will not lose me. I will seek you when the perfumes of fruiting flowers fill the air."

Nuai sat down and looked up into his face. She touched his wild, unwashed hair. What a strange sight he was among her kind. His constant playing in the boughs with the young ones had made him appear like one of them, but he was not. His skin was brown but hairless, and his eyebrows thick. She caressed his smooth cheek, sighing with regret that she would never see him develop cheek pads equal to the other proud males. It was time to let him go, for he had reached the age when he needed a mate.

She said, "You will go out into the human world. If you want to live, you must kill your enemies. Human blood is taboo to our kind. You must not look for me or any one of us."

A long-forgotten grief and memories of lonely nights darkened Bujang's brow. Again he was being abandoned, to be left alone to fend for himself against screeching macaques and hungry pythons. "What shall I do? Who will help me? I have no one if I don't have you," Bujang said.

"Sleep here tonight, at the grave of your father. He loves you greatly, and his spirit will guide you from the world of the dead. At the very least, he will point you either towards the morning sun or away from it."

Nuai passed Bujang a thigh-sized brown and yellow-speckled *cempedak* fruit, which she had brought as an offering to the dead. She tore open the skin to reveal globes of golden flesh between strips of ivory fibre. Its sweet, overpowering fragrance cleared the air of the Rafflesia's pungent perfume. "Goodbye, Uncle, until we meet again in *Sebayan*, the land of the dead."

Then she turned away and climbed up the nearest tree. Bujang watched as countless other apes moved away in different paths and disappeared into the jungle. He knew that it would be impossible for him to find Nuai again, for she recognized his scent and would hide herself at his approach. The young man's brow furrowed deeper in anguish. He could not understand why Nuai did not want to see him again or how she could have said that she loved him and did not want to be with him. He wondered if he was cursed to live his life alone, and if the gods were testing him still. Hadn't he been tested enough?

But anger soon tempered his grief as he decided that yes, he had been tested more than enough. He had gone through more than his share of suffering, for he had been abandoned by his people and then lost his family to headhunters.

Bujang sat cross-legged next to the grave as he thought of these things. He placed the *cempedak* on the ground and divided its flesh into two equal parts before eating his portion of the meal. The light, acidic sweetness of the fruit pacified his heartsickness in this place of the dead.

At the end of the meal, he moved away a few paces and leaned his back against a buttress root as high as a wall, stretching his legs wide in front of him. On studying the area about him, he saw other mounds that were each different in style, formed by animals for the great leaders of their kind. Many odours filled the air, but he only recognized the scent of *Tok* Anjak's fur.

In spite of his grief, curiosity soon overcame him, and he got up to explore the burial ground. Uneven roots led him to the first grave, and there he found two budding branches marking the position of the deceased's head and hind legs. The canine tooth of a clouded leopard, as long as his thumb, pierced through one of the stakes. Bujang kept his distance, not daring to anger a spirit that might have been a terror in its lifetime.

Twenty yards away, layered tendrils of soft grey roots hung down like a thick curtain. He approached the spot cautiously and, on parting the air-roots, saw a moss-covered grave. The thick, dark claw of a black sun bear lay on the old mound. Bujang vaguely recalled his human father's stories about asking for favours from the dead; therefore, he said, "Great bear spirit, protect me against all animals, and may those who look kindly upon you also treat me with kindness."

Away to his left, a long piece of gauze-like material slung on a standing yellow bamboo pole shone like silver under a thin shaft of light. He hopped between the roots of two trees towards it. As he drew close, he realized that what he thought was a piece of cloth was actually the mottled skin of a python. He inhaled sharply as he visually measured the girth of the skin. It was so wide it could have accommodated his large frame with ease. Aloud he said, "May I never be overcome by a serpent."

As the light grew dim, Bujang saw a proud rhinoceros hornbill feather. Mesmerized by its beauty and intimation of strength, he trotted straight to the grave. A sudden sadness filled his heart. "If only I had been born a hornbill instead of a man, it would have been my birthright to wear such a feather. My chest would have been blackened with valour and my head crowned with the colour of the sun. Yet now here I am with my war cap, naked and my chest unadorned. My barren skin bruises on a whim, and my bite can barely break a branch, let alone crush bone."

Spirit downcast and willpower failing, Bujang returned to his father's grave. Fireflies appeared with the dusk, twinkling like stars on a clear night. The young man stared unseeing at the sight as he mulled over his wish at the hornbill's grave.

Finally, deciding that it was pointless to be vexed over his situation, he wrapped himself in his blanket and slept next to the freshly dug earth.

* * *

Hours later, Bujang sat bolt upright in the darkness. The fireflies were gone, but in their place a rotting, moss-covered trunk emitted a soft glow that shimmered like moonlight. He looked about dazedly and wondered what had woken him. Between the cries of cicadas, he made out the sound of an unnatural throbbing, like a slow-beating heart. A lone, distant screech, followed by many hoots and calls reached his ears. He pushed aside his blanket and wended his way towards the source of the sound.

Black night enveloped the jungle. Though he could make out some shapes and forms, he was forced to use his bare feet to feel the way forward. The feel of dry, hard ground was familiar and comforting, assuring him that he would not stumble into a sinkhole or slip on a clay surface. From time to time the sparse undergrowth brushed against him like a caress. Ahead of him, the noise grew louder, and soon an isolated light revealed the location he sought. He crept forward on all fours. Ahead, he saw, rocks of many sizes formed a ring around an open space where a big fire burned in the centre. Bujang hid behind a large boulder and used the shadow of an adjacent rock to conceal his spying face.

In the circle of light, macaque monkeys danced the *ngajat* in a comical imitation of man-warriors. Their frolicking and small stature made them appear like mischievous children. Golden and brown furs glowed in the firelight, and naked pink faces twisted in exaggerated grimaces as dancers tapped their feet, bent their arms and flicked their hands. Long tails trailing on the ground bounced and curled at every third thump on a large hollow log. They danced to imitate warriors hunting for heads, with sticks for swords and wild banana leaves for shields, but throughout, they slashed and missed, slashed and missed. They jumped into the air every few steps – sometimes forward, sometimes backward. Two fell on their faces after being tripped by their fellow dancers and displayed exaggerated death throes which made the audience laugh. The monkeys were cackling so hard they did not hear Bujang laughing with them.

The shrieks and hoots ceased when a female boldly stepped into the firelight. The drumming softened. She bowed to the audience with her hands clasped in front of her face. Gracefully she swung her arms first to one side, and then to the other. Her swollen hips swayed as she walked around the fire. Then she stopped and twisted her body in a circle as she bent her legs and kept her folded arms close to her chest. She turned with a seductive twist to her hips, and the males hooted. Again she went around the fire and repeated the steps. Then coyly she ended her dance, paying no heed to calls for more.

A bard next took centre stage to sing about the foolishness of men. "They waste their energies toiling the earth. Even the smallest animal could ruin their crops and starve their people. Then what do they do when they are hungry? They come and hunt us. Silly, silly fools. Don't they realize that their labours are for naught? They are so ugly they cover themselves with barks of many colours. They feed food to a stranger and then, as the fellow sleeps, they cut off his head. They hang the head on a rafter and give it more food. Ha-ha-ha-ha."

Pebbles rained down on the bard and he was chased out of the circle of light. Dancing continued. Bujang watched in awe as strong macaques exhibited the grace of the hornbill, the strength of the bear and the cunning of the serpent by mimicking their movements with the swing of their arms and bodies and the stride of their feet. While they did so, mischievous youngsters danced the flaws of these same animals behind them. The bear was lumbering and fat, the hornbill proud and arrogant, and the serpent was greedy and reckless.

When the light of the fire grew weak and the predawn dew began to form on the leaves, a male larger than all the rest rose and performed the last dance. He flicked his hands and moved his shoulders in tune with the drumming. His feet stomped the ground, and his legs bent as he turned. Many cried out and challenged him, pretending to be crawling crocodiles or hulking bears, but he was so nimble on his feet that none could touch him. After going round the fire twice, he bent his legs and sank to the ground. Stretching his head down, he used his teeth to pick up a thick branch twice as long as the width of his face. Just as quickly, he jumped up and swung it against his challengers by turning his face from side to side. His neck muscles twitched and rippled, while his free arms twisted like serpents on guard, giving them no opportunity to touch him. The drumming grew more frenzied by the moment.

Dancer after dancer bowed in defeat before his audacity. Loud shouts and calls of victory to the chief filled the night air. Finally the apparent leader lowered the branch to its original position, for it had attested to his strength that night and might again be used to deride males daring enough to challenge his authority. He gave out a high-pitched cry and then ran on all fours into the jungle. The herd rushed after him, and the rock circle was silent.

It was not long before daylight returned to the land, displaying the remains of embers and shredded banana leaves in the small clearing. With the memory of the strange dances still in his mind, Bujang moved away from his hiding place and, after some distance, saw a strangler fig tree which he recognized from the day before. Marble-shaped fruits of green and pink hung down from it like the bead necklace of a noblewoman. He climbed the streaming, thick roots and sat in a busy branch. Below, above and about him were birds, rodents and monkeys. The company there was as merry as that around a table laid out by an absent host.

After eating his fill, Bujang ambled back to the burial ground, but on reaching it, he was dismayed to see the *cempedak* flesh served to *Tok* Anjak gone. He cast about for a clue of the thief and noticed a brown seed lying on top of a tree root. There was no other sign or track. After collecting his meagre belongings and clasping them under one arm, he approached the seed. When he stooped to pick it up, he saw another piece a yard away. He moved to pick it up and saw yet another ahead.

All morning he followed the trail of seeds and placed each and every one of them in an unfolded portion of the red cloth that he had slung over his arm like an open bag. The farther he went, the more perplexed he became because it seemed obvious that whoever ate the fruit had wanted to be followed. He wondered if an animal was playing a joke on him, or if a spirit was guiding him. The empty jungle floor slowly gave way to a covering of fern and low bushes as he moved away from the valley up a slope. Then it thinned again, under the dark canopies of outreaching branches. Even so, because of the thick carpet of leaves Bujang had to put his face against the ground in some places to see where the next seed lay. Although he lost count of how many he had collected, the seeds in his makeshift pouch did not overflow. As the day grew warmer, the sound of fast-flowing water reached his ears. The ground became more compact with every step he took, and soon the jungle faded into a thin spray that filled the air like a fog.

Bujang then ventured where the trees could not. Ahead of him, a shallow stream gurgled delightfully as its water rushed over rocks and bubbled over stones. Ferns, which unfurled like green fountains, drooped over parts of the watercourse and clung onto whatever soil could be found between the rock crevices. On a large flat boulder that hung low over the stream, he found the last seed. But where was the thief?

He heaped the pile in the crook of his arm atop that last seed and placed his things beside them before stepping into the clear water. The coolness swirling around his shins was refreshing. Bujang took off his ragged loincloth and slid into the watercourse. Using a smooth stone from the streambed, he scrubbed himself free of dirt and grime. He washed and combed his wild hair as best as he could with his fingers before tying it into a knot behind his head. Then he reached for the bark loincloth, with the intention of washing it. After rubbing the material a few times, he decided that it was too tattered to be salvaged, so he released it to the stream and the water carried it away.

Indifferent to his surroundings, he lay naked on the rock to dry himself and dozed part of the afternoon away. He knew it was wrong to expose himself on land, for he was no longer a child and would disgust any man or spirit who saw, but he was beyond caring. When the sun had descended midway down the horizon, he rose and unrolled the red bundle. The cloth was twice his height in length and was as wide as his belly. It was a garment fit for a prince. He passed it between his legs and held the front flat against his stomach to cover his navel as he eased out more cloth to the front until it almost reached his ankle. Then he wound the backend of the cloth around his waist and over the front flap three times before doubling the remaining cloth and hooked it under the strip running down his buttocks. He pulled on the loop until he felt a comfortable tightness. Proudly he studied the stripes of white, black and red at either end of the loincloth. Even the most cowardly man could become a warrior if dressed in the colours of a hornbill.

He placed the bare war cap on his head and tied the hanging strings under his chin. It was a perfect fit. Then he took it off again to scrutinize the perfect yellow tinge of the rattan. As he ran his fingers over the knife marks upon its surface, he marvelled at how well the cap must have protected its previous owner. The golden sheen reminded him of his father, Apong, who had shown him how to soak and dry rattan vines to rid them of sap. He touched a finger to every resin stain in breaks between the spiralling strips with awe, all the while wondering how tall the feather that once stood there was.

Next he picked up the sword and, on examining the sheath, realized that it was made out of four broken pieces of wood loosely strapped together. His foster father must have assembled the parts: the ape's short thumb would not have allowed him to tie a proper knot.

Bujang cut away the frayed cord and arranged the fragments on the ground. Squatting down and leaning forward, he pulled a bunch of tough ferns growing on the water's edge. After stripping the leaves away, he beat on the spines with a stone to soften the fibre. Then he twisted them together to form a new cord which he used to lash down the loose pieces. He sheathed the sword to test his handiwork, then pulled it out again. The newly assembled scabbard might still be crude, but it was sturdy. Pleased, he next turned his attention to the sword itself. Its hilt was made from the ivory of a deer's antler. The main horn contained his grip comfortably before it forked in two and was sliced an inch away from the split. Carved upon the lower horn was the grinning face of a monster, and encircling the upper were dancing spirits. The rusty blade upon which it was attached curved slightly as it gently widened to about two inches at the tip.

He ran his fingers over the sword's dull surface. Then he sat down at the edge of the stream with one leg in the water and the other folded before him. He reached into the streambed to select a smooth, flat stone, which he placed in front of him. The iron whined hoarsely and bled away its years of disuse into the stream as he whetted it against the rock while splashing handfuls of water over it occasionally.

When the sword started to shine like a grey mirror and the edges began to eat into the surface of the whetstone, Bujang wiped it dry on his loincloth. He wished that he had some fat to rub onto its surface to keep it from rusting, but since there was none he slid it back into its sheath.

The sun set uneasily in the horizon, veiled behind a strange layer of mist rising from the water. Bujang draped the blanket over his shoulders like a shawl and was soon comforted by the warmth it gave him. After dunking and rubbing the *cempedak* seeds clean in the stream, he sat down cross-legged on the flat rock and began peeling away the soft brown skin. Before long, the brown pile by his side turned milky white.

When he finally looked up, Bujang sensed a strange silence about him. The leaves had stopped rustling, and the stream had stilled. While he was pondering the meaning of this change, suddenly a man dropped from the sky with a loud crack of thunder. Bujang fell back and gaped, wide-eyed, at the stranger. Then, on realizing that this was no ordinary man, Bujang prostrated his body before the stranger. Even in the dimming light, the man's skin shone like a copper sun. A forest of handsome feathers crowned his white head, further emphasizing the proud face that was etched in an expression of war and the golden eyes, which were deep as pools and seemed to portend death. A sleeveless jacket of black fur adorned with rows upon rows of claws and canine teeth covered the warrior's chest. A cloak woven in brown feathers draped over his right shoulder. And hanging over this assemblage was a large, flat shell, whose mother-of-pearl surface reflected all the lights of the rainbow.

As the man straightened to an upright position, he snapped the front flap of a loincloth the colour of a red sky, interwoven with gold and silver light. Bujang dared not look up into his face as he held up his hands and offered the *cempedak* seeds.

The man sniffed in disgust. "I intend to eat your flesh and drink your blood, boy. If you want to live, bring me a wild boar in your place. It must be an adult male with tusks as long as your arm."

Bujang stumbled in his hurry to get up and flee, for he did not intend to end his days in the belly of a spirit. His meagre belongings slipped out of his hands and arms as he tried to collect them, for the terror he felt in the man's presence curdled his blood and stiffened his muscles. He sped to the edge of the jungle, his cap and sword gripped tightly in one hand. On reaching the shelter of the boughs, he placed the cap on his head and fumbled awkwardly with the sword strap as he tried to tie it around his waist.

Turning his head back to the stream once more, to make certain that he was not hallucinating, he saw the spirit squatting on the flat rock he had just vacated. The white head was now turned upwards to the heavens, following the flight of a hawk that soon landed at his feet. In its beak was a piece of bloody meat, which it placed before the being.

A voice of angry thunder shook the rocks. "The Kayan chief shall not be harmed. I have granted him protection before he began his journey. To the man who defies me, I shall send another to end his life." The hawk flew off in a trail of high-pitched screech.

4

Bujang shivered, the cold feeling like dead fingers clawing into his bones. With each step he took, needles of chill stabbed into his leathered feet, and when darkness pursued him, his stomach forced sour bile into his throat. He vomited. He squeezed his eyes shut for a moment then opened them again but saw only black emptiness stretching ahead like an endless tunnel. Not daring to move either forward or back, he froze.

Stars and a faint glow like the glimmer of the moon began to appear, on the ground, in the bushes, and on his arm. A thousand fireflies drove away the black hopelessness in his soul, for he could again see his surroundings and determine that there was no demon anywhere near. Above him, dark clouds relaxed their guard over a waning moon, and the night brightened. As his breathing calmed, the purr of a wildcat reached his ears.

He looked up to the low branch where it rested and said, "Greetings, sister cat. Do you know where I can find a wild boar with tusks as long as my arm?"

The wildcat snarled and sprang to a neighbouring branch.

"Wait!" Bujang called, but the sound of fast snapping boughs continued to move away from him at lightning speed.

Time after time he tried asking the same question of each animal he met, and each, like the cat, ran from him in terror. Yet the all-pervading chill would not leave him. A faint memory, stifled under layers of a carefree life, plagued him. He might have been told about the beast before but had never realized it. The apes had always been watchful of their words whenever they spoke of danger because they believed that the mere mention of a terror would manifest it. He sensed that he knew this beast, but he had no memory of it. For a moment, frustration overtook his anxiety. If only he could remember, at the very least he would know where to start searching.

For the next five days, fear fuelled Bujang. He only stopped to rest when exhaustion overcame him, and even so he expected the terrifying man to appear at any moment to demand for his blood. Each day the ground rose and fell beneath him like ocean waves frozen at their peaks. He searched within the thick forests of pines, eucalyptuses and casuarinas. He found tracks of wild pigs between the buttress roots of *tapangs* and *kapurs,* but none led him to the animal he sought. From the crest of every hill he climbed, he would study the expanse of green land as far as his eyes could see. He explored every shadowed valley and sunny slope his feet led him to, but nothing.

After finding yet another useless trail on the fifth day, Bujang collapsed against a moss-covered log and resigned himself to the fate of being eaten by the spirit. He looked up to the canopies, and his gaze fell on a macaque watching him from a low bough. It was the bard from some nights ago.

Bujang sat up. "Hey, skinny monkey. Where can I find a boar as big as a monster?"

Barks of laughter greeted the question. "Why should I help you? You are the stupid human who offered pig's fodder to Sengalang Burong. He will do us a great favour if he eats you."

Bujang's eyes widened and his heart pounded. He had come face to face with the warpath god and lived! However, despite his fear and amazement, the young man did not like being laughed at by a monkey, particularly one that was barely a fifth his size. He broke a dry branch from the log and pointed it at the animal. "I will throw this at you and break your skull. I will have my meal first, before Sengalang Burong has his."

The monkey stared warily at Bujang and weighed the likelihood of averting Bujang's throw: the youth was well known for his skill at stick throwing. Having observed a few orang utan competitions, he was aware that a well-aimed throw could easily knock him out of the branch and break a bone or two.

To Bujang's delight, he opted to bargain. "I am Simutik, the most sought-after bard south of the world. Nothing is hidden from me, except for the will of the gods and the cunning of demons. If you promise that you and your descendants will never again hunt my kind, I will lead you to the boar."

"My descendants will not hunt yours, if you and your kind leave our planting fields alone."

Simutik scratched his tan head. Then he nodded and said, "Instruct your children to place a *cempedak* seed at the foot of every *teresang* they erect around their field boundary. They must not put the seed into the offering baskets on top of the splayed bamboo poles. The spirits will not be pleased to be offered such a poor thing."

On perceiving the man's blushing face, the bard laughed at his own ingenuity. Bujang Maias's foolishness would now be remembered by both humans and monkeys for many generations to come.

Next Simutik jumped onto the tree trunk and climbed to the top of the canopy. Just as swiftly, Bujang scaled after him. Epiphytic orchids and flowing leaves created a strange, wild garden far above the shaded world. Oblivious to the familiar sight, the two travellers leapt from branch to branch until the sun fell low in the horizon.

On reaching the thick branch of an *engkabang* growing at the edge of a muddy pool, the monkey stopped and said between pants, "There, do you see those tracks? Don't go down lest you leave your own imprint on the soft earth. The demon-boar you want comes here at night to drink from his own filth. You would do well to keep out of the way of his tusks," the monkey said, and with a cackle he scrambled away and out of sight.

Bujang climbed down to the lowest branch of the large-leaf dipterocarp they had been perched in to study the criss-crossing tracks of a heavy-hoofed animal on the ground. Then he clambered away to another tree and yet another, keeping a picture of that place in his mind as he committed the area to memory. The light from a late sun shining down in thin shafts upon the grey, muddy pool revealed a sprouting, thirty-foot rattan vine covered in thick mud. It drooped like unkempt locks of hair only a few yards away. To the opposite side was an inclining tree with tendrils of torn and dirty bark, some of which had been stripped loose and left to drape over a rotting log covered in flaky moss. All about, flies buzzed as though guarding a fetid feast.

Yet above that stench was the undeniable fragrance of the sweet smell of ripe *durians*. Bujang's stomach growled. Nimbly he climbed towards a sub-canopy tree that was about seventy feet high, with branches bending under the weight of thorny fruits the size of heads. On reaching a tree trunk that crossed one of the thick branches of the *durian* tree, he touched the glossy-green leaves with silver underside and sniffed appreciatively. Below him, more fruit peppered the ground. He tested the branch to make sure that the burdened limb would endure his added weight; then he crawled on all fours to the forking. Squatting on the thick bough and reaching up, he placed his right palm under a yellow, spiky fruit and shook it gently. The ripe fruit came off at its stalk, and the hard thorns sunk onto his palm. He leaned it against the trunk and knocked the bottom with the hilt of his sword. It cracked open, and he split it the rest of the way with his hands. Gleefully he scooped out a chunk of yellow flesh and sunk his teeth into the sweet, rich meal. Soft, custard-like flesh clung to his fingers as he licked the seed clean before throwing it to the ground.

It had been six days since Bujang had last eaten a full meal, and he ate ravenously. He ripped the shell, part by part, to get to the flesh, until finally he reached the fifth and last pod. After finishing that fruit, he straddled the empty husk on the branch before wiping his hand on a peeling bark. Longingly he stared at a second fruit, but his right hand went to the hilt of his sword instead. He must not weigh his body down with too much food now, as it would slow his movements.

He returned to the grey *engkabang* tree that faced the pool and climbed down to its second lowest branch which he hoped was high enough away from the ground to elude the boar's sensitive sense of smell. He twisted the long flaps of his new loincloth and pushed both ends into the waistband. The moist, cold air made him wrap the blanket over his shoulders. Then he leaned against the trunk. Before settling down, he unsheathed the sword and rested it across his thighs.

Incessantly the jungle chirped and squealed, as monkeys shrieked and owls hooted in response to the symphony of cicadas. While Bujang dozed, night advanced like a swift black tide. Soon the darkness became so thick that a man could barely tell which way was up or down, and the jungle fell silent. In that blinding hour he woke.

He smelled rather than heard the huge mass moving beneath him.

Bujang's stomach cramped, and sour bile burned his throat. He forced it back down. He trembled, for he couldn't escape the wrath of a god, and the beast below terrified him. Still, he had come here to seek it.

He flexed his stiff fingers and wiggled his cold toes. The sound of guzzling reached his ears. Slowly he removed the cloth from his shoulders, letting it hang over the bough and hugged the trunk, as his feet felt their way down the smooth bark.

A dry leaf crunched when he stepped onto the ground. A snort, a lifted head, and instantly the boar pivoted on its hind legs. It shook its head as though to rid the air of the smell of ripe durians. Then its body stiffened.

Bujang gulped air like a drowning man. Another gulp, a deep breath and he stepped away from the tree trunk, all the while keeping his eyes firmly on two red points of light, which were the animal's glaring eyes.

The boar bellowed. The young man lifted his sword and stood akimbo to steady his shaking knees.

The boar snorted and growled. "Who are you, mortal man, that you should dare face me alone?"

Bujang talked back to the red points of light. "I am Bujang Maias, son of *Tok* Anjak. I am here to take you to offer to Sengalang Burong."

"You are not the first human he sent to kill me. You shall also not be the last. Your scalp will make a fine trophy on my tusk."

"Prepare to die, demon," said Bujang – more bravely than he felt.

The boar snorted and bayed out a laugh. "I am Taring Ai. I am death to many a hapless warrior. The warpath god uses me for his own purposes."

Taring Ai backed up until his hind legs sank into soft mud. Then, with almost no hesitation and barely enough time for Bujang to draw his breath, he charged like a bucking boulder.

Bujang jumped out of his way. A tree took the onslaught, and half of its trunk splintered. The animal swung back and again charged.

Bujang dug his feet into the ground. He yelled and instinctively stretched out his arm as though to brace himself against a falling wall as the animal crashed into him. As he grabbed onto one of the tusks, Taring Ai lifted him off the ground and threw him back down. Bujang slipped and fell on his back, though one hand still clung firmly to the tusk. He tried to turn Taring Ai's face to the side as rough whiskers and hot putrid breath assailed him and the edges of sharp teeth pinched his chest. But his hand slipped, and a tusk dug into his left shoulder. With the hilt of his sword he beat a red eye. The boar grunted, and they separated.

As he scrambled back to his feet, Bujang wondered if he would end his life in the belly of the beast that night. Again the ground rumbled. Pain, like a burning hand, pushed Bujang's shoulder and threw him to the side on his knees with the sword gripped uselessly in his fist. Taring Ai brushed past him.

Instinctively, Bujang twisted his body to the side, pushed himself up and ran on all fours. He clambered over the log and tumbled into the shallow pool. Bujang's frantic memory searched the dark surroundings as he jumped out of the water. He scampered towards the rattan bush and made a sudden turn to his left, but not in time to stop the sharp thorns from scratching his flesh.

The storm behind him crashed into the vines. Taring Ai tore himself free with an enraged squeal. Bujang stood to face him on bended knees, though his thigh muscles shook in spasms. Taring Ai charged. With all his terror-filled strength, Bujang hurled the sword at the pair of red eyes. The boar's head jerked back, and his forelegs bent. The man leapt to the side, but was too late to avoid the momentum that crashed into him and battered his body against a standing trunk.

Bujang had to crawl his way out from under Taring Ai. Then he gripped his side and writhed as he willed the pain to stop. Gradually his hard breathing slowed and his body curled in exhaustion.

* * *

He had no idea how long he had lost consciousness for, but he was alive, at least. A leaf speckled blue sky returned Bujang's pain-drenched gaze. The morning was too quiet. He coughed to clear his throat, sat up and saw two rows of macaques watching him. He jumped to his feet and reached for the sword that had remained embedded between Taring Ai's eyes. That was when he saw his foe, a beast the size of two grown men. The pair of long tusks, which were carved with white spirits dancing against a yellowed background, was adorned with human hair. Quill-like strands of hair covered the boar's body, and the heads of fifty macaques circled the demon's neck like beads. Even dead, the stench of terror around the beast was suffocating.

The macaque that had danced (how many hours, or nights ago was it, Bujang wondered?) with a branch in his jaw, stepped forward and said, "Greetings, Bujang Maias. My name is Kayu Batu. I am the chief of this herd. I have come to commend you for killing Taring Ai and to ask you for the return of the heads around his neck."

Bujang studied the size of the carcass and gingerly handled the aching bruise on his side. "I will give you back the heads, if you and your troop help me carry him back to the stream carved in the hill of rock."

Kayu Batu stared at the raw lesion on Bujang's side. He looked up to gaze into his face. Then the chief lifted an arm and shrieked a signal, and males, the largest of their kind, came forward and lifted the beast. A youngster even climbed up the *engkabang* to collect Bujang's blanket and cap for him. As they moved through the jungle, twenty monkeys at a time took turn carrying the carcass. Taring Ai's stench went ahead of them and drove away any jungle creature that crossed their path.

In Bujang's bruised and beaten condition, the journey seemed to take forever. When evening fell, they placed the carcass in the middle of a clearing and stopped for camp. He was grateful for the rest. The herd scattered into the surroundings and returned with dry bark, wood and twigs. Kayu Batu placed a white rock on top of a pile of shredded, dry bark. Then he gripped another rock with both hands and screeched as he struck down on the first. Sparks, like short-lived fireflies, flew down. Again he struck, with a louder shriek, and a third blow soon followed. The pile began to smoke. Monkeys hooted and jumped about like children who had lit their first fire. Two of the animals teased the embers and added more wood under the watchful eye of their chief. When the tongues of flame began to leap and wave, the older macaques broke into a dance which eloquently mimicked Bujang's duel with the demon-boar. It was like their dance of the earlier night, but now a man was the hero, not a fool. The bard, Simutik, sang about Bujang's bravery, and this time the herd listened in awed silence. Many eyed the hero with disbelief as he slouched against a trunk and munched on soft leaves and jungle fruits. But the wonder did not last long, for soon only the sentries remained awake. The day had been laborious, and a new day promised more labour.

* * *

On the third morning, the troop breathed great sighs of relief at the sight of the rock stream. Finally, they had arrived. Sengalang Burong was nowhere to be seen, but a large fire with an iron stand placed over it proved to Bujang that he had not imagined his encounter with the god. Rice wine in twenty tubes of one-foot bamboo cups had been arranged in rows on the flat rock.

The macaques laid the carcass next to the stream, after which

Bujang cut the rope around Taring Ai's throat and released the heads to the monkeys.

Kayu Batu bowed, both hands clasped in front of him. "Thank you, Bujang Maias, son of *Tok* Anjak. May you live a long life and may your harvest be rich. For this deed, your children shall sprout around you like wild fern, and none shall lose their heads to hunters in the night."

With little ceremony, each skull was handed back to one of its kin, so as to be buried and to have the spirit returned to its proper body in the land of the dead. Then the monkeys turned back to the jungle and melted into the foliage. Bujang scratched his left shoulder absentmindedly, watching them until they were out of sight. When he looked down, he saw that his torn scabs had begun to ooze transparent yellow pus. He ambled to the stream, washed the wound and covered it with mud that he had dug from the streambed to reduce the irritation. Then he turned to look at the wild boar, and his mouth began to water with memories of charred meat and sweet runny juices, for it had been seventeen harvestings since he had last eaten cooked flesh.

His eyes scanned the area. There were bunches of elliptical bamboo leaves fluttering in the breeze on the other side of the water. Propping the sword over his shoulders, he crossed the stream and trod a short distance into the jungle where he chose two of the thickest stems to cut down. Once that was done, he looked about him and realized that he was standing in a small, abandoned garden. He explored, and collected palmate tapioca leaves. There were ginger roots, which he soon dug out, and two wild pineapples growing by the edge. On returning to the other side, he prepared the bamboos by cutting them just below the septum. Having made two long tubes, he split the remainder into skewers.

Then he stepped into the stream and splashed water on his kill intermittently as he scraped away grime and hair with the sword. Clear, speedy water turned cloudy grey and carried Taring Ai's scent downstream. That done, Bujang reached for a bamboo tube and held it steady as he carefully sliced open the boar's throat. Blood spewed out into the tube, over his hand, on the stone and into the stream. He grunted, pleased to see that the fluid had not congealed. The meat would still be good. Next, he gutted the animal, cleaned out the intestines and stomach by turning them inside out, and cut them into bite-size pieces. This went into the second tube, together with the chopped ginger and wild pineapple. The opening of both tubes was then sealed with twisted tapioca leaves and the tubes leaned against the iron rod placed over the flames. He stabbed the liver, kidney, heart and lung with skewers and planted them around the fire. Next he cut the meat into thick strips, which were pierced with two or three bamboo sticks and laid over the iron rods. The large head, with its protruding tusks, was also placed atop the fire. Beneath them, the flame cackled as if with delight, as fat dripping from the skewers sent sparks flying.

A thin mist began to form over the water. Again Bujang stepped into the stream and splashed the rock to clean its surface of blood and grime. Finally he dipped himself in the watercourse and bathed. Dripping wet, he returned to the fire to tend to the cooking meat. Soon the warmth against his cool skin made him drowsy. Sweet smelling smoke swirled upwards, and the sun released its gaze over the land as it set in the horizon.

But this peace did not last for long. Once more, the loud stomp of a god falling from the sky shook the ground. Bujang was startled out of his doze and, on seeing Sengalang Burong, immediately prostrated himself. A loud crack made him look up. The deity had snapped the front tail of his loincloth and turned his face upwards to the sky as a screeching hawk flew over.

Far too soon, the glaring gaze turned down again to Bujang. The god approached the fire and sat cross-legged before it. Bujang reverently offered him a skewer of meat, hoping that his error with the *cempedak* seeds would not be used against him. The warpath god took the food without a word. Then the youth poured out cooked bamboo contents onto two large yam leaves, making the god sigh with delight on beholding the offering of blood and rich innards placed within his reach.

When Bujang offered him the choice liver, the deity asked, "Why are you not eating with me? This is your kill. Do you not know that I eat with humans worthy of my company? I dance and make merry with them when they feast in my name."

Bujang dared not utter a word in response, terrified lest he say or act in a displeasing manner. He bowed and, like a shy boy being made to eat with a venerable guest for the first time, selected the lightest skewer. He chewed slowly. The fat was sweet, and it ran down the side of his face. He struggled to contain his hunger, for he had not eaten since the night before. His hand reached out for more meat, and soon his full attention was on the meal.

Sengalang Burong laughed, and the ground shook with pleasure at his mirth. They washed down their meal with rice wine from the house of heaven. The milky *tuak* brew was male, and its bitterness made Bujang so giddy that after his second cup, he began to feel all strength leave his body. He tried to get up from his cross-legged position to offer more food but fell on his back instead. The drunken haze, however, did not stop him from feeling the stabbing pain on his right shoulder. He opened his eyes and saw the deity beating him with sharp thorns but he could not resist, for he was paralysed in place as though held down by four men.

When the jabbing stopped, Sengalang Burong glared into his terrified eyes and said, "I am sending you to vanquish one of my own. This mark is proof of my will to the spirits. Then, you shall either become mine or be destroyed."

Bujang tried to beg for mercy, but the only words that came out from his mouth sounded strange and alien to him. They sounded as though he was pledging his life and soul to the god. He tried to protest against those promises, but his mouth seemed to have a will of its own. The harder he struggled, the more he worshipped Sengalang Burong. Exhaustion soon overwhelmed him, and he lost all will to fight his fate.

* * *

The wind howled a storm, insects shrieked an uproar and waves crashed on rocks. Bujang woke up to a clear, sunny day. Branches waved lazily in the breeze, and across the stream a mouse-deer cautiously lapped water. It dashed back into the jungle when Bujang sat up. Nausea shook his frame, and he was forced to take deep breaths to hold the bile down. In front of him, the rock surface was black with ashes and littered with empty bamboo cups.

His shoulders throbbed and burned like a spreading fever. The need for coolness made him drag himself to the stream, where he splashed his head with ice-cold water. Again nausea flooded his throat, and he vomited the night's revelry into the swift watercourse. He splashed more water onto his face to wake his sluggish senses. Then he rolled into the stream, and let the water run over his full length. Once the pounding in his head lessened, he sat up and stared down at the two raw, circular wounds on his shoulders before slapping mud over them.

The ground beneath him swayed and rolled as he got up on his feet. Carefully he picked up his sword and blanket. He wondered over the white carved sheath of his sword, for the pattern of dancers looked familiar. Thinking, however, made the hammering in his head worse. He turned to reach for his war cap and stopped to finger the two hornbill tail feathers stuck on the crown, each more than two feet long. He picked up the cap with difficulty and almost lost his balance as he placed it on his head. Shading his eyes from the painful rays of the morning sun, he wobbled into the cool shade of the jungle.

5

A sea of sunlit cogon grasses rolled along a steep incline down to the edge of a river on one side and a wall of thicket on the distant other. Within it, burnt stumps of giant *kapur* trees that had once reached to the sky lay scattered. A young stag paused and stared before ambling away to the river. Humans had once been here, Bujang thought as he recalled how the men of his longhouse had slashed and burned whole areas during the dry season so the women could plant rice and maize on the patch of land. For months and years they would continue to plant on the same patch of ground, until their crops could no longer gain nutrients from it. When that happened, the land would be abandoned to be taken over by hardy weeds and deer or buffaloes. It would be many years before trees or shrubs would once again grow, and during that time there would barely be enough food to sustain a single ape.

Bujang, however, was searching for human company not food. He knew that most longhouses only moved a few miles away from the land they had abandoned: the river would lead him to the closest settlement. The waist-high grasses brushed against him and scratched his exposed flesh as he made his way down the slope. He hoped that he would be welcomed by any settlement he found and not be chased away by them, for after the scabs on his shoulders had fallen off, they had formed rosette patterns, marking him a headhunter. The raised scar on his left shoulder was dark copper, and the tattoo on the right was black, but in the centre of each eight-petal flower swirled the eye of a dragon-dog.

He was thinking about the marks, what they might mean to any humans he encountered, when a loud honk startled him. Two hundred yards away, just in front of where the river disappeared into a bend inside the jungle, he saw a rhinoceros hornbill throw back its black head and point a curved ivory beak to the sky before letting out another series of honks. Bujang jogged towards it, wondering why the bird had called, "Here, here, here." Natural sinkholes and protruding roots covered in layers of weeds forced him to proceed more slowly than he wished. However, when he was but an arm's length away, the bird leapt into the air and flew off with a loud roar of its wings.

As he stood pondering over the significance of seeing the omen bird, a sudden human shout shook the air. Then more war cries erupted, scattering wild pheasants from within the jungle into the field. The sound of clashing irons reached him. Each blow he heard was preceded by a yell, and some were followed by cries of pain. Bujang stooped low and darted into the jungle of young, sparse trees towards the skirmish. Just before reaching the trail where the fight was taking place, he bent down, crept forward and crouched behind a shrub covered in a thick veil of ivy.

In front of him were four Kayans who stood facing an Iban party of three men. Feathers in the war caps of the Kayans shivered as they moved, and blood glistened on their vests of wild animal fur. Two bodies lay at the feet of a frail old man, whose skin was as fair as an eggshell where it was not covered in tattoos. The canine teeth of a wildcat which decorated the shell of both perforated ears suggested the grandfatherly man had had a valiant past. He stood straight and tall, with a fighting sword gripped in his steady hand. Three young warriors stood between him and their attackers, though the fact that they were using their oblong shields more often than their swords revealed them to be the weaker party.

The Ibans, made bold by the weakening defence put up against them, played with their victims. Their hornbill- and argus pheasant-feathered caps twisted from side to side as they taunted the young Kayans. Sweat trickled down their bare backs and glistened under the bright midmorning sun like drops of dew on sprouting leaves. One man thrust his shield forward and laughed as his victim stepped back in fright. The tufts of human hair clinging to its surface danced as he swung it about. He gave out a loud cry, raised his sword and arched it down violently on his victim's shield, splintering the soft wood and forcing the youth down on his knees.

As the aggressor hunched over his victim Bujang flinched. The loincloth the man wore was his cloth of swirling water, the cloth that Sika had woven for her son Menjat. He recognized the coil of the head and the undulating form. He saw the serpent in the dance of the water, and he recalled the spiritual battle his mother had fought with it and lost. Rage made him pull out his sword: rage at both man and cloth. His hands gripped the handle so hard, his knuckles turned white. With a loud cry he jumped out of hiding, appearing like a demon incensed.

The attacker turned to show his scowling, monkey-like face. On seeing Bujang, he laughed with glee and stuck out a tongue which reached down to his chin. *Ilang*s were brandished, as one after another the Ibans rushed for Bujang's head.

The Kayans stared at the stranger whose eyes shone like an angry hornbill's and whose war-frown was more terrifying than the carved face of a monster. They wondered if the gods had hewn him out of rock or hammered him out of bronze, for his skin was as dark as red soil after the rain and his voice sounded like thunder before a storm. His iron moved like water, the blade so sharp that his labours appeared effortless as he meted out blow after blow on their enemies. Urged by his war cry, the young Kayans gathered their remaining courage and charged to join the fray.

Bujang fought with blind rage, and with each blow forced the monkey-faced man to retreat out of the jungle into a fading trail along the foot of the grassy slope. He tried to wrench the grisly shield with one hand, while the other met each oncoming stroke with equally hard blows from his sword. In spite of that, his opponent jumped nimbly and moved out of his way faster than he could strike. They parried and evaded each other's swings until sweat drenched the clay ground about them.

A strong wind blew over the land and filled the air with a swirling storm of white, feathery seeds from the cogon grasses. The day darkened and thundered in a low growl. The Ape Man sensed the brewing thunderstorm. He must act before the spirits interfered in this fight, for he had to kill his family's murderer with his own hands.

From the corner of his eye, Bujang saw a three-foot chunk of wood lying by the side of the path. Channelling his full strength into his hands, he hacked the lashed frame of the monkey-man's shield until strips of rattan came loose. Then he struck a heavy blow right in centre of the convex surface, twisted the blade and split the shield in half.

The enemy retreated a few steps, dropped his mutilated cover and flexed his shoulders. With a cry, he charged. Bujang squatted and bit down on the rim of the chunk of wood. He jumped to his feet in time to meet the man's swinging blade, and then, with their swords locked, he swung his burdened face towards his adversary. The monkey-faced man howled, covered his bruised face with one hand and moved back a step. Bujang swung his sword hard, slicing through the man's throat and hand. The head thudded to the ground, but the body remained standing for a few moments. Then, slowly, it fell forward on its knees and sprawled on the path.

Bujang lowered the wood to its original position before standing up to face the other two attackers. The larger man turned and ran; he was soon followed by his companion. A white light streaked through the sky, and was immediately answered by a clap of thunder. Large droplets of rain pelted the earth like a cascade of waterfall. Soon an instant stream poured down the slope and swirled around Bujang's feet.

The Kayan warriors moved away from him, taking their position once more around the old man. Their swords were ready to meet him, but their eyes were unsure. A muffled sob burst out from the youngest, a teenage boy too young to be called a man.

Bujang's scowl softened, for he remembered what it was like to be afraid. He sheathed his sword and turned to expose his back to them. Grabbing the cloth covering the enemy's loin, he unwound it and left the body naked where it lay. He rubbed the cloth under the pouring rain and tried as best as he could to salvage the last remnant of his childhood. But it was impossible as the cloth had been soiled beyond repair by his father's murderer. He stared at the separated head, strode forward to pick it up and wrapped it in the cloth. The downpour quietened to a drizzle, and the sky cleared.

The old man let out a long *uh-ha* under his breath as he suddenly realized that this could be the Ape Man the Penans had spoken of. The rosettes on his shoulders were strange, and his long hair unkempt. The young warrior's unplucked eyebrows and sideburns made him look like a man in mourning. If so, then the taking of Terbai Lang's head should more than nullify him of the curse of his loss, for it meant that the gods now blessed him and that a powerful spirit would henceforth protect him. The old man said to Bujang, "I have heard tales from the birds, of a man who killed the evil spirit

Taring Ai. Is this the man who also killed Terbai Lang, the truce breaker who disregarded the wishes of the gods because of his lust for blood?"

"I am Bujang Maias, son of *Tok* Anjak. Here is one of Taring Ai's tusks, carved into a sheath for my *ilang,* the sword I received from my orang utan father."

The old warrior nodded. He did not seem surprised. "I am *Tuai* Laing," he said, "the headman of a humble Kayan longhouse in the upper reaches of the Batang Balui. My party and I had been to the Tiau River, which is on the other side of the hills you see to the south. Our home is only a half day's run from here. Come and be my guest."

The chief instructed his warriors to hide their fallen companions, for trying to carry the two men back would only hinder them, and since the place was not far from the longhouse a larger party of men would be sent to collect the bodies for burial. In the meantime, they had to prevent wanderers from taking the heads and claiming heroism when such trophies were not earned with courage. The body of the enemy, however, was left lying where he fell.

As the sun reached its noontime summit, they resumed their journey on the jungle trail. After a short while, the level path gave way to a lazy slope before running across a shallow valley. For the next two miles, straight-bole trees interspaced between burned buttress roots the size of boats filled the landscape about them. Eventually the way turned steeply uphill and cut into the colder, denser shade of ancient canopies. They jogged steadily on a well-trodden path.

Bujang ran next to the old chief and timed his speed to the light slap of a small mat tied to the back of his companion's loincloth. When they reached a small clearing that had a fresh pool of rainwater, they stopped to rest. Bloated land leeches fell from their exposed flesh one by one, while those that remained were rubbed off with chewed tobacco spittle. The Kayan men arranged buttock mats on the damp ground before they sat. Bujang, however, sat directly on the moist earth, and the sight was a wonder to the party, for his attire appeared princely, and his iron shone as though polished with the fat of great conquests. Yet he was without a buttock mat or even a small basket to carry tobacco and an extra loincloth.

Bujang's childlike manner satisfied the old man's belief that the Ape Man was indeed sent by the gods to protect him on that expedition. Before his party had set out for the journey, the augur had predicted danger by observing the flight of the omen hawks. As a consequence, the wise men of *Tuai* Laing's community had elicited an omen from the spirits that promised his safe return. It was critical for the chiefs of settlements about the upper and lower reaches of the Rajang to meet every three harvestings to renew their peace pact. Particularly so when the meeting itself was one of the conditions. If no witness from his group had been able to return and report that Terbai Lang had attacked them, his son would be required by customs to seek out the murderer and thus jeopardize the fragile peace bargain.

After listening for some time to Bujang's tale of his experiences since leaving his childhood longhouse, the youngest warrior, Jau Rong, asked, "How could you have survived meeting the strange spirits if you are unaware of the proper conduct and sacrifices?"

"I am not sure. I had always been empty handed, although I was never turned down. Only one spirit asked for an offering. After I offered him the boar he asked for, we ate and drank together. Then he pierced my flesh and made this mark on it."

On hearing this, *Tuai* Laing smiled and said, "I do not think he asked for an offering. He wanted you to prove yourself. Is it not the way of your people to send a boy out hunting alone in the jungle and to have him return a man? The mark on your shoulder is a gift to mark your future conquests, and it tells everyone that you have pleased him. What will happen to the world if the spirits only receive but do not give? No one understands their actions. Yet we should always remember the *adats*, the ceremonial customs, so as not to anger them. The wrath of a god is like a terrible storm: it will not harm only one man but also many who are living close to him."

Jau Rong eyed Bujang Maias with dread as he wondered if this warrior's presence would bring disaster to his people. *Tuai* Laing's smiling face, however, calmed the boy, for the headman was so old that some believed his wisdom was an open-eyed vision into the netherworld.

The chief stood up and said, "Come, let us go now. We shall have much leisure to learn more of each other once we are in my house."

The party resumed their journey at a slower pace, for the trail next went through an area thick with thorny rattan vines that clung onto their baskets and loincloths like hosts urging them to stay for a moment longer. The speed picked up when the way before them again cleared, and they jogged until their shadows grew long on the ground.

At length, *Tuai* Laing halted the party at the edge of a low cliff.

Bujang looked down and saw the largest longhouse he had ever seen in his life. It stretched for over a mile and stood about thirty yards away from a winding, swift river. Even from that distance, he could appreciate the thickness of the eighteen-foot pillars that kept the inhabitants safe above predators and floods. In patches of an open field about the perimeter of the house where fruit trees of tiny or wide or palmate leaves fluttered in the breeze, men and women toiled. Across the river, and some twenty yards' distance behind the building, a jungle dense with vine, figs, soft barks and resin grew. Glistening like a jewel a short distance away, stood a low hill cleared of trees and lush with green stalks of rice.

Tuai Laing squared his shoulders with pride as he gazed down at his home. "It was only one hundred sixteen family quarters five harvestings ago. The river grew wider to bless us, and we moved the house to higher ground. Now we have one hundred eighty-six *bileks*."

Agilely, the chief picked his way down a slippery white clay path cut into the slope ahead of them. People looked up from their work when he called out a greeting and responded with joyous voices that rang through the clear air. A large crowd thronged out to the open veranda of the longhouse and then poured to the ground. *Tuai* Laing made his way towards an old hut squatting along a path between the house and the river, where the trophy head and other items for travel were placed. Then the party trudged to the river for a bath as children ran behind, beside and ahead of them.

Split logs that stretched to the edge of the low-tide river created a footway across the muddy yellow bank. The men followed it down to a large wooden platform that floated on more logs. A haven of calm water surrounded it, for a wall of rocks stood in the way of the oncoming river. To the downstream side of the platform, five dugout boats were moored to stakes erected in a row. A sixth craft, manoeuvred by a robust boatman, stopped by the pier to disembark three passengers. Each of the two women – one young the other old –and a bent old man wore a wide-brim mushroom-like hat made of overlapping dried palm leaves. Their long-sleeved work shirts were caked with dirt and sweat.

Bujang stared at the burdens they unloaded from the boat. One wide, three-foot-high burden basket was so full that its side flap seemed about to spill out *cempedak*s, bananas and the glossy white pith of mature palm. Fern, maize and bamboo shoots brimmed over two other smaller baskets.

Bujang was not surprised when the old woman took off her hat and sang a song of praise to the spirits for the safe return of her chief. The song seemed worthy of his stature:

Who is this standing over our swift river? Is it not the son
   of the land?
Many long days has he been gone, many long days have we
   not caught the scent of his tobacco.
Blessed are the spirits that returned him to us.
Blessed are the gods that lit his way home.
Tonight the people shall eat without trouble in their hearts
   and watchmen need not strain their eyes in the dark for
   him.

The woman's hearty song brought out a chortle of joy from the young boatman. He paddled to the end of the row of boats, moored the craft and deftly clambered over the other vessels to get to the platform. With the help of the two women, he lifted the largest burden basket onto his shoulders and slipped a crown strap onto his brow to steady the pack. As he hastened along the wooden-plank path, the women slung a basket each on their shoulders and followed him. The frail old man remained behind, squatting by the edge of the platform as he chatted with the chief.

Lush green branches on either side of the dusk-soaked river reached down to touch its naked banks. Children swam close to the platform, splashing pale droplets and inducing squeals of delight from naked toddlers. To one side, three young women beat cloth with flat pieces of wood as they did their laundry. The fronts of their dark skirts were hitched between their legs to the back to keep the fabric dry while they squatted over their labours. Their elongated earlobes stretched along pale necks until the brass, bell-shaped ornaments lay to rest above nipples as dark as the red of a ritual cloth. The intricate tattoos that crawled and swirled on the backs of their hands and along their arms also showed that they were not common women within the tribe. Every now and then, their doe-like brown eyes would turn to Bujang and just as quickly dart away.

Bujang unwound his loincloth and dropped it in the middle of the platform before diving into the icy cold river. The women gasped with wonder, for they had caught sight of his unperforated penis. Before jumping in after their guest, the other young men of the returning party also stripped, and made sure the women noticed that unlike the Iban hero, they were not boys.

Tuai Laing turned his attention to one of the young women, his granddaughter Dau, and asked her to wash Bujang's loincloth. He instructed his young grandson to run back to the house to get a fresh piece of cloth for the guest to wear. He added, "Tell the people that Grandfather has brought home the great Ape Man warrior. He saved our lives and took the head of Terbai Lang. Tell your father that he must get the people to ready a feast worthy of our guest."

Excited naked children clambered out of the river and ran back to the house, shouting and yelling for a feast the whole way. *Tuai* Laing watched their rowdy progress until his grandson disappeared into the house. Then, as he dipped himself into the river, five elderly men came onto the platform and squatted at the edge where he bathed. He gave them news from the other villages and recounted the tale of Terbai Lang's attack. They squinted at the visitor and let out long breaths of wonder at his girth, for he was certainly the wild man the Penans claimed to have seen walking among the apes.

The sound of men calling out for tools and bamboo drifted towards the river as a swarm of people clustered over the old hut, which had not been used for many harvestings and was in need of repair. Some of the men had been teenage boys when the last trophy heads were brought to the longhouse and could barely recall seeing any being roasted in the hut. Two men climbed up to the roof and added fresh palm leaves. Another carried a thick lump of fresh clay inside. Others tested the building by shaking parts of it, then re-strapping rattan strips or hammering in wooden pegs where necessary. More men brought firewood. Soon, smoke could be seen blowing out of an opening in the roof. Young palm leaves were also brought into the hut.

Bujang stepped out of the river with one hand over his loin and was dismayed to see a young woman beating on his cloth. A small boy handed him a fresh but shorter dark cloth. He thanked the child and proceeded to put on this newly borrowed garment by twisting the fabric around his waist once. The same child passed another cloth to *Tuai* Laing. Then he hugged the old man's thigh and stared wide-eyed at the guest. *Tuai* Laing chuckled when the boy stood, unmoving, even as he tapped the child's back twice with the cloth.

Once the freshly washed travellers had returned to the hut, they found three old men and two old women waiting for them around a clay fireplace. Each eyed the bundled head by turn, and talked in low voices among themselves. They recalled Terbai Lang's terrible deeds by turn. If the chief himself had not witnessed the truce-breaker's death, they would not have believed that his head was now in the hut with them. When Bujang opened the cloth, the elders recoiled in horror, for dark purple veins stood out on the trophy's forehead and the bloodshot eyes shone with living rage. A long tongue trailed out of the mouth, from between a pair of sharp, fang-like teeth that protruded out of the lower gum.

Tuai Laing squatted in front of the head and said to Bujang, "Give me your sword, my son. You have done a heroic deed when you took this demon's head, and everyone living in the land of Sengalang Burong shall know of it."

The chief used the blade to cut thick strands of hair from Terbai Lang's head. Then he forced thin bunches into slits in Bujang's sword handle, after which he stuffed wood resin to keep them in place.

Five young boys, between the ages of seven to nine, were brought in for an initiation rite. The old warrior took out his own sword and clasped his hand over theirs as he helped them strike the trophy. To each boy he said, "See you have struck an enemy. You will be a great warrior one day."

After the children left, an elder handled a small knife, picked up the head and started scoring out strips of flesh, which he set aside on a palm leaf. The clinging vertebrae were pulled away, and brain matter was extracted from the hole under the skull with a large hook before the head was burnt over a slow fire. Young men brought in more fresh firewood. One of them, a beautiful warrior whom the chief introduced to Bujang as his son Baho, was instructed to ready a party to collect their dead.

When the first scent of cooking meat and rice wafted into the hut, the travellers left the elders to their gory work to join a crowd of men around a campfire set outside the longhouse. A bard sang songs of their bravery, turning every action by the heroes into poetry to be passed down to the next generation of singers. Middle-aged women tied strips of palm leaf on the men's left wrist. Boys who had struck the trophy were also given leaf bracelets. Bujang, who struck the death blow, received more palm leaves in his war cap. Then finely chopped tobacco was rolled up in dry, square banana leaves and lit at the fire. As the men smoked, a fragrant perfume filled the air and mingled with the smell of cooking food. Soon after dinner, the tired men lay down to sleep on the dew-covered ground with their travelling blankets over them.

* * *

The next morning, the crows of persistent roosters woke the people before sunrise. Children swarmed about the camp, wide-eyed and curious as to why the travel-weary adults had not spent the night in the longhouse. Eight men, two of whom straddled toddlers on their laps, had brought food and water for their breakfast and stayed and kept them company. Others erected a long bamboo pole next to one of the two altar-posts, both of which were thick, black timber with staring faces carved at the top.

After satisfying himself with the general progress of works at the altar of the One Supreme Being, *Tuai* Laing strolled to the hut to see how much had been done in the preparation of the trophy. All flesh that had not been scraped off the head had been burned off, leaving only the grinning skull. He watched the elders pierce a hole in the crown. Once that was done, a strip of rattan was tied on one end and threaded through the foramen, then through the man-made hole. More strips were twisted around the lower jaw to strap it firmly to the skull.

Finally they covered the whole head in palm leaves, and an ancient man placed it on his shoulder before carrying it to the altar post. The long bamboo pole, decorated with more palm leaves, now had a rope dangling from the top. The old man tied the end of the rattan strip to it and left the skull hanging. Pieces of shrivelled flesh that had been stripped from the face and smoked were skewered atop short bamboo stands planted before the altar-posts, and all those present looked up to the sky for a hawk to come down and accept the offering of flesh.

And so the celebration continued until, after four days of noisy merrymaking before the altar, the old man again placed the trophy on his shoulder and stood at the head of a grand procession. The men trailing behind him all wore rich loincloths that reached down to their ankles, carved bones or canine teeth that curved out of the shells of their ears, and feathers that fluttered on their heads. Vests of animal fur covered their chests, and some wore large, shiny discs of shell or iron over the vests. The women were dressed in dark skirts and jackets embroidered with all the colours that the rainforest could offer. Fine embroidered caps decorated with beads or clumps of bristling fur graced their heads and, around the waists of some, were strings of beads and shells.

The procession were led to the altar posts and proudly presented themselves to their god. More than ninety pigs were either laid on their sides or tied to posts about the area, for every family that could afford to do so had offered an animal to be sacrificed. The air was saturated with squeals when the pigs were speared, and the ground became drenched in puddles of blood as each was cut open. Elders studied the livers and pronounced their findings to the concerned families. The chief collected blood from one pig in a bamboo cup and sprinkled it on his people with a shredded palm leaf as he blessed them.

The sun blazed through the morning coolness, adding to the day's heat layer by layer as it climbed to the cusp of noon and down the western horizon. Finally, when the day began to cool, the procession, led by the old man, climbed the common ladder to bear the trophy into the house for the first time. They sang and stomped and shouted down the whole length, shaking the building from end to end. And as though to show that the tumult they were making did not do justice to their joy, some brought out rice pestles from their *bileks* and pounded the floor to add to the commotion.

Bamboo and bark doors swung open and shut as squealing children ran in and out of the rooms whose walls were decorated with drawings of birds and animals in colours of red, white and black. Piercing through the wooden floor across the whole length of the common gallery every four or five yards was a long line of strong pillars, all covered with woven cloth and encircled with food and rice wine.

The men stomped their feet in tune and turned fierce faces to their left and right. Old and young arms waved tattooed hands in the air, reminiscent of serpents beckoning in the breeze. Children ran ahead of the procession and shrieked with delight as adults teased them with exaggerated, scowls.

After the procession had danced through the whole length of the house twice over, the trophy was brought to the chief's *ruai*. Elders and proven warriors poured into the common gallery in front of *Tuai* Laing's quarters. The people sat along the length of the gallery facing each other while they waited for a group of men and women to serve them food and wine. Then six women, bare breasted and dressed in loincloths like the men, came forward and took possession of the head. They imitated the men's war dance as they swung the trophy to and fro. Finally the head was handed to a pair of ancient men who hung it above the principal column, among eighty other trophies that had been handed down from one generation to the next.

The noise of festivity subsided when the chief once more recalled how the head was taken. Men eyed Bujang in awe, for no party had ever survived Terbai Lang's attack, yet here now, in this longhouse, was his head. They all nodded approvingly when the young visitor was given a seat next to the chief. It was a place of great honour, for the old man had been a feared warrior in his heyday, and his enemies continued to speak his name only in whispers. Many believed that Terbai Lang's arrogance in attacking him had aroused the wrath of the chief's guardian, the macaque spirit. Yet others recalled that the hawks had promised a safe passage to him before he embarked on the journey.

Once the chief ended his tale, the augur of the house, a bent old man, was lifted up by a warrior as he offered wine in a small bamboo cup to the head. This cup was hung next to the trophy. Then pig fat was shoved into its mouth. He called upon the spirit of the slain warrior to bless and protect the house. If his presence brought good harvests to the people, he promised that the head would be kept warm for many generations. He rejoiced because the house had acquired a strong and feared guardian; then he blessed the hero with the strength and courage of the enemy he had felled.

Bujang felt proud, yet bashful at the same time. He kept his eyes focused on the tip of his toes as the chief again recounted his courage and skill. Each time the old man patted his shoulder, he would look up, startled, and quickly look down again like a shy groom. He barely ate when food was placed before him, and he chuckled each time someone called him a hero.

After dinner, the people thronged about the chief's gallery and craned their necks to get a better view of the strange guest. Young men wondered over his unmarked fingers and hands, and elders gawked at the rosettes on his shoulders, for the shades of black and brown were unfamiliar to them. Two old men separated themselves from the crowd and, in a dim corner of the house, drew invisible patterns on their palms as they discussed the tattoo design to give the hero.

Before the sun lit the horizon of a new day, they took out a wood block each and began carving. By the time the women had begun to mix an ink brew of soot, sugar-cane juice and water in a shallow bamboo cup, the finer details had been added unto the blocks. This tattoo would prove to Maligang, the guardian of the bridge of souls, that Bujang was a brave warrior, an accomplished man, and that he deserved to cross into the glorious place in the land of the dead. If Maligang were to see the tattoos, he would let Bujang pass without trouble. He would not shake the bridge and cause Bujang to fall into the river of suffering, where he would be consumed by the giant fish Patan. Bujang and Jau Rong, the only two persons of the returned party who did not have tattoos on their hands, were made to sit cross-legged side by side. The back of Bujang's hands and fingers were marked and stamped with designs from the carved blocks, while Jau Rong only had his thumbs coloured in the ink, since he had been part of the scuffle but had not taken any trophy. Two women took up their positions in front of each man. One tapped a striker on the tattooing rod, which had thorns glued to the end, while the other assisted her by stretching the skin of the man who was to receive the pattern.

And now Bujang Maias learned what he had not known before: that there were spots of flesh on the back of his hand more sensitive than he had ever imagined. To make matters worse, his design was elaborate, and as black as the chest of a hornbill, so he had to suffer through a lengthy session. *Tuai* Laing gave him some *tuak* in a long bamboo cup. He drank the wine in one gulp, which earned him the admiration of the men. The women worked from morning to late afternoon over him, after which, the freshly tattooed man went through another bout of drinking and eating with the people.

The feasting continued for days, and even Bujang was caught up in the revelling, yet each night a group of men would not drink. A few inebriated revellers teased the sentries and described every single sweet sip of their cup, but the warriors minded them not because revenge would come soon enough, when the shift changed the following night.

The festivities to thank the gods for their blessing and protection lasted so long that the inhabitants were exhausted by the end of the fifth day and slept where they had fallen on the common corridor.

Late that night, the chief's son, Baho, heard a fowl on the ground below give out a single squawk. He put his face against a crevice in the floor. Below was total darkness and absolute silence. He signalled to his companions that there could be trouble, for a wild animal would have frightened many fowls, not just one.

Just as the men unsheathed their *ilangs*, a loud rumble filled the air. It was so loud it shook the house to the rafters from end to end. Sleeping occupants woke up in fright and rushed out of their *bileks*. It was the children's laughter that brought the sentries to the source of the disturbance – Bujang Maias's snoring. The young man was so drunk that the noise of the whole house laughing did not wake him.

* * *

Under the building, men held their breaths and froze where they stood. The torches in their hands had not been lit. The leader wondered what the roar above was and why the people were laughing. The scouts had waited for many days for the longhouse to lie in stupor from their festivities because that was the only way to attack such a formidable group of warriors. The heads of Kayans from the house of *Tuai* Laing would have made his house and the house of his accomplices the most feared in all the land, but now all his careful plans had come to nothing. The leader hooted a bird call and his warriors retreated in the pitch dark.

A hornbill that had perched on the roof flew off.

6

Baho stepped out onto the veranda. A new morning blew down the river, both urging and following the crows of roosters. Soon, a hint of light appeared in the distant horizon. Armed with a sword each, Baho together with five men went under the house to learn whether their fear of the night before was real or imagined. Everything appeared normal, the idle boats lying bottom side up and bundled tools hanging on the pillars undisturbed. A pig snorted at Baho for peering into its pen, and the scavenging fowls that had been frightened off by their appearance returned to peck incessantly on seemingly empty ground. The hard, greenish clay surface yielded no sign.

But soon a man who found a line of trampled grass called out from the back of the building. He pointed to a path that only a large party moving in single file could have made in one night. Baho and the others followed the incoming trail for two miles through the jungle. Traps which the people had laid out to ward off unwelcome visitors had been set off but appeared to be ineffective, for sharpened sticks lay on the side untainted, and across from them, springpoles stood away from the loops of vines that had held them down the night before. Baho suspected that a clever scout had released the cord triggers with a stick, which would explain why the group had walked in single file and risked creating a path through the jungle.

The group trod over the track until they reached the edge of a low cliff and looked down. Involuntarily, their legs bent and their swords rose, for the empty, muddy bank below had been scored by dozens of boats.

Biting his *ilang* between his teeth, Baho grabbed a vine hanging on the side and scrambled down. As the men climbed down after him, they each made sure not to release the creeper or root until their feet touched the ground because mischievous spirits tend to play hallucinating tricks to make one believe that the ground is nearer than it really is.

Softly Baho said, "Stay close; there are only six of us. Scouts may still be here."

They counted eight small campfire residues hidden in niches along the bank. A beam, resting on two platforms, stood not more than five yards away from the scored bank. Baho approached it and counted the notches cut into the wood – two hundred and sixty headhunters. He wondered who would have the gall to attack them. *Tuai* Laing had made a pact of peace with the other leaders in the region. The peace pact had been so successful, there had been no war expeditions in the area for the last five harvestings.

The back of every hand that held the *ilang* was dark from tattoos, yet anger turned to dismay as each man realized how close he had been to losing his life and his offspring to the enemy. Sensing their panic, Baho lifted an arm to warn his men not to voice their fear because the invaders might have left a spy to guard the area. The chief's son next studied the ground behind the beam, a place where a leader would stand to welcome his warriors. One set of prints had three toes missing on the left foot. He scowled and signalled with a tilt of his head for the men to return to the longhouse.

They climbed back up the incline and ran home like the wind, though each stride they took seemed to take them farther from their families. When they finally heard the laughter of children coming from the back perimeter of the longhouse, the relief that washed over them felt as cool water to the thirsty.

No sooner had they reached the children then Baho called out angrily, "Don't play here. Hungry spirits prowl at the edge of the jungle. Go find your parents." Startled, the children ran off in fright from the usually mild-mannered Baho.

As the men walked under the house to the front, Baho said, "Tell the other sentries what we saw. We will double the guards and get the youngsters to help set more traps."

On reaching the front of the house, Baho climbed up the nearest standing bamboo ladder. The lively sound of laughing and teasing made him pause midway, and he watched as Bujang Maias walked towards the river with a throng of children running about him. They were telling him to change his name to Bujang Guntor, "Thunder Man" or Bujang Palau, "Drunken Man."

Baho called out, his voice ringing to the heavens, "Stop your foolishness. That is no way to treat a guest!" Or a god, he almost added.

The hair on his nape stood as the thought crossed his mind. He clambered the rest of the way up, crossed the veranda and pounded down the common gallery, making planks shake under his heavy and swift footfall. He threw open the door to his father's *bilek*, making *Tuai* Laing look up with a start. The old man was unadorned and wearing only a simple dark loincloth. Dried gourd loofahs and fresh twigs clasped in his hand showed that he was about to go out for his morning bath.

Baho said, "Father, we found strange tracks and a large camp some two miles from here. The headhunters' crossbeam indicated a large party of two hundred sixty men. I saw Salang's footprint. He was here last night."

The chief's face crinkled into a scowl. "The truce breaker. He must be here to avenge his uncle's death some twelve years ago. Why did he not attack?"

"I think Bujang Maias's snore must have frightened them last night. Maybe they thought his presence a bad omen."

Tuai Laing chuckled until he noticed the anxious frown on his son's face. "What else did you see?"

"It is not what I see father, it is what I feel. Bujang Maias. The children were rude to him this morning and the whole longhouse laughed at him last night. Father, he may be a god or a guardian. There is too much uncommonness in his manner and bearing. What are we to do to take away this curse from us?"

The old man nodded thoughtfully. "Call for the *Tuai Burong.* Ask the augur to learn from the spirits who this man really is. We must not call him what he is not. It is taboo. I will talk with Bujang and find out if we have offended him. It will not do for him to part from our people in anger. A great warrior who is not a friend will become an enemy."

The chief thought about his son's worries as he walked out of his quarters and smiled at the men and women who had gathered in his *ruai.* His face revealed no concern, though, and this untroubled demeanour calmed the people enough to persuade them to return to the work that had been abruptly interrupted by an agitated sentry.

As *Tuai* Laing walked down the gallery, he called for his grandchildren. "Where are you, my little Flower? Where is my Rock? Where are the little Bird and the crying Hawk? Is my Bear awake, is my Bamboo Shoot playing on her bed? This old grandfather is ready to bathe. He will be lonely without them."

Little faces poked out from different *bileks,* and each child rushed out after the grandfather. The old man called out again, "Come, wind, and blow gentle breezes on these children. Come, rain, and shower on their crops. Jungle, be good to them and give them food and vines. Lengthen their days that they may be wise before they begin their journey to the land beyond this world."

The older children ran ahead, down the steep ladder, and bolted towards the river. Their younger cousins, however, crept down the steps on their buttocks under the gentle urgings of their grandfather. They followed the path to the bathing place, greeting and returning the greetings of everyone they met. The land about *Tuai* Laing reflected the fragmented rainbow colours of the sun from a thousand drops of morning dew, and from the jungle behind him came the barks of hornbills, the twittering of sunbirds and the screeches of macaques that blended with the *kreet-kreet* symphony of insects.

When he reached the bathing platform, he let out a long sigh of displeasure on seeing Bujang swimming naked in the river with a rowdy group of children. They jumped about him and splashed water into his face with full abandon. The young man laughed and lifted a boy above his head before throwing him back into the water.

Tuai Laing had seen enough. "Hoi, do not show such disrespect to a guest. Let him bathe in peace, else I will call out the crocodiles. Go home, go home. Go to the fields with your mothers and fathers."

Wet children squealed as they scrambled up the platform and ran back to the house, for the chief was well reputed to be a man of his words. They were not ready to face crocodiles yet.

The old man dipped into the river after his grandchildren, making sure that the youngest two clung onto the sides. He scrubbed the toddlers with a loofah and made them giggle with surprise tickles from his fingers. At length, the two men heaved themselves out. After donning dry loincloths, they squatted to one side of the platform. *Tuai* Laing passed a fresh twig to Bujang and proceeded to chew on the other well-used stick and to scrub his teeth with it, all the while keeping an eye on his grandchildren.

Gradually the platform began to fill with people who had

returned from their morning toil in the fields, and the calmer side of the river came alive with splashing youngsters. Adults scooped cold water with coconut shells to pour over the heads of their struggling infants. Young women exfoliated their skin with yellow turmeric root that gave them a golden glow. Some did their laundry, and the air began to resonate with the sound of cloth slapping on timber. Those on their way back to the longhouse filled bamboo tubes with water from the oncoming current and carried them back in wide baskets slung on their backs.

This went on, until *Tuai* Lang became aware of how much time had passed. It was time to eat – and time to closely observe Bujang, to discern whether he could be the reason for Salang's attack plan.

After persuading the most active of his grandchildren that it was time to return, *Tuai* Laing made them march or race ahead of him. The chief then invited Bujang to his quarters for breakfast. His granddaughter Dau unrolled a wide mat for them in the middle of the spacious room. *Tuai* Laing sat down facing the door and indicated with his hand for Bujang to sit next to him.

Though Bujang had stayed with them for close to a week, this was the first time he had been inside the quarters. A square patch of sunlight beamed down from the open roof onto a dark wooden floor that shone from constant scrubbing with dry coconut husks. Five tall jars with paintings of red, blue or green flying serpents and long-tailed birds lined one wall. On the other wall, spears, swords and shields stood side by side behind a row of overflowing baskets. At the end of the row hung a flat, wide piece of copper sheet which looked like a peaceful, clear pool that reflected everything it saw.

A slave served them rice, wild vegetables and broiled fish on wooden plates. Bujang washed his hand in the bowl she placed before him and asked her to eat with them. The old woman shyly replied that she would breakfast with her mistress. Then she passed them a tube of illipe butter, which made the chief grin wide. He stamped the slender bamboo tube over their hot rice to grease the grains with it, releasing a tangy aroma that further whetted their appetites.

In the middle of the meal, Baho entered the room with the old augur clinging onto his back. Three middle-aged men trailed behind them, and more food and drink were served to the new guests. In a soft voice, the augur asked Bujang about himself, from as far as he could remember. He smiled and nodded at points of interest in Bujang's story.

When the young man reached the end of his tale, *Tuai* Laing instructed one of the men to crop the front of Bujang's hair and to pluck his eyebrows and sideburns. His time of mourning had ended, for he had killed his father's murderer.

Perceiving how young Bujang's knowledge of the manners of men was, the chief said, "Remember to make sure they burn your cut hair, my son. Do not allow anyone to take it from you even for a keepsake. You are a friend of this house, not an enemy for my people to use to decorate their swords."

Bujang thanked the old man for his advice; then he got up and left the room with the other man. After some moments of thoughtful silence, *Tuai* Laing asked, "Well, augur, who do you think the man is?"

"He is no god. Neither is he a guardian," replied the augur. "His being adopted by *Tok* Anjak is a point of great interest, since I have never heard tales of an ape adopting a human. Would the gods allow such a thing?"

"His story seems to create more questions than answers. Who was the man that gave him the sword? And why did the spirit he met at the river not introduce himself?" Baho asked.

The augur said, "A wise warrior keeps the source of his strength hidden, and he guards his terrors close to his heart. Did he tell you who made the sheath for his *ilang*?"

Tuai Laing shook his head.

The augur reached for a clump of tobacco, rolled it into a ball and rubbed it over his gum and the few remaining teeth. Finally he said, "A great spirit watches over his iron. The two rosettes on his shoulders are strange, for Terbai Lang's head was his first. Could they be a sign of future expeditions? It is hard to say. I have never heard of anything like this before."

"Do you think he will harm us?" *Tuai* Laing asked.

"You have added his enemy's hair to the hilt of his sword, and the people of this house have tattooed the back of his hand. If he survives the test of fate, your kindness will be remembered and this house will be rewarded with a strong ally."

Baho asked, "Should we invite him to stay with us, then?"

The augur shook his head. "I sense that this will not become his home, for this house is blessed with many strong men. The gods will send him to another place, maybe in answer to a prayer or as the harbinger of a curse. Yet as is the way of a wanderer, it shall be a woman who will provide a home for him."

Tuai Laing nodded, "Yes, you are right old friend. His eyes have not strayed to any of the women of this house, though many of them can trace their ancestry back to the beautiful daughters of the god of heaven."

Baho said, "Then we shall give him a gift fit for a hero. We shall make him a shield worthy of a man whose very presence saved our lives."

After saying those words, Baho stood up and strode out of the *bilek*. He took four men with him: Uta the woodsman, Ngipo the storyteller, Mawan the farmer and young Jau Rong.

Each man collected his trusty *parang*, a two-foot-long machete, and tied the blade around his waist with a cord. Uta slung two coils of sturdy rope on his shoulder, while Jau Rong unhooked an axe hanging on the wall outside his quarters.

As he stood on the high veranda, Baho shaded his eyes to study the land about him. Beyond the frothing waters, on the other side of the river, the white branches of a honeybee tree stood out against the empty sky. The sub-canopy beneath it was lush with young red leaves. Thrusting out of their foliage like stout mushrooms were the fluting branches of Merantis. He realized that he would have to travel far into the jungle to find wood as good as those on their side of the river, so he made up his mind to do his search on the opposite side.

The men piled into his boat, each carrying a personal paddle. Once they'd left the calmer waters and approached the fast-flowing low tide, Baho stood up on the stern to scan the waters ahead and called out his instructions. A storm rose in their bellies to match the water swirling against the rocks that lay in their path. The boatmen roared above the sound of the rapids to subdue it. At Baho's signal, they swung left, then made a sharp turn right. Again, Baho called and was answered by a sharp left swing. A rock as large as two men scraped against the side, and wave after wave of water rolled into the boat. Again and again they turned and twisted their way between rocks that protruded out of the water or lay just beneath its surface, so that when they finally reached the calmer currents close to the banks, they let out a triumphant shout.

Baho pointed to the lowest part of the bank, and the men rowed in that direction. The shallow draft slid over soft yellow mud and loose pebbles; then the boat was pulled ashore into the underbrush. Once satisfied that the craft was well out of the reach of a full tide, the men collected their gear and trudged into the jungle. The leaves were so bright that they seemed to reflect the little light that filtered through the canopy. Barbets of striking green and blue called from the branches and flew off. Startled out of its sleep in the tree, a black bearcat leapt away from them. The men said nothing among themselves, but they each recognized the omen as one which meant that their work that morning would be blessed by the spirits.

After a mile of hacking through thick foliage, they stopped to survey their surroundings. Baho approached the grey buttress root of the honeybee tree that was as tall as forty men. One side of its roots was stained golden. Shading his eyes, he looked up, and sure enough, high above the ground was a giant beehive that spanned the whole length of a straight branch.

Jau Rong came to stand next to him, being not much help to the others, for he was still unlearned as to the manner of wood that would make a good shield.

"I don't think the five of us can carry this one back."

Baho chuckled. "No, it is not wise to fell a tree that gives us sweet honey and grubs."

Jau Rong slapped his arm and legs restlessly as he watched one particular man. Then, as if unable to contain his curiosity, he asked, "Why did you invite Mawan with us?"

"He is a strong and hard-working man. It is good to have one like him in our party."

"But he was a slave, and he stole your love from you."

Baho smiled. "He did not steal her from me. She chose to go to him, and she paid the full price for his freedom. I was only a boy, and she a woman when I loved her. I have no regrets. I have my wife, my children and my fields."

Jau Rong responded with more nervous slapping and scratching. Baho pointed up to the branches and said, "See this *Tualang* here? It is a symbol of ever-growing strength. It reminds us that the bloodline of a man is not important. His roots may be shallow, but if he is like this tree, even his weakest origin will grow into buttresses and hold him up as he reaches for the heavens."

Jau Rong was not convinced. "Is it the same for Bujang, then, cousin? He came from the loins of a common man, a man whose virtues have never been heard of in our land. Even his mother's name is unknown to our weavers. He grew up with apes, which neither live in houses nor work in fields. How can he become greater than you, a prince of our people?"

Baho gazed skyward. A hawk soared far above the tree, while another perched on the highest branch. He turned his gaze back to Jau Rong and said, "Because this is the land of Sengalang Burong, and in the customs of this land, the title of chief is never inherited, it is earned. No man can claim greatness from the labours of another."

Suddenly a call from eight yards away made them turn, "*Apai* Dana, this tree here looks good."

Baho approached the tree and nodded with approval on seeing the straight-bole meranti with branches that stretched ever upwards to the sun. Its smooth bark was covered in moss and creepers, giving it a flaky aspect. It was still young at about two feet wide and fifteen feet high.

On reaching the spot, Baho patted the trunk and was pleased with the thick, soft thumping sound it gave out.

"This is good wood. It will make a good shield."

He took the axe from Jau Rong and swung it at the base of the trunk. The iron sunk into the wood and became stuck. His muscle strained as he pulled out the blade. He took another swing. Again it became stuck. This time he could not pull it out.

Baho leaned one hand against the trunk and said to the tree, "It is not for myself that I strike you. Neither is it for any man of my house. Your wood will be used to make a shield for Bujang Maias, the son of *Tok* Anjak. You will shield him from his enemies and grasp their swords for him. You will be his companion and carry his trophies for him. Children will speak of you, and men will cower before you. I take you down today, so you may go before him in war to herald his courage before his enemies."

Once more he put his hand on the axe handle, and the blade came unstuck. The other men stepped back with eyes wide and mouths gaping. Again Baho swung the blade, and a large chunk of wood fell to the ground. He swung another time, and a piece as wide as his hand came loose. Three more swings and the tree began to sway. He stepped to the uncut side and sunk the axe into it. A groan filled the air. He pushed. The soft wood cracked like thunder, and the branches of adjacent trees whipped the air as it fell past them.

The men swarmed over it to cut away the branches. They burnt every single loose piece, including the leaves. None dared to use the fire, not even to rid the leeches stuck to their calves, because it was obvious to them that the tree had only yielded to the axe after Baho explained that its wood was to be made into a shield for Bujang. They were unwilling to test their souls against its spirit.

After the trunk had been cut down to a length of six feet, four men heaved it onto their shoulders and, with Jau Rong walking ahead of them, they started the trek back to the boat.

On reaching the river, they saw that the tide had risen as they'd hoped it would. They lashed the log with ropes and rolled it into the water. Then the boat was carried in, and the men paddled their way home, dragging the log behind them in the quiet tide.

The trip back was uneventful, and finally they arrived at their point of departure. Except for a few men who had returned early from fishing, the pier was almost empty. Three more men helped them drag the log out of the river. Once more it was hitched to their shoulders as they wound their way back to the house. As one, they climbed a common ladder (this was made by cutting away parts of a log at regular intervals) and placed their labour on the chief's open veranda. Baho took out a wide piece of floor mat from his quarters and rolled the log onto it.

A middle-aged man asked, "Why are you doing that? Our rough work will ruin your mat."

"Not a single piece of wood will go to waste. Every part of it shall be only for Bujang's use. Remember, every single piece, even the chips must be burned, and only his food may be cooked over the fire."

An old man wondered aloud about the instruction, for he had never in his long life heard of such a thing. Taking delight in the attention he was getting, Ngipo recalled the incident of that morning to the people. Each retelling of the tale to new audiences had new details that grew ever more vivid and frightful. Only two of the most experienced carvers were allowed to hack on the log as the people kept their distance. It was the most difficult wood they had ever worked on, and every now and then they had to stop to sing or to talk to it. Though working on it put a sore strain on their experienced hands, both men marvelled at how well the wood grasped and imagined that it would hold captive every enemy who would dare cut into its surface.

Neither Bujang nor *Tuai* Laing was in the house that afternoon because they had gone to inspect the rice field. Hence, on their return, they were surprised to see people milling around the open veranda.

After placing their overflowing baskets and tools in the *bilek*, they joined the swelling crowd. Bujang watched the activity with curiosity and was astonished when told that the shield was for him.

He said, "I would like to carve the surface myself."

One of the carvers looked up from his squatting position and said, "We can pass the frame to you after it is done. I will lend you my carving knives." True to his words, after he had strapped down rattan strips to reinforce the top and bottom of the shield, the carver brought out his best carving knives for Bujang.

Tuai Laing provided Bujang with a piece of charcoal which he used to draw on the new hexagonal frame. Bujang etched upon it a boyhood memory of the monster head he had seen strapped to Keling's *terabai*. So engrossed was he in his art that he became oblivious to his surroundings. When he looked up, a row of frightened eyes returned his gaze. Some whispered that he was arrogant and callous for invoking the spirit of a raging demon to protect his shield, while others marvelled at the strength of his soul and his ability to make this spirit submit to his will. Baho parted the crowd and squatted next to him. "Where is this design from?"

"I saw a live head once when I was a boy. It is only a pattern of what I saw."

Shyly, Baho asked, "Will you draw on our walls? I know that I should not ask this of you, but you appear to be so gifted by the spirits."

"It is a great honour to do as you ask. You and your people have been kind to me. It is a gift I cannot refuse to give."

The following morning, uproar spread like a surging tide in the common gallery. In charcoal, Bujang had drawn over its whole length a rude relief of the pattern he envisioned for the house. He had done it while the people slept. Only the sentries had seen him at work. On *Tuai* Laing's wall was the outline of a man who sat with arms stretched and branching out to his left and right, thus becoming part of, or entwined with, the original drawings of plants and animals decorating each family quarters.

It was a tree of life for a house that would never die: the Ape Man's gift to the people who had welcomed him. The great length of the fig vine showed health, and the thick stems held promises of many fruitful seasons.

Eager to complete and make permanent the rough outline Bujang had made, the people collected soot from hearth, rust from iron and limestone chalk from the hills. Nobody went to the field that morning as each dyed his own wall. Children ran about and older folks sang praises to the spirits as the people painted.

While they worked, Bujang finished carving a pattern in low relief on his shield and painted it in black and red, leaving the teeth and background untouched. All admired it, and again there was dancing and eating.

However, the revelry subsided when Bujang announced that he intended to resume his journey come first light. Men and women gathered in the veranda that night and cooked rice, roasted meat and boiled eggs on makeshift hearths. They used up all the remaining wood that had been left over from his shield. And, eventually, they slept.

All too soon, a faint breeze brought the scent of a waking day. The land was unusually quiet that morning as the people bid farewell to Bujang. Baho passed him a new burden basket with dark shoulder straps. The rattan canes, woven to resemble overlapping gourds, shone yellow under the dim morning light. Cooked rice wrapped in leaves and smoked meat filled the *selabit* for his journey. Every family that could afford to give had supplied him food. Baho had also added a short piece of dried rattan to help him start his fires.

In honour of his departure, *Tuai* Laing gave him an extra dark loincloth and a small buttock mat. The young man who had saved his life would no longer need to sit directly on the moist jungle floor. *Tuai* Laing helped tie the mat to the Ape Man's backside.

Bujang twisted back to look at it before asking, "Must it hang there? It is strange to feel it slap against my buttocks."

Many laughed as the chief patted his shoulders. "You are as precious to me as one of my own. I have never let any of my children sit directly on the wet forest floor. If they don't have mats, I tell them to sit on a large, dry leaf. It is not wise to get your loincloth wet for long periods of time. And there are also small creatures that will bite. Always they will bite in the wrong place."

Baho grasped Bujang's hand and said, "Farewell, my friend. We will always have you in our hearts."

Bujang added in return, "And I shall never forget this house in the valley of raging waters."

He turned and walked up a path to the hills. The women sang a sad farewell as he climbed the track. Their voices blended with the breeze and floated up to him, but he did not look back, for the years and inevitable losses had taught him to never regret his partings.

7

A trail of fruiting trees led Bujang farther and farther south, over sandstone hills and limestone mountains. He travelled mainly in the trees. Life in the canopies was never quiet, and many a creature asked him for news of *Tok* Anjak's passing. At times he was forced to climb down to the ground for solitude. Yet even there, a stray two-horned rhinoceros or a black sun bear would join him. He did not mind their company, for unlike the chattering monkeys and birds, they were of few words. However, each time he lit a fire, the bear would climb into the trees and the rhinoceros would amble away, for the light threw a strange, hulking form on a wall of roots and trees.

Day after day, Bujang trudged under moss-covered trunks that stretched straight and tall like pillars or hiked along the clay banks of winding rivers that bore the tracks of hidden crocodiles. Above him a waxing moon timed his journey.

* * *

One evening, after he had travelled a great distance, Bujang propped his shield against a buttress root. As he lowered himself, he adjusted the seat-mat tied from his waist so that he was sitting square on it when his hips touched the ground. He leaned back against the tree and stretched out his legs, and a small, brown frog leapt out of its camouflage of dead leaves. Mosquitoes buzzed and bit persistently, so he crushed a handful of soft leaves by the side to rub over his skin. As he did so, a bloated lowland leech fell off his ankle.

He dug for the last packet of food from his basket. A pungent aroma of stale rice assailed his nostrils as he unwrapped the leaf package. By the time he had finished dinner, the day had begun to dim, so he searched about the area for wood. After collecting an armload of twigs and branches, he took out the rattan and another piece of stick that he had dried over the fire from the night before. He rubbed the patina surface of the rattan hard against the shredded surface of the stick. The wood started to smoke. He blew, and the ember spread over its surface. He placed dried moss and bark over it and, once these caught fire, he added wood and twigs, so that soon he had a warm fire burning.

It was not too long before a brown, thirty-foot reticulated python slithered down from a vine and coiled itself on the opposite side of the fire. Bulang admired the hexagonal patches of black and yellow over the whole length of its body. But beautiful or not, the snake could be dangerous.

"The sun you brought down is good and warm. May I sleep here tonight?" the python asked.

Bujang studied the snake's swollen stomach and said, "Will you still hunt after this?"

"I have eaten my fill. It will be another week before I need to eat again. Fear not, son of *Tok* Anjak. Your shoulder has been coloured with soot from the house of heaven and your loincloth woven from a red dawn. I shall not harm you, lest the gods put a curse on me."

In the firelight, the python's orange eyes glittered like dew on hawk feather. They stared into his face, as steady as the eyes of a blowpipe hunter.

Unsettled, Bujang said, "I shall not harm you, either, for I have eaten my dinner. There is no need for you to eye my every move."

"You misunderstood. I do trust you, but I am hard of hearing. I need to look at your face to know what you say."

"Are all snakes like you?"

"Yes. Even warriors guarded by our spirits are spiritually deaf."

"Does that mean that I can creep up to a snake without it realizing my presence?"

The python's throat widened, and a long hiss shook its forked tongue. "A young, inexperienced snake, maybe. Elders like me, however, are highly tuned to our surroundings, and we can sense the slightest change."

"What if I lay in wait for one?"

"You are wise, Bujang, like your father *Tok* Anjak. Even the most experienced will not notice your presence unless you move or it sees you."

Bujang smiled, grateful for this lesson that the snake had taught him. As they talked into the night, he also learned that pythons were at their most ferocious after moulting.

His companion explained, "A python's might is in his size. The quickest way to grow is to swallow something larger than oneself while the new skin is still soft. Some of us moult three times between harvestings. Even the humans we guide will use such seasons to grow in strength, though not often and far in between. Some humans, however, are insatiable and insist to grow at every change. Instead of swallowing one, they devour many. It is unnatural, and the gods are not pleased."

He was speaking of men's warlike nature, Bujang knew. "What happens to such men?" he asked.

"Most times, nothing, for their guardians grow from strength to strength through their bloodlust." The snake's unblinking eyes stared at Bujang, and it continued, "I see you have a presence about you, in the form of a man, yet not a man. Neither hunter nor warrior..."

It stared for a moment longer before curling into a resting position. As it slowly dozed off with eyes wide open, it said, "The fire is good, old one, yes, yes, the fire is good. Tomorrow I will return to the river and tell her that I have met you. She will rejoice greatly. May the father serpent bless you and the boy."

* * *

Two days later, Bujang found himself in a sparse jungle walking on a fading path. He studied a long-forgotten man-made ridge ahead. A tree covered in greyish bark, with brown splashes and lush green leaves, caught his attention. He breathed deeply and grunted appreciatively when he picked up the strong scent of ripe *cempedak* fruits. He was hungry.

Patches of sunlight beat down on the jungle floor, enticing saplings to reach ever upwards. Although the heat drenched Bujang in sweat, the moisture that ran down his back barely cooled him in the humid air. Even his blanket was soaked, and he had to hang it over the front of his shield to rid it of dew.

Dogs bayed in the distance. Maybe there was a hunt in progress, he thought, for the dogs sounded as though they were nipping at the heels of their prey. Then he heard a child scream. He sprinted, nimbly dashing across stumbling roots and jumping over hiding sinkholes. He bounded down a path carved into the soft yellow earth until he reached the place from which the screams had come and saw what had caused them.

A woman stood with her back against a tree, while a naked three-year-old boy clung to her. The thick stick in her hand quivered. Five wild dogs surrounded them from all sides. Mud had spattered on the woman's dark shirt and on the waist-length hair that hung limply around her face. Between sobs of rage she heaved short, rattling breaths.

Throwing down his shield and empty basket, Bujang pulled out his sword, dashed forward and chopped the spine of the closest animal. The pack turned and attacked him. He swung his arm down and tore open the abdomen of one animal. Then he sliced the neck of another, almost severing its head. A fourth received a wound right between the eyes. The last wild dog ran into the jungle with its tail between its legs.

Overcome with a combination of relief and terror, the woman collapsed to the ground. The boy grabbed her shoulder as he scrambled into her lap. She hugged him close to her chest. Her gratitude at being saved had quickly turned to horror at the sight of a tattooed hand that held a bloody *ilang*. She pleaded for mercy with her eyes.

Bujang drew in a sharp breath. She was the most beautiful woman he had ever seen. Her brown skin was as golden as early dawn, and her hair was as black as soot. Red dye stained her thin and callused hands, while tied to her waist was a cube-shaped small basket that was finely woven with triangle patterns of the bamboo shoot. He took another deep breath, but could not seem to draw in enough air. He felt suddenly lightheaded.

Suddenly, he felt shy. It was a new emotion, and he did not know what to do or say. So Bujang turned his gaze away and wiped the bloody sword with a leaf. He sheathed it. After a minute, he squatted down in front of the woman, but still his eyes looked away from her.

"My name is Bujang Maias. I have travelled many hills since I was young. Who are you and the boy?"

"I am Upa, and this is my son, Baling. We are out looking for food."

Bujang looked about, but there was no one else in sight. "Will you take me to your people? I have roamed for many days, and I miss human company."

The woman got up, still carrying the boy. "Yes, my old father and mother will welcome you. Allow me to collect food first for our dinner tonight," she replied with a quivering voice and looked about her, ascertaining that he was alone.

She picked up a thin piece of bent iron rod from the ground. Twisting her hair into a bun, she stuck the skewer into it. Then, with the boy still clinging to her, she began to fill her small basket with young fern as quickly as she could. She would look up once in a while to check her surroundings like an anxious mouse-deer.

Bujang stood watching her for some time, thinking about the sound of her voice and smelling her scent of betel vine that still lingered. He longed to say something to her, so she could say something in return to him, but no words came out of his mouth. The boy turned and stared at him, and the young man saw how underfed he appeared. He looked down at the woman's feet and noticed the sharpness of her ankle bones. The cause of their thinness was no mystery to him, and he knew something he could do.

He turned, picked up his empty burden basket and climbed back up the path. He hacked his way to the *cempedak* tree, which was bent under the weight of its fruits. After picking one ripe and two green fruits that filled half of the basket, he opened another path to reach a cluster of bamboo. With his sword, he dug up two bamboo shoots. His callused hands peeled away the furry brown skin; then the white flesh was also placed into the basket.

As he turned to make his way back, his eyes fell on an eight-inch feather that lay on the ground just beyond the bamboos. The round eye-like spots against a sandy brown background showed that it had once belonged to an argus pheasant. Thinking that it would make a fine gift to endear himself to the boy, he picked it up.

Upa watched him tread down the path from the corner of her

eye. She drew in a sharp breath when he raised the cloth-covered shield upright, for the design of footsteps was the most unusual she had ever seen. Cautiously, she studied the man's sheathed sword and saw that it was encased in aged ivory. The human hair trailing from its hilt appeared to have been taken from the head of a warrior in his prime.

She called to Bujang, indicating that she was ready to lead him back to her longhouse. He approached and held up the golden feather. Her son's squeal of delight comforted her, for it was fitting for a headhunter to give a warrior's token to pacify the boy's fragile spirit. Her child was still too young to be frightened or spanked, as the hurt would leave a mark on his soul and make him susceptible to sickness that would eventually lead to weakness or death.

They walked under the shade of sparse trees for half a mile, until they came upon an open field where herbs, edible plants and weeds grew side by side. A few aged men and women were going through the field, collecting food. They turned their faces away when he called out a greeting.

Upa said, "Please do not be troubled by their behaviour. We are almost there."

Bujang raised his face and saw a longhouse of about twenty doors' length. As they drew near, he noticed that parts of the open veranda had rotted away. Black, underfed dogs barked on seeing him but stayed out of his way. He climbed the notched steps with care, for the log bent hazardously under his weight. The common gallery was also in a bad state, with fractured bamboos jerking under the feet of children as they chased each other about the place. The disastrous scene was rendered even worse by the sight of young men who lay sprawled on the floor, some next to their own vomit, obviously from drunkenness and dissolution.

When they reached the third door, the boy, whose name was

Baling, climbed down from his mother's back and ran into the family quarters yelling, "*Akik*! Someone is here. He is strong, Grandfather, he killed many bad dogs."

Bujang was taken aback when Upa held the door open for him, but not wanting to appear rude, he stepped into the narrow room. Numerous rice baskets lined one side of the wall, many of which were empty. One part of the thatched *atap* roof had been pushed upwards with a stick to allow in fresh air and an overcast natural light. In one corner, a finely woven pattern cloth hung to cover an offering to the spirits.

The tap-tapping sound of a stick on the bamboo floor was soon followed by a bent old man whose wrinkled brown skin was free from tattoos.

Bujang put his things down next to the hearth just inside the door and said, "Good evening to you. Forgive me for intruding upon the kindness of your family. What I have brought to compensate for your trouble is menial, but I hope you will accept them."

"Please, come, sit. I am Pamun, Upa's father and Baling's grandfather. People here call me *Akik* Baling."

He turned to his daughter and said, "Tell your mother to cook rice for our visitor. We shall have good food to welcome him."

Bujang attempted to carry the basket to the back, but Upa would not let him. She explained, "My mother is outside collecting herbs. She will help me prepare dinner."

Akik Baling called out, "Come join me for a bath in the river. You have done your part by providing food. Let the women cook the meal."

Bujang followed the old man outside, and a more affectionate Baling grabbed his hand as they walked down the ladder. A few older folks responded to *Akik* Baling's greeting as they made their way down a muddy path to the river. The sight of an old man in the act of patching parts of the bathing platform with pieces of wood made Bujang stare. He wondered why the younger men back in the house, at least one of whom would have had the strength to split timber, were not doing the work. With trepidation, he watched children jump from branches into a debris-filled dark river. He kept Baling close to him as they bathed, treating each passing branch as a submerged crocodile.

* * *

After she emptied the contents of the basket at the back of the quarters, Upa returned to the family room and leaned it against a soot-covered wall next to the hearth. She looked down at the low pile of dry twigs and firewood, praying that she had enough fuel for that evening. She blew on the smoking embers that lay on the clay hearth, then added fresh wood, before going to the back and climbing down a bamboo ladder. A row of maize blocked her view, but she knew that her mother must be digging for tapioca roots since she was not cooking rice. Fragrant leaves and herbs brushed against her as she hurried down a short path.

She found Punai, or Baling's grandmother as she was known to her people, bent over the ground and digging at the base of a tapioca plant. She called out, "Mother."

"Yes, child, what is it?" *Inik* Baling said and pushed away palmate shaped leaves as she looked up. She became alarmed on seeing Upa's face. "What is wrong? Has something happened to Baling?"

"We were attacked by dogs in the jungle, and a stranger saved us."

"Where is this stranger now?"

"Father has taken him down to the river for a bath. Mother, he is a headhunter. I was afraid not to bring him here. I was afraid that he would hurt me and my son."

"What did he say to you?"

"He said his name is Bujang Maias, but he did not say where he was from, and I dared not ask too much."

Punai stooped to scoop up soil-covered tuber roots, and Upa did likewise. As she stood up, the old lady asked, "Was he unfriendly and arrogant?"

"No, he was very kind. He even helped me collect food for dinner tonight."

"Such things are simple generosity from a man."

"Should we set the sentries of the house on him then?"

"Let us learn more about him tonight. The visitor may have been sent by the spirits to protect you in your distress. To scorn their providence will bring a curse down on us."

They climbed back up the ladder, and *Inik* Baling gasped when she saw the *cempedak*s and bamboo shoots waiting to be prepared. He was a generous man indeed, for there was food enough for many days.

Upa said little; she simply returned to the hearth, reached for a wide bamboo tube, put one end to the ember and blew into it. A few breaths later, a fiery tongue appeared and slowly licked the wood she had placed earlier. She scooped precious grains of rice from a basket, went to the back and washed the dust off with rainwater collected in wide bamboo tubes. Then she poured the grains into a fresh bamboo and filled it with more water.

Another tube was filled with fern. She chopped half of a bamboo shoot and put it into a clay pot with brine water that she had boiled from the stem of *Nipah* palm. She picked up a long stick and poked open another part of the roofing above the hearth to let the smoke out.

As her mother watched over the cooking, Upa picked up a tube of water and a hard coconut brush. She opened the front door a crack and looked up and down the common gallery, which she was relieved to see was empty except for three intoxicated men. Then she hurried to the guest portion of her gallery, got down on her knees and scrubbed the floor as fast as she could, pausing now and then to listen. It did not take her long to finish the work, for her part of the *ruai* was narrow. She returned to the *bilek* with relief, and Baling's chatter soon alerted the women to the returning men.

* * *

Bujang was pleased to see the *ruai* freshly scrubbed. At least his sleeping area for the night was clean. However, he was surprised when the old man led him back into the *bilek*, for it was customary for a male visitor to be introduced as soon as probable to the head of the longhouse, usually after he had washed himself.

Next Upa unrolled a large mat on the floor as *Akik* Baling invited him to sit. When *Inik* Baling was introduced to him, he saw that she was old, and beautiful like her daughter. Her wrinkled skin was as fair as pale soil, and her flattened breast hung low over her chest. Her grey hair, streaked with black, was as lovely as the feathers of a hornbill. Yet the most beautiful feature was her gentle dove eyes, and he thought it fitting when he learnt that her name was Punai, which meant "dove" in their language. While they waited for dinner to be served, they talked about Bujang's travels and his life in the jungle. Bujang made sure to leave out the uncommon aspects of his tale, particularly his ability to speak to animals, for he did not want to be chased out of the longhouse like an unwanted dog.

"How many people live in this house?" Bujang asked when their conversation died down.

Akik Baling said, "Including myself, fifty-two adults and sixteen children. Many have left, because the land has provided poorly."

"But why has the house not moved?"

The old man fiddled with a loose strand on the mat and answered evasively, "We do not have enough strong people to do the work."

Bujang thought better of asking about the men he had seen snoring noisily in the common gallery. Just then, Upa placed a wooden bowl of bamboo shoot in the middle of the mat, followed by the rest of their dinner. Both men smiled boyishly at the meal of boiled fern, soft bamboo shoot and young *cempedak* cooked in broth. Fragrant rice was portioned out of a bamboo tube that had been split open, and the rice-filled banana leaves were passed around. They ate with their hands, expertly picking up food with the ends of their fingers and pushing these into their mouths with the thumb.

At the end of the meal, a bowl of water was passed around for them to clean their hands in. Then the banana-leaf plates were slid through breaks in the bamboo flooring and dropped to the ground.

Upa cleared the bowls and served rice wine to the men. She also peeled the ripe *cempedak*, which was a rare treat for her son.

Bujang had seen the condition of their kitchen. There was barely any firewood, and the smoking racks were empty of meat or fish. There was also no raw rattan in the room, only the soft water reeds for mat weaving. Seeing how impoverished the family was of jungle materials, he asked, "Is Baling's father away hunting?"

A sad silence followed his question. Finally *Akik* Baling said, "Kumat died before Baling was born. He was teased and ridiculed by some men in this longhouse for marrying Upa without giving her a trophy head. Many consider her to be a gifted weaver, and because of that, these men believed that he did not deserve to be married to her. He followed a *ngayau*, a head-hunting expedition, to prove himself and was killed by the enemy. Like me, Kumat was no fighter."

Abruptly, the noise of playing children outside turned to muffled silence as men called out boisterously, many not steady in their speech. *Akik* Baling stared at the front door until the noise receded to distant laughter. Then he got up and burned a clump of shredded bark. The room was smoked to clear it of mosquitoes. He placed the fumigant on a flat stone to one side of the room and left it smouldering there.

The quiet did not last, however. Without warning, the front door suddenly slammed open and a large man stomped in. Pale, tattooed flesh sagged over his hulking frame. His handsome face was clear from facial hair but marred by red blotches. In a loud and angry voice he asked, "Why have you brought a stranger to this place? Are you fools? He could be a scout sent to count our heads."

Upa faced him defiantly. "He saved my life this afternoon. He is only a lone traveller."

The man lifted up his arm to slap her, but Bujang's hand shot up and gripped his wrist as it came down.

Akik Baling half rose and said, "This is my *bilek*, Raung. You may be the chief of this house, but you cannot come in here and insult my guest and my daughter. He saved Upa and Baling from being eaten by wild dogs."

Raung pulled his hand away, glaring into the face of the stranger as he rubbed his wrist. "So you were the one who killed those mongrels." He turned to Upa. "If you had agreed to marry me, you would not have any need to scavenge in the jungle. I have slaves to do the work for you. They will do anything you ask them."

In a ragged voice Upa said, "You led my husband to his death. Baling is now without a father because of you."

Raung spit on the floor and strode to the doorway. He called out from the entrance, "Pamun, bring the stranger out. He is not your son; neither is he your son-in-law. It is improper for him to sleep in the room of a widowed woman."

Bujang made to get up. He had seen what kind of man Raung

was, but he was still a guest here, and Raung was correct that his sleeping in the family's *bilek* would harm Upa's reputation. But Upa grabbed his arm and pleaded, "Please don't listen to him. Sleep here tonight. It does not matter to me what the rest of the house thinks."

The young man smiled. "It matters to me. You are a good woman. I am not afraid. I have slept with pythons before. My spirit father will protect me."

As he stepped outside, he saw that Raung was making his way towards eight other men who were sitting in a circle around a large jar of rice wine. Above them, like globes of dark fruit surrounding a timber column, hung over two hundred and fifty human skulls of many sizes. Each head was wrapped in a loose, round rattan holder and kept warm by a fire burning on a hearth at the foot of the column. Bujang passed six intoxicated men as he approached the chief's gallery.

Raung offered him a bamboo cup and made him drink the sweet female brew in one toast. After he had drunk from it, Bujang passed the same cup to the man next to him. Getting drunk in a friendly longhouse to honour the gods for their blessing was good, but Bujang could see no reason for thankfulness in that house, so he was on his guard as he studied the drinking men. Raung did not refill the cup when it reached him, although he made a show of drinking from it. Six men were genuinely drinking, but two, like the chief, were still sharp.

Each time the cup was passed to him, Bujang would refill it and pretend to drink by letting the main portion of the *tuak* dribble down the side of his mouth. Soon he began to smell as potent as the jar of wine. Once the gallery was empty of curious children and working adults, and the lamps darkened, Bujang feigned drunkenness by slurring his words as he said, "Good chief, great chief...I must now be to bed. Goodnight, for I must wake early tomorrow."

He tottered to his feet. His legs bent and his feet stomped as he swayed like a passenger tossed about in a boat riding on white-water. Hoots of laughter followed his gait. When he reached *Akik* Baling's *ruai*, he rolled onto the bare planks, spread-eagled on his back, and closed his eyes.

With his eyes still closed, he heard Raung laugh loudly. "Look at him. He only looks big, but he is stupid. His tattoos must have been painted for the heads of children."

Amidst the roar of his men's laughter Raung stood, picked up a folded cloth and strode towards Bujang. He shook open the red cloth used to receive trophy heads and covered the visitor with it. Omen birds lined the vertical border, and serpents slithered along the horizontal margin. Warriors, discoloured by blood, pranced in the middle of the cloth. Bujang could not know this, but it had been woven by Raung's grandmother, a woman whose virtues he had not inherited.

Now Raung brought his face down to Bujang's and said, "I will wrap your head in this *pua*."

Inside the bilek, Upa and her family had been listening, and now *Akik* Baling rushed out with his walking stick tapping urgently on the floor. "Do not do this. It is wrong."

He went down on his knees and tried to pull the patterned cloth away, but Raung kicked his face. "Go away old man, or I will have your grandson's head in his place."

Akik Baling tottered back and fell; he saw one of Bujang's eyes staring at him. It was alert, but then it closed. He got up shakily and returned to his *bilek*. Now Upa stepped out of the door, meaning to go to Bujang's side but her father stopped her. He whispered, "The warrior Bujang is only pretending to be drunk. Do not be a fool, do not incur Raung's wrath."

"I am not afraid of Raung. I will fight him, I am not afraid of him," she said.

Akik Baling shook her shoulders, "Do you think his rage will stop with you? He will hurt your son, too. He will hurt my grandson."

Upa's legs gave way beneath her and she crumpled down to the floor. Her hand fell on the shield. She pulled the cloth away and recoiled at the grimacing image.

Akik Baling reassured her. "He will be fine. You should go to sleep."

"No, Father. I will keep watch tonight."

"You cannot go outside. It will cheapen you. A woman does not sleep outside with unmarried men."

"I will keep watch from this crack in the door here."

"But what good will it do?"

"Raung will wait for him to flail in his sleep. He will use that as an excuse to take his head."

"If the spirits say that he is an enemy of this house, then he is an enemy. Even if he were to have saved your life moments ago, he may still return to kill you in the future," the old man advised.

Upa refused to look into her father's face and squared her shoulders stubbornly. Finally, the old man shook his head and walked away.

Pressing her face against the bamboo door, Upa spied through the crack while one hand gripped Bujang's blanket. She knew that she was being unreasonable and that she had put everyone's life in danger by inviting the man to the house. Yet she could not help herself because his presence was comforting, and the more time she spent with him, the stronger she felt. The dim light from the fire under the trophy heads cast strange shadows in the quiet longhouse. Her usually hungry stomach now feeling warm and full made her drowsy. The chirping of cicadas was like a lullaby, and every now and then a cricket would join the symphony. The cloth slipped out of her hand.

She did not know how long had passed when a shout from the gallery startled Upa out of her doze. She was too late. Raung had lifted his sword to strike. As the blade came down, Bujang's arms shot up and crossed above his chest to check the deathblow. Raung jumped back, and immediately two men positioned themselves behind him.

Bujang raised himself to a sitting position and threw the cloth to the side. "What is wrong, *Tuai* Raung? Did you have a bad dream and could not sleep?"

Raung was furious. "I am the chief of this house. You are an enemy."

Bujang stood up and faced him. "How do you know that I am an enemy?"

"You were having a nightmare. The spirits showed us that you have evil intentions. I have two witnesses to prove it."

"The spirits are witnesses too. Will these two men swear on the *Antu Pala*, will they swear on the trophy heads, that they had truly seen me flail in my sleep?"

"Yes, they will," Raung replied with assurance. But his confidence was shattered when a loud crash shook the gallery. Raung turned and was horrified when he saw that all but one of the trophies had dropped from the ceiling. Shattered bones lay scattered on the floor, and not a single skull remained whole.

Raung's soul chilled when he recognized the head that had not fallen. The people threw open their doors and, on seeing that the spirits they had called upon to bless the land and to guard the house had abandoned them, they wailed.

Bujang carefully stepped over the broken bones and approached the principal column. He scrutinized the single remaining head. Reaching up, he unhooked the rattan holder and took it down.

Turning the skull in his hand, he said, "There is no spirit in this one. Why would a spirit not want to live in the vessel you cherish?

Whose head is this?"

Raung loudly said, "It is the head of an enemy. You have brought ruin to our house."

A gust of wind shook the sparsely woven walls of the house, fanning the slumbering fire into a bright flame. Bujang balanced the skull on the tips of his fingers, and when he lifted it up to the height of a grown man, a shadow cast against the wall. It was the shape of a man with neither shield nor war feathers. His sword was small, and his right shoulder, which was more developed than his left, showed signs of carrying countless loads of heavy firewood and logs.

Upa had emerged with the others when the trophies crashed down. Now she cried out, "No, no, it is *Apai* Baling. It is my husband!"

She wailed, and those who heard her words cried out in horror. An old woman shouted, "How could this have happened right in front of our eyes? How could such taboo have existed among us? Is it any wonder that our crops have been poor and our children hungry?"

Raung roared, "That is all a lie. This man is a sorcerer. He must be the spirit that has stolen our food from us."

Bujang scowled, and the people gazed in wonder at the furious beauty of his face. He called to Upa, "Bring a cloth to shelter your husband's remains. Kumat was a true man to the end of his days."

She sobbed her way back to the *bilek* and came out with a delicately designed *Pua*. After she had covered the head in the folds of the cold blanket, she hugged it tightly to her chest and wailed.

The longhouse women sang their grief.

Will the spirit of the paddy, will the spirit of life-giving rice, ever return to this land?

Will fish swim again in our waters?

Will the gods ever again bless the seeds we plant in the ground with life?

Raung bellowed for his men. Eighteen rallied behind him, although sixteen of those stood quite unsteadily. The tyrannized people of the longhouse, old and young, rushed to get knives and any hard metal or wood they could lay their hands on.

Raung knew that he could not fight the angry crowd, since most of his warriors did not even have their wits about them. So instead he called out, "Hey, ungrateful people. My presence has blessed this house bountifully."

Inik Baling threw a piece of firewood at him. "You have brought a curse to our house," she accused. "You have ruined us. Everyday we live in fear of being attacked because of you. We tremble when we search for food in the jungle. We sleep with one eye open at night, waking up at every strange noise. The nomadic Penans sleep in their simple shelters with more peace than us. We were right to be fearful. The enemy is not outside; he is the chief of this house."

Raung glared at the circle of angry eyes. He signalled for his men to retreat and whistled for the hunting dogs. A man lowered the common ladder and Raung and his men climbed down, all the while pointing their swords at the people.

When his feet touched the ground, Raung glared up at them and shouted, "I declare that this house is now my enemy. I shall return for your heads." His men roared drunkenly behind him, and then they disappeared into the night.

Bujang watched their dark forms retreat into the encroaching jungle. He knew that the wine would wear off, but the anger would not. He instructed the people to bolt down every door and window, warning them that the ousted chief and his men might return that same night.

Then Upa brought out two sleeping mats, one for Bujang and another for her father. She placed her husband's head next to a column in their gallery. How could they not have read the signs? When their crops had failed and when they returned empty-handed from the jungle or the river, how could they not have asked why the spirits had abandoned them? Then Upa questioned her own blindness and derided herself for not sensing her husband's spirit. Even if his head was hidden among the hundreds at Raung's gallery she should have recognized him.

Upa studied Bujang from the corner of her eye and wondered who he was and what power he had that he was able to reveal the violation of taboo that had cursed them.

The people came out, and the augur, who introduced himself as Mendakap, picked up the covered skull and placed it in the centre of the crowd. They kept watch for the rest of the night as wailers sang ceaselessly for one of their sons. Meanwhile the augur and elders of the longhouse discussed what rituals should be performed, but none had ever heard of such a taboo being committed before, and the group could not reach a conclusion as to how to right the wrong based.

It was after their discussion had finished, with no solution offered, that Geramun, a strong one-arm man addressed as *Apai* Gamit, approached Bujang and asked if he would go together with him into the jungle to find a trunk to carve for Kumat's final resting place.

8

Morning dew had barely dried on the leaves when thirty-five sombre men, women and teenage boys trudged down to the river and filled three longboats. One boat carried the skull of Kumat, while the other two bore three baskets full of shattered bones between them. A rising tide slowed their progress as they paddled downstream.

When the light began to feel warm upon the skin, the leading boat turned towards a muddy bank lined with upright breathing roots that jutted out of the water. Approach by paddle was impossible, so four boys jumped into the muddy water and waded towards a tree, dragging a boat between them. They moored it, and the passengers climbed out into the ankle-deep mud. The same favour was offered to the other two boats, and the boys received thanks and blessings as the work was carried out.

Once everyone was on dry ground Mendakap instructed the eldest boy, Gamit, to show Bujang the way into the burial ground. No one had visited the place for years, and it was now overgrown with vines and creepers. Bujang found traces of a disused path and started hacking his way in, while Gamit and his friends trailed behind him with hoes over their shoulders.

The thick foliage soon gave way to a clearing under the shade of a latticed canopy, and they passed three carved pillars that held up the coffins of great men. Gamit stopped before a mound, knelt and spoke into a bamboo tube embedded in the earth. Then he unhooked a gourd-bottle tied to his waist and poured rice wine into the same tube. Behind them, the main procession of mourners placed the three baskets of bones next to one of the carved pillars, together with meagre offerings of food and wine to the spirit of a chief.

When the boy was again on his feet, Bujang asked, "Who was that?"

Gamit sauntered to his side and said, "That was Nanjang. He was a great farmer during the time of my great grandfather. Everything he planted bore abundant fruits. Not a single seed was ever wasted. I am going to be like him one day."

He pointed out a few more famous graves to Bujang and urged him to ask for favours from each one of them. Bujang, however, shook his head and said, "I did not bring wine with me. I do not wish to offend their spirits with empty-handed requests."

The boy shrugged and strode ahead of the group like a proud rooster as he brought them to the site picked by the augur. Though he had only been there twice before, and only for short spans of time, he had memorized the names of every person buried there. Finally he stopped next to an unmarked grave and stuck his hoe into the soft, dark soil next to it.

Bujang scored the ground with his sword and drew out lines in the exact length and width of the child-sized coffin that he and Geramun had carved. They started digging from the middle, being mindful not to slip into the hole. The earth was loose, so that by the time the slower funeral procession had reached the site, the grave was ready. The box that held Kumat's remains was deep enough for a single head and wide enough for the dead-man's worldly belongings. He would neither be shamed nor naked in the spirit world.

From the side of the gaping hole, Bujang lowered the casket. It was a perfect fit. A sigh rose from the people, for the earth would not demand for another body anytime soon. Bujang nodded to the boys, and they pushed the disturbed soil back into the opening.

Mendakap laid out rolled cigarettes and poured wine on a large leaf. As he placed the meagre offerings on the grave, despair poured out of his spirit like water from the side of a cliff during a thunderstorm. He had not been able to find a single egg in the whole longhouse, as the fowls had been barren since the last full moon. Day after day, the people's traps remained empty, and the women were forced to go farther into the jungle to look for food. Crops that did not rot from the roots had been attacked by insects, while fruit trees sprouted flowers that withered and fell before their time. Underfed children roamed the common gallery, looking as uncared for as the hunting dogs, while their mothers cried over empty pots. Mendakap did not dare to pray for new land, for they had only the strength of old folks and inexperienced boys. He could simply beg that the gods show mercy and allow them more time to survive in that place.

The rest of their party must have also felt the same despair, for the return trip up the river was silent. As the slow current moved them along, lush greenness reached down from either bank. Old folk wiped tears from their eyes as they scanned the steep incline and barricades of underbrush. There had once been a time in their life when such obstacles had meant nothing to them. But times had changed.

When they reached the pier, only two women with fresh bundles of clothing were there to meet them. The children had been sent back to the house and admonished not to come out to meet the group because bad spirits that brought death and sickness might have followed them home. The mourners bathed and scrubbed everything that had been used at the gravesite. Every piece of clothing was stripped and washed before they again donned dry clothes and returned to the longhouse.

Now *Akik* Baling invited the community to sit in two rows facing each other in his part of the common gallery. He patted the mat next to him as he waved to Bujang, and made the visitor sit between himself and the augur. Children held their banana-leaf plates high as six men and women walked up and down between the rows to distribute a meagre meal of tapioca roots, yam, wild fern and *cempedak* fruit. They all ate in silence.

As Upa ladled boiled yam onto the plate before him, Mendakap said, "Raung has taken all our warriors with him. The rest who are here are either too old or impaired or without experience. Will you lead us, Bujang Maias?"

"I am a wanderer, and I am not of this longhouse. Your people may not agree to the suggestion."

The group of elders nodded with satisfaction on hearing his answer, for his words proved that he held the people's opinion in high regard and was not proud.

The augur explained, "We have discussed this among ourselves, and we all agree that you are the one. The people would prefer peace, but seeing as how Raung had attacked so many houses before this, we need a warring leader to teach our young boys to protect us from the vengeance of strangers."

Bujang fiddled with an unlit cigarette between his fingers. He turned his head and watched lovely Upa serve more brine-flavoured yam into the raised plates of bright-eyed children. He said, "I will stay and lead, as long as your people wish it."

* * *

Just days since his arrival, the old longhouse began to resonate with the sounds of knocking, chopping and scraping. That bright, clear morning Bujang, together with Gamit and his friends, walked under and around the structure as they searched for portions in need of repair. Then they went into the jungle and returned in the evening with back-breaking loads of bamboos.

The following day Bujang showed the boys how to halve the wide bamboo tubes and to cut a sharp point at one end. They dug around the perimeter of the house, planted in the bamboos with the sharp edges pointing upwards, and twisted strips of rattan between the pieces to hold them together. Inside, the old folks split and sharpened more bamboos into light spears. They taught their young grandchildren how to throw those simple weapons down at enemies on the ground. In the evening, the older boys sat around Bujang as they cut more bamboo halves and learned to strap them together into new floorings.

Within the first month of his stay, Bujang ha⟨...⟩d a new hardwood log to replace the old common ladder. It v⟨...⟩urdy that even Baling was no longer afraid to climb down by ⟨...⟩although he still asked to be carried up. Inside the house ⟨...⟩budding artists had carved out forms of animals and plant⟨...⟩relief on the crossbeams. Laughter rang about the gallery as ⟨...⟩ple made unkind jokes about each others' handiwork. Childr⟨...⟩d mischief until the wiser folks found ways to put their energy ⟨...⟩d use.

The weeks rolled by and brought rain, accompanied by thunderstorms. On one such day, Baling dashed down the gallery and crashed himself into Bujang, who lifted the boy up on his shoulders. Then to Baling's delight, Bujang turned in circles and swayed from side to side as though to toss him off his shoulders. Upa, who was pounding the last of her rice grain in a wooden mortar, looked up and smiled, which made Bujang suddenly imagine his own child suckling her breast, and a flush spread over his face.

Gamit's grandmother peered his way from under her plucked eyelids, while her hands worked deftly over the warp and weft of

a half-done mat. She knew that look on his face because she had seen the same look on two sons. She turned to her eldest, Geramun, who was in the midst of laying new bamboo floorings and lashing them down with his good left arm. The stump that was his right arm dangled purposefully as he pulled on the cord strapped to the shoulder.

She called out, "*Apai* Gamit, come over here."

Gamit's father turned and raised an eyebrow at the mischievous look on his old mother's face. Experience had taught him that it was pointless to ignore her, so he released the cord and went to sit by her side.

"I think he likes her," she said, nodding toward Upa.

"Of course he does. Everyone knows that."

"But why doesn't he do anything?"

"He brings food, repairs their quarters and watches out for Baling."

Then, as though a great thing was revealed to her, *Inik* Gamit said, "He doesn't have a backyard of his own. He has no betel vine leaves to roll for her. I don't think he even has lime-chalk."

"Do not pry, Mother. We have only buried Kumat's head three months ago."

"*Apai* Baling has been dead for over three harvestings. Upa's period of mourning for him ended since before Baling learned to walk." After some moments of silence, she continued, "It will also persuade him to stay. If he does not get a wife from this house, he may want to travel again."

That afternoon, the old lady took it upon herself to bring the matter up to the augur. There was much bantering, and finally Mendakap agreed to supply a little of his precious lime-chalk on Bujang's behalf.

That night after his evening meal, Mendakap approached Bujang a little bashfully. He found the young chief threading a wide tear in a fishing net that hung from the ceiling with fibres beaten out of wild vine.

The augur spoke of minor matters with *Akik* Baling, but when the rolled palm lamp started to sputter, Pamun excused himself and stepped inside his quarters to get a new bundle of dammar resin for light.

Mendakap cleared his throat, "*Tuai*, I do not wish to pry or to decide on matters for you, but have you given any *sireh* wraps to Baling's mother?"

Bujang blushed. He recalled watching a cousin from his old longhouse roll one for his lady-love. His eyes dropped self-consciously. "No, I have not."

"Then come to my gallery after *Akik* Baling retires for the night."

No sooner had he said that, Upa's father returned with a lamp. Mendakap said his goodnight and left them to their labours.

One by one the lamps in adjoining *ruais* were put out, and shadows stretched to mingle with the faint lights of two flames. Teenage boys climbed into their plank beds, where they snuggled under warm blankets prepared by their mothers.

When he caught sight of Bujang's silhouette approaching him, Mendakap tapped his ankle with impatient glee. He fingered the items in a small, flat basket for the tenth time that night: green betel vine, white lime-chalk, shredded red tobacco and sliced betel nuts.

The moment Bujang sat next to him, Mendakap placed a fresh *sireh* in the chief's hand and showed him how to brush a dab of lime-chalk onto its surface. Betel nut and tobacco were lumped in the centre of the leaf, which was then folded into a square bundle.

Bujang returned to *Akik* Baling's *ruai* with the two tiny bundles grasped in a trembling hand. He blew out the lamp. After taking a few deep breaths to calm his nerves, he tiptoed to the door and placed his palm on its surface. It yielded under his touch. Embers from the fireplace showed him where she lay. Baling slept next to her, while her old parents reposed at the far end of the room with their backs turned to the front door. He squatted next to the boy as he debated over whether he should wake her or not, because he was afraid that her screams of protest might wake the whole house. He gazed into her face for the length of a hawk owl's song. Then, taking a deep breath, he got up and turned to head for the door.

A tug on the back flap of his loincloth made him reach down to loosen whatever had caught the cloth, but instead he clasped her hand. Upa was awake.

Her gentle prodding forced him back down on the floor. Shyly he passed her a rolled *sireh*. She smiled, lowered her eyes and received it from his hand. Bujang's chest filled to bursting. It was so wonderfully full, he almost forgot to eat his *sireh*.

* * *

While a misty fog still hung over the dim morning, Bujang lowered the common ladder and climbed down with an empty burden basket slung on one shoulder and a borrowed spear gripped in one hand. He trekked into the jungle alone. He scrutinized the floor, scanned the boughs and craned his neck to listen but found nothing. As the day grew older, his spirit dropped, for he had not found a single track, not even that of a mouse-deer.

The chirp of a cricket drew him to a low bush. His hand whipped out and snatched an airborne brown insect, which was as long as the width of his palm. He grunted, then peered around the bush for more.

"Kreet, kreet. Let me go. Let me go," the cricket called out.

"Why should I? I have searched the whole day for meat but

found nothing. I do not wish to return to my future bride's family empty-handed."

"How could there be meat? The animals are terrified of this place."

"Why are they afraid?"

"Because the guardian spirits of your house are vengeful and angry. Men ate their food and drank their wine. And most days they don't even have a fire to keep them warm."

"The spirits are gone. Their skulls have shattered into pieces."

The cricket kreet louder, "What a terrible omen! They have cursed the house and the people living there. It would have been better if no trophies had ever graced the house."

"How do I lift this curse?"

"Do you not know your own customs? You will need new trophies. Ask the gods, and if they look upon you favourably, they will show you the way."

Bujang squeezed the cricket in his hand. "I still need meat to feed my people tonight."

Chirping loudly for mercy, it said, "Please, wait, wait. Go down this way and follow the trail of *sago* trees. You will find a mud hole. An adult boar goes there every afternoon to cool himself from the heat. He is far too arrogant to heed the warning of the spirits, and they will place him in your hands to punish him."

Bujang thanked the cricket and let it go. Immediately it disappeared into the vegetation. He parted vines and leaves, which he made sure not to break, as he made his way down the slope. The mud hole was exactly where the cricket told him it would be. One tree at the edge of the puddle was particularly muddy, and part of its bark clung to the trunk in tatters. He climbed an adjacent gum tree and hid behind a layer of leaves to wait.

The burning heat of the day slowly gave way to gentler warmth, and he began to nod. A rustle in the undergrowth, followed by heavy grunts, cleared his head instantly. Before long, a tusked boar stepped into the small clearing. It was about half the size of a man. Bujang flushed with glee as he quietly positioned his spear.

The animal stepped into the shallow mud hole, lay down and began to roll from side to side. The sudden swish of iron was immediately followed by a loud squeal. Bujang clambered down from the tree as the pig struggled to pull itself out of the pool. The spear fell out of the wound on its back, and blood gushed down the side. Bujang stooped to pick it up just as the animal made a dash for the underbrush behind him. He thrust the spear down, aiming for the back of its throat. The boar fell on its side and struggled to free itself from the impaling force that held it back. Bujang pressed down hard on the shaft until it was still. Then he shook it and, after he was satisfied that the animal was dead, pulled it out. More blood pooled under his feet. He opened the side flap of his burden basket, strapped the beast down, and heaved the basket onto his shoulders and head. With a light heart, he trudged home.

* * *

Chattering children trailed behind Bujang as he made his way to the bathing platform. Some had never seen a boar in their short lifetime, and they wondered if the animal was a monster.

Gamit called out as they passed. Bujang shouted back. "Bring along some of your friends to look for firewood. Ask your grandfathers to come down to the river and help me clean this boar. We will have a feast tonight."

The teenage boy sprinted up the house and came back down with a group of machete-wielding youngsters. They rushed into the jungle, shouting like hunters at the heels of a deer. Old men climbed down the ladder at a slower pace, though with the same eagerness, and made their way to the river. There Bujang gutted the boar and chopped it into large chunks with his sword, while the old men scrapped bristling hair off the skin and cleaned the organs. The women came out with fresh bamboo tubes to collect blood and pieces of the internal organs.

The boys soon returned and, under the watchful instruction of Mendakap, they built a large fire on the ground, which was placed a few yards away from the house. Capering children raced to the river and offered to carry the meat back to the blaze. The augur carefully lined full bamboo tubes along the edge of the fire and taught the boys to turn them at intervals. The boar's head was roasted slowly in a clay pot, then the flesh stripped off. Mendakap cracked the skull open and extracted the brain, which was stuffed into a bamboo tube filled with brine and herbs. All the larger bones were cracked to release their sweet marrow and cooked in wide-mouthed pots with water, banana pith and more herbs. The skin was singed to a crisp.

While each family cooked their own rice or tapioca root in anticipation of the feast, the smell of cooking meat filled every nook and cranny of the house. By the time *Akik* Baling was ready to announce the chief's engagement to his daughter, an expectant crowd had already gathered in the common gallery. The people shouted with joy, and youngsters were encouraged to beat on gongs to drown out the calls of bad omens that might come from the surrounding jungle.

They all ate, and none were left hungry. After the feast, men and women went about the gallery to collect bones to carve into knife handles and needles or awls for weaving. That night, the augur presented a thank offering of meat, fat, rice, eggs and wine to the spirits. Tears rolled down his cheeks as he thanked the gods for giving them more time.

Bujang observed the goings-on with an unfamiliar contentment in his heart. Finally, he had found a home. He watched Upa as she walked into the *bilek* and closed the door, all the while gazing meaningfully into his face. She had washed his blanket for him that morning. He covered himself with the *pua* that was still warm with sun, lay down on his new plank bed and fell asleep.

* * *

Bujang leapt up into a crouching stance. There it was again, an infant's scream.

He ran out to the veranda and jumped. Cold wind whistled past his ears as he fell down the side of a steep cliff. He splashed into a lake of blood so thick he could barely kick his legs to bring himself back up to the surface. On reaching it he choked and gagged as he tried to fill his lungs with air. Still struggling to stay afloat, he stretched his arms out and found a rock to cling onto. Again he heard a shriek. Then he looked up and saw an old woman sitting on the dead body of a child and crying like a babe. Her face began to melt. Fat dripped, and flesh fell off, revealing a blackened skull. Even then the old-infant would not stop crying.

The scene horrified him, and he looked about for the shore. A tall, red man stood at the bank, and he resolved to swim towards him. Suddenly he was standing on the bank, and he saw his father's face.

Tok Anjak pointed towards the middle of the lake. Bujang turned and saw a large black bear tearing flesh off an old man. Then he saw a hornbill crushing the heads of children, and not far from it, a black python ripped heads from men and women in a feverish frenzy.

Tok Anjak shook his head from side to side. His throat sac swelled and he roared, "Taring Ai has betrayed you, Tama Ramun. Here is my son, and he sees your face."

The bear threw a human leg, and as it flew in the air, it turned into a twig and fell at Bujang's feet.

Again *Tok* Anjak called out, "The warpath god has abandoned you, Salang, for you have debased your warrior feathers."

The hornbill shouted curses in return and, as it spread its wings, a strong wind blasted against it.

The python turned its head to face Bujang, and there was so much hate blazing out of its eyes that it made the young man's skin crawl. Then it laughed. "A boy!"

Bujang looked down and saw that he was naked, his unperforated penis exposed to mockery. He tried to cover himself, but his hands would not obey him.

The python hissed, "I will drink his blood and vomit his bones on a mound of excrement."

Bujang turned to run. His legs jerked against the plank bed. He grabbed his sword and sat up. Looking around the dimly lit gallery, he realized that he was back in the longhouse. Sweat drenched his body, blanket and wooden bed. With heart pounding and legs shaking, he walked out to the veranda. The night was cool. He breathed deep, but the stench of blood and burnt flesh would not leave him.

Finally he said, "Yes, Father. I will go," and the air changed to the sweet scent of herbs and fruiting trees.

* * *

The following night, Bujang called for the people to gather. "A great darkness still hangs over the house," he told them solemnly. "As chief, it is my duty to bring back prosperity and to annul the curse placed on our heads. Your sons are brave and your fathers wise; you are more than able to protect the house without me. It is important that I go, or the house will not prosper. I will walk again in the jungle,

140

and I will marry Upa when I return."

A stunned hush fell upon the people, for no one had ever heard of a lone war expedition. Mendakap's heart sank as he realized that they did not even have a small domesticated pig to send as a messenger to the warpath god. Allowing Bujang to leave without seeking for permission from the gods was akin to sending him to his death. Only a blood sacrifice would make the gods look upon his quest favourably, and it was his duty as *Tuai Burong* to appeal to them.

The augur's voice shook as he said, "*Tuai* Bujang, let us wait for the proper time for you to go. We have nothing to offer the gods now. We cannot let you leave without getting assurances of their protection."

The people murmured – the augur was right. And it saddened them to be so impoverished that they could not even assure their chief a safe passage for his journey.

Bujang read their minds, and his heart went out to them. He decided that it was time to end their suffering and to reverse the curse that the fighting men of the house had brought upon them. "The jungle was my home. I shall seek the spirits of each land to get advice."

"But that is against customs."

"Yes, that is so, Mendakap. However, you must agree that the suffering of the people is also because of the *adat*. The head of a man from this house had been treated like an enemy, and that is a terrible violation of the law. For that reason I must go. On my return you shall have fish in the river and pigs under the house." He smiled reassuringly and continued, "I have come a long way from the day I was born. I have faced many death-threats and lived."

Upa gave voice to what all the people were thinking. Her eyes were fearful as she pleaded, "You need not go. You must not go.

What will we all do without you?"

Bujang gazed into her beloved faced and said, "There are many houses that are vengeful towards this one. My spirit-father has shown me that I must get the heads of three violent headhunters to hang at the principal column. It will make our enemies pause in their steps and secure the longhouse for generations. I cannot live forever to protect this place."

Old men nodded as they grudgingly agreed with Bujang. Such heads would make the chance of being attacked less likely because nobody would deliberately attack a great hero or his descendents.

Upa knew that it was pointless to argue with Bujang in front of the people. Turning her eyes away from her betrothed, she returned to the *bilek*. She folded her legs beneath her and sank to the floor. She did not want to be near him just now; she could not bear to listen to his voice, all the while wondering if she would ever hear it again. Heartsick, she wondered if she was destined to lose every man she loved to the warpath.

She looked about her. The indoor hearth was now filled with fresh clay and sand. Dry firewood piled high on the side of one wall and smoked fish lay on the smoking rack above the fireplace. Two straight rods of iron lay parallel over the fire, their distance wide enough to hold a new earthenware pot. A gourd jar filled to the brim with honey stood next to the hearth, while blocks of new wax rested next to her mother's weaving loom. Green salt, boiled and extracted from the stem of *nipah* palms, packed a coconut bowl. Each object she saw was a demonstration of his love, and with that in mind she decided that that love must be returned: he would carry more than tobacco and salt for his expedition.

Two coconut shells' worth of precious rice were scooped and washed, then poured into a fresh bamboo, together with some water. She stopped the opening with fragrant leaves so the grains would not spill as they boiled. Placing the tube over the fire, she leaned it against one of the iron rods; then she climbed down the back ladder to collect wide leaves to wrap the food in.

Upa cooked tapioca root and a simple broth for the family while she busied herself at the hearth. Rice and smoked fish rolled in large leaves and unpeeled boiled eggs were lovingly arranged in a medium-sized basket. By the time she was done, it was late and she had not had her dinner. She waited for Bujang that night, but he did not come to her. Then she realized that he could not, for he was going head-hunting. She held Baling tight as she cried herself to sleep.

* * *

Bujang woke before dawn cracked through the horizon and silently went about his preparations. His face broke into a smile when *Akik* Baling passed him a basket filled with food, tobacco and a fresh loincloth. Only Upa could have prepared such a thing for him. He had despaired the night before because she had not joined them for dinner, but the basket proved that she still thought kindly of him.

The old man patted Bujang's tattooed shoulder and said, "Come home to us soon, my son. We will all watch for you at every sunrise, and a plate will wait to serve you every evening."

Gamit and his father lowered the common ladder as Mendakap blessed the one-man expedition in a low voice. The people watched from their individual galleries. After Bujang had left, the augur walked the whole length of the longhouse and, in hushed tones, reminded the members of each room to continue their daily routines and to not speak of the chief's expedition among themselves because the birds and animals might be listening.

9

Insects hummed like a throbbing pulse in the heart of the jungle. A lonely frog croaked, and doves answered from the branches. Bujang paused each time he saw an omen bird and inquired the way from them. The spider-hunters and woodpeckers cocked their heads wonderingly, for they had not received instructions concerning his expedition from the house of heaven.

An old hawk, however, was familiar with the will of the warpath god and advised, "Continue along this way and watch out for the tracks of Ribai, the river god. You shall find a friend by the banks. Explain your quest to him, and he will tell you where to go."

Bujang listened to this advice and followed a faint trail used by four-legged creatures, where giant ferns brushed his face and thorny rattan vines grabbed his basket. Steadily the thick undergrowth gave way to a carpet of dead leaves as the ground became filled with writhing roots, like wrinkles on sun-baked skin. His eyes darted warily to all sides as he crossed the space, for its emptiness exposed him to open view, and he knew that he was not the only traveller in that part of the jungle.

Towards noontime, he approached a giant strangler fig. Its core, which had once been a thick-bole tree that the fig roots had clung to and choked, was now empty. Standing like a guard next to it was a four-foot-tall, moss-covered grey stone streaked with the colour of the sun. Rain had chiselled the top surface down to a shallow natural basin. Carefully, Bujang pushed aside the moss and fern covering before dipping in his cupped hands. He drank his fill. After finding a comfortable spot to sit on inside the natural hollow of the tree, his eager hand reached for the basket and took out a meal pack. When he thought about Upa preparing this food with her own hands, it warmed his heart and satiated his appetite. After his meal, again he drank, then splashed his flushed face and head with the same water. Refreshed, he continued his journey.

Dimmer the day grew, as the shadows of the canopies conjoined the approaching darkness. Underbrush closed in around him, and the ground began to slope. Scraggly roots kept his feet from slipping as he trotted down the moist jungle floor. Before long, the sparkle of a river piercing through the coverings of palm leaves caught his eye and Bujang jogged towards it.

In the distance a torch glimmered, and flames began flaring to either side of it one after another, stretching for as far as the eye could see. Men. His steps slowed, like an animal sensing the presence of a hunter. As the odour of the muddy banks reached him, he called out to announce to the sentries that he had come in peace.

Two men met him, each with his hand resting on a sheathed sword handle. Their skin was rough and cracked, like drought-cursed earth. Neither had ears, and the bridges of their noses seemed almost flat on their faces. Except for rough strips of bark that encircled their waists and covered their loins, both men were free of ornaments.

The sentries stared at Bujang, for his face shone like a god's in the dim light. Without a word, one man turned his back to the visitor and walked ahead with his back bent into a crouch. The other cocked his head to indicate for Bujang to follow after his companion. This second man took the rear, all the while turning his head left and right as he eyed the dark surrounding. The deep, guttural calls of crocodiles greeted them every few yards. The men clambered over the stilt roots of *nipah* palms and were scratched by the thorny leaves, until finally they sunk their feet into shin deep river mud.

Bujang caught his breath at an unexpected sight; he stared up in shock at a longhouse built right at the edge of a deep river. There were no boats to be seen. He watched with dread as young children jumped from the house windows directly into the water. The columns holding up the building were covered in green slime mottled with shells and snails. Mudskippers, looking like giant tadpoles with legs, observed him with eyes bulging from the sides of their heads.

Now a large man approached them. He was a head taller than Bujang, though his clay covered limbs were thick and short. He lifted a claw-like hand armoured with nails like thick brass to stay the other men of his house, who had begun to circle Bujang.

"Greetings. My name is Bujang Maias. I have come to beg for your hospitality."

The man answered in a raspy, strange voice. "Greetings to you too, lone traveller, son of my blood-brother *Tok* Anjak. Come up to my house and be my guest. I am Semaga, the chief of this village."

With a start Bujang realized that he had stumbled upon the crocodile people, for his ape-father had often spoken of his blood-brother, Semaga. He also remembered how the other apes would tremble and keep their distance while *Tok* Anjak told his tale.

Tuai Semaga led him up a ladder made out of the ribcage bones of deer and bear roughly strapped together with dried tendons. They walked down a wet gallery with floors formed out of crudely sliced palm trunks. Fowls, at various stages of decomposition, hung from the rafters, while the bare bones of animals in prancing or sitting poses decorated the walls of each *bilek*.

The chief sat down cross-legged in front of his family quarters, where the head of a deer, with horns so enormous they pierced through the walls and roof, watched them with empty eyes. Skulls of crocodiles hung down from the principal column, looking potent even in death.

As Bujang looked around, marvelling, a man came up to the chief and asked, "Why do you welcome a human into our house? It is not our way."

Semaga growled and said, "He is son to my blood-brother *Tok* Anjak. You never liked the old ape, Dimang. Was there a reason? I do not recall ever hearing your explanation."

Dimang lowered his glowering eyes. No crocodile of the house dared to insult *Tok* Anjak, not even in a whisper, for the ape had saved Semaga's life while he was still young. Next to his great-grandfather *Tok* Mangom, Semaga was the greatest crocodile warrior to ever have lived, and he was chief to two thousand adult reptiles.

The arrival of *Tok* Anjak's son was an occasion for hospitality and celebration, and soon Semaga called for a feast to honour his guest. Raw meat and fish were brought out in plates and bowls formed out of dried animal skulls. A female placed a jar of murky red wine in front of the chief, and eight elders joined them to form a circle around it. Bujang asked, and was told that the wine was made out of yeast and yam soaked in blood.

"Where do you get the yeast from?" the young man asked.

"The elders can change into men even in the daylight. They will go and meet with traders at the mouth of the river. We skin the finer animals we catch and exchange the furs with yeast or trinkets we fancy."

Bujang steadied his stomach. It would be rude and perilous for him to decline the meal his host presented. However, the kindness of Semaga and the brusque friendliness of the elders encouraged him. So he ate their food and learned to imitate their gusto as he drank.

Music, beaten on dry turtle shells, soon began to fill the air. A female bowed to the chief and started the first dance. She kicked her floor-length bark skirt with her feet, making it snap at every turn. Her arms waved gracefully, but her long torso was hard and unyielding. The onlookers called her "princess," first female among all crocodiles.

Bujang watched, amazed, as the dancer turned her wrists and clawed the air. Her hips swung hard to one side and then to the other. She tore down a rooster hanging from the rafters and bit off the head. Then she squeezed black blood into cups, forcing those who sat about her to dance and drink the heady brew. Many took up her challenge to prance on the floor. Their necks and chests glistening with the aftermath of a bloody feast, they swung and jabbed torches in the air in tune with the beat.

After watching the spectacle for some time and shouting encouragement to a few dancers, Semaga turned to Bujang and asked, "Why are you travelling in this land, my son?"

Bujang peeled his gaze away from the revellers. "I am on an expedition, Uncle. My longhouse needs a reason for celebration. We also need the presence of strong guardian spirits."

"You are aware of the pact between humans and crocodiles?" On seeing Bujang's nod, he continued, "Good, then I will explain no further. I have to warn you though, that the crocodiles of the Klauh River interpret the pact differently. They believe they have a right to kill any trespassing human."

The chief turned his gaze to the horns of the deer and said, "To the east is a hillock. On its peak is a standing grave. The bones of a great Iban war leader reside within. I have seen men going there asking for guidance from his spirit, though few received any. The chief is known to be proud, like the hornbill. You will need the help of the gods to get his advice."

As Bujang took in Semaga's directions, a tottering man thrust a pungent rooster in front of his face. The young man involuntarily pushed it away. With a slur in his voice, the crocodile-man asked, "Is the traveller so high-minded that he finds our drink beneath him?"

Bujang responded as deferentially as he could. "No, my friend. I am a human, raised by orang utans. My spirit is not strong enough to take too much of this drink."

The man snorted, "The spirit of a child." The throng around him, including Semaga, bellowed with laughter. Within moments the uproar spread to the rest of the people, most of whom were unaware of the reason for mirth.

Abruptly, the chief stood up and pulled Bujang after him. He needed to test the young warrior because he wanted to give him a gift, but customs required that he gave it to someone worthy. The host began the first step of the *ngajat bunoh*, the dance of war.

Undaunted, Bujang bent his legs and lifted his arms, making the crocodile-women murmur on seeing his strong bare thighs. His shoulders and arms parried Semaga's moves confidently, while his own movements remained fluid and sure.

Their shouts shook the roof, and their stomps rippled to either ends of the longhouse. Warriors rose and joined the dance, grotesque in form but beautiful in valour. These dances were occasions for the men to display their attributes, and many used the opportunity to show their prowess to the women who caught their fancy.

The night grew deeper and darker, swallowing all signs of life outside the longhouse. Exhausted, Bujang wanted to stop, but the revellers would not allow him to.

Then he observed something strange happening. It was not a surprise, yet he had never seen it before; their faces changed. Their teeth grew jagged, and their heads flattened as nostrils elongated to form jaws. They crawled on the floor on all fours, then jumped into the air and banged down hard. The music was consumed by the noise. Only Semaga remained standing on two legs.

A crocodile roared, and Bujang twirled so that, unintentionally, the tail of his loincloth lashed out and slapped the reptile on the upper jaw. The enraged creature charged, and Bujang leapt out of his way. He swung around in time to spring on the reptile's back. He twisted the front flap of his loincloth around its closed jaws. The crocodile jerked, twisted its body and whipped its tail savagely in its effort to roll. But Bujang's iron grip was tempered with terror, and it could not be loosened.

Semaga's laugh clapped like thunder. The reptile submitted.

Bujang released his grip and unwrapped the flap, then stood up on shaky legs. Thick smoke began to fill the house. He coughed to clear his lungs, but the ever-thickening billows forced him down on his knees. He peered about for a way out but found himself fenced in by flames. The smoke weighed him down like a log.

Then darkness overcame him.

* * *

Cool water licked his outstretched arm. Bujang opened his eyes and tasted mud in his mouth. He tried to turn, but a paralysing chill held him stubbornly in its grip. He gazed towards the eastern horizon and was relieved to see the face of a red sun, for the light was a promise of warmth, heat.

Slowly he turned his neck and realized that one of his arms was pinned under the body of an open-mouthed crocodile. The creature, however, was snoring noisily, evidence of too much wine.

Bujang pulled out his stiff arm and pushed himself up. Pain shot up from the back of his right leg and made him bite down on his lips to stifle a scream.

He turned to look at the source of the pain. Dark crocodile-scale patterns had been burnt onto the sensitive flesh of his thigh, and a charred stripe circled his calf like a bracelet. More of the same pattern had been drawn on his other leg. A large male saurian lay next to his left side, holding a smouldering thorn in his jaws and snoring softly. The sight galvanized Bujang to action. He had no intention of waiting until his host wake up to continue the artwork.

He looked about the bodies of basking reptiles and was relieved to find his belongings unscathed by the fire of the previous night. As quickly as his stiff limbs would allow, he stumbled out and into the jungle of *nipah* palms and ran towards the morning sun.

Ordinarily he would have relished the new day and looked forward to resuming his quest. But now his muscles were sore from his cold bed, and his right leg smart from the burns. Giant roots appeared wider apart than usual, and he had trouble skipping from one buttress to another. Previously apparent sinkholes became invisible, and mischievous roots tripped him, some even making him fall flat on his face. He was so angry with himself for being slow that he would not stop to rest. On he went, fortunately encountering no enemies.

After a long while of this gruelling travel, the last remnant of the day led Bujang into a small glade. He fell down in exhaustion, his chest heaving as he tried to catch his breath. After a while, he caught a familiar scent in the air, mingled with the aroma of his favourite fruit. He picked himself up and saw half of a peeled *cempedak* in the middle of the clearing. He sat down before it with his left leg crossed and the other lightly stretched in front of him. A great longing filled his heart, for it had been many moons since he last shared a meal with Nuai, his beautiful niece.

He looked about as he ate, hoping to catch a glimpse of her, but other than the symphony of insects and the shadows of fluttering bats, he heard and saw nothing. Still, he thought, she had been here and left this food for him. After his meal, he rolled in his blanket and slept like a child for the remainder of the night.

* * *

Bujang woke up renewed to a fresh sunrise. A pile of soft, wild guavas and red, soft leaves lying next to the consumed *cempedak* indicated that Nuai had come and gone. The fruit was sweet, and pink juices ran down the side of his mouth as he ate. Recalling how Nuai had always insisted that he finish his meals, he rolled the leaves and chewed down on every single piece. After again searching the surrounding for her to no avail, he cut a bamboo growing at the edge of the clearing and carved patterns in low relief onto it. The eyes of doves decorated the top border, with bamboo shoots sprouts in the bottom margin. Square motifs of two adults linked by two children on either side circled the row between them. He placed the bamboo message on the ground, picked up his things and continued eastward. Nuai would be pleased to learn that he had found a mate.

Jogging steadily until the sun set behind him, he stopped to rest and attended to his growling stomach. He opened a food pack and ate an egg. Memories of Upa revived his spirit, and since the moon was out, shining brightly that night, he decided to continue his journey to make up for the time he had lost from the day before.

Giants stood out black against the silver light of the moon, and fireflies shone like stars in the blackness of the rainforest. The air swirled with tendrils of mist that rose from the ground like smoke from a dying fire as he ran past. Gradually the shadows of buttress trees shrunk before him. A hornbill called, which made him turn his head. There to his right, about a mile away in a straight line, stood a low hill.

A warm sensation, like mature wine, coursed through his veins, and he sprinted towards the hillock. He ran so fast that the wind whistled past him. Logs that lay in his path broke like twigs. In the time it took him to take ten breaths, Bujang found himself standing on the summit. He stared up at a massive log that rose straight from the ground like a column pointing the way heavenward.

The carved trunk was so wide that two men could barely touch their fingers together if they were to embrace it. It was as tall as five brave men, and it raised the bones so high that no outstretched bough could hide the remains of the warrior from the gods. Under the light of the moon, Bujang could see that the colours of the coffin-sized wooden hut set on its peak had faded away. Plants, rivers and scenes of life were etched onto the surfaces of the hut and the column, both to reflect the greatness of the chief and to cover the bodies of his slaves. Bujang ran his hand over the surface of the carved log and felt the resin used to seal the covering. He reckoned that there were at least two slaves sealed within. Then he looked up and wondered if there were more. Bujang bowed before the log and asked for permission from its spirit to spend the night there. "I am alone, great chief, and I have nowhere to sleep. I hope that you will agree to my company."

He took out two packets of rice and some smoked fish and egg. One portion was placed at the foot of the log, while he ate the second. Then he poured rice wine on the ground and drank a mouthful, as a sign that he dined together with his host.

Seeing that there was no tree nearby that was wide enough to protect his back, he leaned against the log and yawned loudly. It was a warm night. Above his head, a young hornbill flew down and perched on the roof of the coffin.

A sedative-like drowsiness fell upon Bujang, and he dozed off. Soon he was snoring so loudly, even the gentle spirits in the jungle were annoyed. A sharp jab poked him in the chest, waking him up with a start.

A silver coated deer with intricate white horns and brass earrings glowered down at him. The animal said, "Who are you? What are you doing here?"

Bujang yawned and stretched. "I am Bujang Maias. I have come seeking guidance from the great chief."

The deer snorted contemptuously. "There is no guidance for the likes of you here. Go away, Iban."

Bujang rubbed his eyes with his fist. He squinted at the deer. "Could you at least tell me where to go for guidance? I am looking to take the heads of three evil men. I want someone to tell me where I can find them."

The deer ignored his request and simply turned up its nose and trotted back into the jungle.

Again, Bujang leaned back and fell asleep. Once more the surroundings shook with his loud snore.

For the second time, the lone traveller felt a jab on his chest. The deer had returned. "Go away, I say, there is nothing for you here."

"Tell me where to go."

Fur bristling with irritation, the deer said, "Very well. I will tell you what the spirits say. Twenty harvestings ago, four men swore to serve Keling but turned against him when they received the spirit of the warrior. Tama Ramun was given the strength of a bear, Salang the grace of a hornbill and Burak received the speed of a python. Terbai Lang, who rumour declares was killed by you, was given the agility of a gibbon. Each warrior was meant to represent Keling, to protect the rituals and to act as guardians. Each had become proud and bloodthirsty. There is nothing that whets their appetite more than the smell of human blood."

"How do I find them?"

The deer ambled back to the jungle as it called to him, "I wish you luck."

Bujang watched it go with frustration. But he was tired and could not think properly. Once more he leaned back on the standing log and slept. Again, his snore tore through the area. He was awoken by a third sharp jab on his chest.

The deer's nostril flared. "How can you call yourself a warrior? You are so loud even a blind man could find your head."

Bujang grunted. "Do you know how I can find these three men?"

The deer shook with rage. Then it stabbed the log with its antlers and broke off a horn. It kicked it towards Bujang. "The creatures of the jungle will tell you where they are. Put this horn on the ground whenever an animal crosses your path. It will be obliged to show you which direction to take."

The young man called out his thanks as the deer walked away. When the animal turned to observe what he would do next, it was annoyed that he had chosen to go back to sleep.

Just then, a loud flapping of wings made it look up in time to see the shadow of a bird cross the moon. No more snores came out of Bujang, and the jungle resumed its usual symphony for the rest of the night.

10

Vigour returned twofold with the new sunrise. Bujang scanned the horizon from the top of the hillock and breathed in the scent of the land which shone like the face of a new bride. Around him, fruit trees blushed red with new leaves, and at the foothill, yellow flowers tumbled like a waterfall from the bough of a black cassia.

He jogged down the slope and approached a medium-height tree. Its branches were laden with pink, bell-shaped water apples, which made it droop over the ground. He picked some to eat, and the juiciness of the fruit quenched his thirst, while the grubs growing within added sweetness to his breakfast.

He trotted farther down and caught sight of a squirrel scurrying in the branches. As he dug into his travelling basket for the deerhorn, he called out, but the animal only picked up speed.

Bujang crashed into the undergrowth after it. He did not expect what happened next: the ground opened. He flailed and grabbed for the nearest branch, but the limb broke, throwing both him and the squirrel down to a bed of fern four feet below. He dropped the horn on the ground and called out, just as the squirrel turned tail to run in the opposite direction.

"Hey, brother squirrel. I only want to ask for direction. Why do you run?"

The squirrel trembled, but its feet appeared to be frozen to the ground. "I can smell meat on your breath. Please don't harm me. I am not even worth a mouthful of food to you."

"Tell me how to find Tama Ramun, and I will let you go."

The squirrel stood on its hind legs and eyed him warily. Then, with tail straight up and muscle taut, it crawled forward, touched the horn and pointed it north. It drew back with increased haste, turned and scurried away with lightning speed.

Bujang called out his thanks and went in the direction pointed out to him. For three days he travelled in this manner. Sometimes he would not meet an animal for a whole day; other times he would meet four or five between the periods of two meals. Each pointed him steadily northward, with some slight detours where the jungle was difficult to traverse.

On the fifth day, after a rhinoceros told him to go east, Bujang heard a sound like the howl of a tempestuous storm. What, or who, was making that sound? Ignoring his quest for the moment, he approached the source of the noise, and as he got closer he could hear an angry male voice mingled with the sound of wailing.

Bujang proceeded carefully, for he did not want his presence to be misunderstood.

A Penan man and two teenage boys, each carrying spear-tipped blowpipes, stood in a half-circle with their backs to him. Though their yellow skin was free from tattoos, palm leaf bracelets encircled their naked arms and shins. A wailing woman sat on the ground rocking herself to and fro, and a young girl clung to her neck. Strapped to her back, in a seat basket, was a crying infant. The ground before them lay soaked in blood.

Bujang pushed aside the undergrowth and revealed himself. Instantly the man and boys turned and pointed all three blowpipes his way. The woman dragged her daughter and disappeared into the foliage.

Bujang spread wide his empty hands and said, "Greetings, brothers who walk the jungle. My name is Bujang Maias, son of *Tok Anjak*. I come because I heard weeping."

The man snarled, showing dark, strong teeth.

Again Bujang spoke. "I mean you no harm. I am looking for a man called Tama Ramun."

"What is he to you?"

"I want his head for my pillar."

"That is too good a fate for the demon. You will have to find him first before my poison dart finds his cheek."

The Penan man moved aside and revealed the broken torsos of three men, two women and five children of different ages. Bujang's soul chilled at the sight of the hacked body parts. Blood was everywhere, as though the killer had meant to bless the ground and every single plant in the vicinity with his victory. The remains of a fire lay next to the bodies.

The man said, "My name is Iot, and the old man was Mon, my father. He went ahead of me a day earlier, with my sisters and their family. This was Tama Ramun's work. He takes the heads and then he mutilates the bodies. He always mutilates the body."

Bujang studied the tracks on the soft dark ground. One pair among the many criss-crossing prints was wider and deeper than the others. He placed his foot next to it and saw that the length of the footprint was one and a half of his own.

He looked around him and ascertained that the headhunters had not hacked through the underbrush. He lowered his face to the ground and saw that their tracks headed east.

Evening rose like a mist around them. Sensing that the stranger could be trusted, Iot called back his wife and daughter, telling them to set up camp a hundred paces from the site. They covered the bodies with leaves. Then the teenage boys went out to collect firewood.

Bujang vanished into the bushes with his sword and soon returned with two gibbons. Iot took the kill from him and passed it to the woman at the other camp. She cleaned the meat and roasted it until it was dry. Then she cooked wild sago in pitcher plants over the fire. One of the boys sent the food over to his father and their guest, while the other brought fresh firewood and used a burning stick to build a fire for the two men. Then Iot sent them back to their mother's side.

For the whole time, Iot remained squatting on the ground, ready to sprint the moment he sensed danger. After their silent meal, he asked shyly, "I have heard much about you Bujang Maias. Were you really raised by the apes?"

"Yes, I grew up among them. A chief of their kind adopted me as his son."

"This is a strange thing to hear. How did they treat you?"

"As one of their own. The adults chastised and disciplined me like any young ape. In the evenings I sat with my father and learned many things from him."

"The spirits looked upon you with great favour. Did they also tell you to take Tama Ramun?"

"I heard his name called in a dream."

"Then you shall be successful in your quest. Be careful, though, for I hear the demon has many men."

After a thoughtful silence, Iot continued, "But I also hear that his men don't stay long with him. He is too cruel, and few can remain loyal for long."

"Will they run if I tell them to?"

"Look at my frail father and the children that could barely fend for themselves. Is there courage in men who strike down a group such as this?"

Iot knew that any information he possessed would help Bujang in his quest; he searched his memories for things he had heard about the assailant. "Many said that Tama Ramun's sword is so thick, it looks like an elongated axe. His blows are heavy, and he has broken many swords in the past, even ones made by the most experienced Kayan blacksmith."

Bujang said, "I have heard tales that the Penans are knowledgeable in the ironworker's craft."

"I also heard that you took Terbai Lang's head with only one stroke of your blade. May I look at your *ilang*?"

Bujang unsheathed his sword and passed it to Iot. The blade gleamed red, gold and black in the firelight.

Iot tasted the iron with his tongue and declared, "Ah, this is the work of not just any Kayan. I have not come across such iron for many harvestings. This must have been forged by Baloi Un. Strange, I know where every single one of his swords are, I know all the families that inherited them."

His brow creased as he stared at Bujang. "It is said that he forged his last sword just before he died. The ore was burned in fire fed with black coals so hard they were like rocks and white limestone so pure it was like powder. The forged blade was dipped in pig's blood and cooled in icy water. After the sword was completed, he took a boat out in the middle of the night. When the vessel returned the following morning, the people found his body covered with a *Pua* so beautiful only a perfect woman could have woven it. Where did you get this sword from?"

With his father's advice ringing afresh in his ears, he replied, "My ape-father gave it to me at his deathbed. He told me nothing of its origin."

Iot was not convinced by this story, yet he hoped it might be true. If Bujang had stolen the blade in an offhanded manner, he would die at the hand of Tama Ramun. That much Iot was sure about.

Bujang parted company with the Penans when daylight once more revealed the tracks to him. He spread wide the underbrush and followed the giant prints on the soft ground. Three miles later, he came upon the gutted entrails of a deer. The cuts clearly showed that knives had been used. As he pursued the trail of fresh blood, the jungle stretched onwards, monotonous in its thickness and assorted in its foliage.

Much, much later, fading light brought with it the smell of cooking food. Bujang crouched low and was creeping forward when a deep-throated laugh and a burp that sounded like the call of a bear reached his ears. He peeked through breaks in a wall of five-foot ferns and saw a large, big-bellied man sitting on a rock, contentedly chewing on a betel vine quid. Every now and then, he would spit out the red juice onto the ground beside him. The rest of his company sat around a fire, some tending a bubbling pot and others sharpening or wiping their swords. Bujang counted four burden baskets, and two of these were filled with human heads.

The large man, whom Bujang discerned as Tama Ramun, said, "Jau, your *selabit* is becoming empty. We cannot allow that."

Roars of laughter greeted the comment.

The charred face of a child, not older than Baling, stared out with dead eyes from the nearest basket. What kind of courage did it take to kill a child? What reason was there for such an atrocity? Bujang's hand shook with rage, and he gripped his sword handle to steady it.

Suddenly, a deep cry resounded high in the canopies. The men jumped on their heels and pulled out their weapons as they looked up with frowning faces.

Tama Ramun laughed. "It is only the hornbill, the guardian of great warriors like us."

His men's shoulders shook with self-conscious laughter as they returned to their cross-legged positions in front of the fire. None of them thought much of the fact that it was the first time they had heard the call of an omen bird so close.

Bujang's eyes narrowed. The bird had said, "Now, now." Gripping the handle of his shield, he unsheathed his sword and stepped out of the hiding place into the circle of light. Ten startled men jumped up and again reached for their weapons.

Tama Ramun's hulking form rose as he bellowed, "Hey, who are you to come to our presence like a thief?"

"I am Bujang Maias, son of *Tok* Anjak. I have come for your head. It will make a good ornament for my house."

The call of hornbills filled the jungle, making Tama Ramun's men stare up in terror, wondering what the calls meant and who the omen birds were empowering. They knew the Ape Man by reputation because reports abounded that he had killed, in his prime, Terbai Lang, a warrior gifted by the gods.

Bujang recognized the fear in their eyes as superstition mingled with self-preservation. He had seen it once before in the eyes of his people when he was a boy. Yet he had come only for Tama Ramun. He did not want to kill the others, and he shouted a warning to them: "When was the last time you heard the hornbills call out on your behalf? You have all strayed from the *adats*, the rituals passed down by the gods. They are here for my sake, not yours. I will only have Tama Ramun's head, but I will not allow anyone to stand between me and my prize."

With their weapons drawn, the men backed away. Seeing this, Tama Ramun roared, "I will kill you, lone traveller, and I will prove to my men that the war god has not abandoned me."

His thick sword arced through the air and crashed with a loud clang on Bujang's blade. Bujang stepped back and removed his sword from the lock. Tama Ramun advanced against him in a slow lumber, using his weight and strength to try to cut Bujang down, but each blow he swung after that first one only met with empty air. His frustration seeped out of him like the red saliva he sprayed out of his mouth as he shouted the war cry. The dark veins on his furrowed brow grew darker by the moment, and his face flushed to a ripe red. Though Bujang twisted, turned or rolled away from his blows, Tama Ramun could sense him watching, studying, and that made him swing even harder and wider.

Then, with a great shout, he heaved his sword back and instantly realized his mistake. Bujang's sword swung in from the side and cut across his exposed belly. Tama Ramun roared in pain and doubled over. He covered the gaping wound with one hand, holding back the entrails from spilling out. Raising his *ilang* once more, he charged.

Bujang threw his shield down and bent his knees with legs apart. As Tama's tottering form drew near, he twisted his body out of the way and struck. The blade swung through air and ploughed into the thick neck, severing the head and dropping it to the ground with a loud thud. But the body charged onward until it tripped over a log and fell down writhing before finally lying still.

Above, hornbills called, like princes drunk on the blood of their enemies. Tama Ramun's dismayed men kept their swords pointed at Bujang, while their eyes looked up, and about them. After staring for a moment at Bujang's hulking form, one man turned tail and ran. With him gone, the rest of the group's bravado crumbled like a sun-baked clay jar left to soak too long in the river. Bujang glared after them until they disappeared into the darkness.

Once he could no longer hear them, he picked up Tama Ramun's head and charred it on the fire. Then he hung it over the flames. Though tired and hungry, he would not eat from the pot of his enemy. He took out the last packet of food from his basket and ate as he waited for the head to be dried. The fire was warm, but he did not linger after his meal, for he was alone and needed the cover of darkness to hide in while he slept. He put out the fire, picked up his trophy and moved away for a mile. That night he slept in an upright position with his back guarded by a tree.

* * *

The loud honk of a hornbill startled Bujang out of his sleep. He jumped to his feet and looked up to see the adult bird perched on a high branch in the early dawn canopy. It reached down, plucked out a tail feather and released it. The plume twirled like a white, winged illipe nut as it dropped a hundred feet to the ground. Bujang reached up his right hand and grabbed the prize, and, at that same instant, the hornbill cried out with wings spread wide. It flew off with a loud roar, like ritual cloth being flapped dry in the wind.

After covering the tip of the quill with a lump of resin that had oozed out of a nearby tree, Bujang stuck the feather into his war cap. He picked up Tama Ramun's head and grimaced at the protruding purple and green veins snaking over the darkened brow. After he had strapped the snarling head to the front of his shield and stepped back to look at it, a fifteen-foot brown python slid past, all the while eyeing the trophy warily.

Bujang thought the snake might be able to help him in his mission to win the next trophy. He called out, "Hey, brother, could you point me to where I can find Salang?" He placed the deer's horn on the ground.

The snake circled it and turned the horn eastward.

* * *

Bujang ran for four days, stopping only to rest and to sleep. When the world above the canopy rained, water poured down from leaves to refresh him, and if none was forthcoming, he would cut the *lemaksawa*, a thick creeper, and drink from the pale vine. The water gushing out of the "python's fat" was as refreshing as a serpentine river. Steadily he moved, over hills and valleys and flat lands.

On the afternoon of the fourth day, as he stood on a low hill, he saw smoke billowing in the horizon. He climbed a tree and moved towards the sign of fire, hoping to find a settlement. As he approached the edge of the jungle, the sound of mourning drifted his way in snatches. He climbed between the branches cautiously; then, looking down from the top of the highest tree, he saw the burned remains of a longhouse. He counted eighteen headless bodies that were either too young or too old to have the strength to put up a defence. Broken corpses of infants lay next to the pillars, smashed against the very timber that had once sheltered them. A man tore his hair and beat his chest as he screamed hysterically. "*A curse on Salang, a curse on his seeds. May our souls never rest until he is destroyed.*"

The scene brought back vivid memories of Bujang's own childhood. He had lived because he was chased out of the house. He should have persuaded the people to leave with him. He should have insisted that he had made no pact with a demon. They might have believed him, and if they had, they would have read the omens or interpreted their dreams differently and been saved. The smell of rotting flesh and the taste of residual terror returned and filled his lungs and mouth. He had seen enough.

He had no will left to approach the distraught people, so he moved away from the carnage with no direction in mind. His only thought was to get as far away as possible. A long-forgotten grief like rock weighed down his belly, and his legs felt weak. Every bough looked like the other, and he felt as though he was moving in circles.

Finally he stopped to stare towards the horizon. A dove's cooing reached his ears, and he looked down. The green bird shone like a jewel in the bright daylight, while its pink crown moved from side to side, playing with him as though he was still a boy. Bujang smiled. The breeze still carried the smell of smoke, but it also carried the sound of cooing doves and reminded him of the day when hope had returned to him. He took a deep breath. Slowly, strength returned to his limbs. He climbed to the lowest branch and studied the ground below.

The rose apple dove cooed, "You cannot find him that way."

Bujang said, "Salang has killed many. He will be heavy laden and will leave a trail."

"Yes, he will. And he knows that. He will kill you before you even sense him."

"What should I do then?"

"Move three miles away from this place. Then build a fire. Omen birds will lead him to you."

"How many men are with him?"

The dove cocked its head to one side and was quiet a moment. Finally it said, "More than one."

"How do I fight them?"

"I have never killed before, but I am very good at protecting my nest. I always pick an open branch that will give my pecking and flapping a good advantage."

Bujang thanked the dove and moved back into the jungle. He picked a space with an open canopy and hacked down any surrounding undergrowth around it that was thick enough to hide a man. Then he left the site to hunt for his dinner and to get firewood.

On his return, and after he had chopped the meat of a monitor lizard that was unlucky enough to have crossed his path, he started a small fire. As the meat cooked, he rubbed his blade with a piece of soft bark. Darkness surrounded the camp now, like a wall. He placed the *ilang* under the cooking meat and caught drips of fat on its surface. Then he rubbed the blade down again.

At that instant, a hornbill called out. Bujang rose, sword ready in his grip. High above him, the bird had said, "One man, two men, four men."

Bujang called out, into the darkness, "Show yourselves. Don't you know that it is easier to hunt for your own lizard? I don't let anyone take my dinner away from me."

Fierce shouts filled the air as seven men jumped into the circle of light. Oblong shields carved with the faces of monsters or covered with scaly pangolin skins stood between him and the men. Bujang laughed – seven men against one! He picked up his shield and waved it in front of the men, and the attackers faltered on seeing Tama Ramun's head.

The leader, Salang, shouted curses at his men and then said, "May you all die here tonight."

Three men grinned, and their eyes burned with a maniacal light. There was no shame in a warrior's death, as good things awaited them in the other world. They were not afraid of dying. They circled the Ape Man.

Bujang yelled with the hornbill's call. Three men rushed at him from behind, while their leader attacked him face on. Bujang twirled with one leg in the air, kicking one man away. He crouched as the hornbill above him stooped. He arched his sword as the bird sliced the air with its feathers and cut open the chest of one man. Then the blade shot out and pierced the heart of another. His left arm lifted to deflect a blow coming from his side. A sword smashed into his shield, and was caught in the softwood. Before the man could twist his blade free, Bujang yanked his shield to the side and struck the weapon-deprived man's face with the edge of the shield.

Again the bird called out. The three remaining men faltered. They looked fearfully to their leader with eyes pleading for an explanation, for they could not understand why the bird was helping Bujang. After all, Salang was protected by the hornbill spirit, and it was he who had told them that his spirit guardian had promised them a great reward that night.

Salang trembled with so much hate that his scowling face turned dark with the strain of controlled rage. He threw his shield to the side, lifted his sword with both hands and charged. Bujang did likewise, and their ear-splitting shouts preceded the clash of iron. The jungle shivered, and animals screeched, horrified with the violence saturating the air. Bujang leapt back, and the hornbill dropped onto a log behind him, its black wings stretched to the length of a grown man's arms. The red, horn-like casque on its crown shone like fire as it threw back its head. A loud honk shook the branches and sent the other three fighting men away from its presence in terror.

Salang sensed now that this night would be his last, that the warpath god had sent another to kill him. Anew he charged, not to kill but to die. Bujang's *ilang* swung straight for his neck, and suddenly the jungle spun around him in a swift blur. His head fell into the flames, and fire scorched his eyes.

Bujang stood mesmerized as Salang's headless body hurtled forward and crashed into a tree. After breathing deeply to calm his passion, he trudged towards the fire, picked up the head and roasted it over the flames after impaling it on the end of a stick.

A loud swoosh filled the air as the hornbill flew off. Standing upright on the log was a single tail feather. Bujang picked it up and jabbed it into his war cap. Then he pulled out the stuck blade from his shield and strapped the newly seared head below Tama Ramun's drying face. He made no attempt to take the other men's heads. He could not carry so many, and they were lesser trophies.

Now, finally, he remembered that he was hungry. Quickly he gobbled down his dinner, rolled the leftover meat in wide leaves and stuffed the food inside his basket. Then he put out the fire and moved some distance into the pitch dark. He decided to sleep in the high branch of an emergent, a tree so tall that it rose above the jungle canopy like a tower, for Salang's men might recover their courage and look for him.

The stars shone brightly that night, and the higher he climbed the old trunk, the brighter the night became. Finally he found a leafy bough that was sturdy enough to hold him and his belongings. After shaping the branches into a nest, he lay on his back and drowsily watched the twinkling points above him. The lights made him recall his human father's admonishment to never to count the stars, for there were too many, and an endless pursuit would only weaken a man's soul. He fell asleep, lulled by the sound of fluttering leaves.

11

As the morning, dawned, Bujang gazed dreamily into the pink hues of a cloudy sunrise. Before him, the canopy lay open like a field of waking green, and the air there was as fresh as the cool, clear waters of *Tuai* Laing's land. It had been many days since he had felt so at peace. His legs hung down the sides of a bough as he straddled it, while his right hand caressed its moss-covered surface. It was warm and soft like Upa's thigh, and the headiness of the memory made his face flush. He squeezed. The softness under his hand crumbled. Startled, he stared down at the crushed moss in his palm.

A woodpecker cackled. Bujang replied with a guffaw as he bashfully swung his legs back and forth like an embarrassed child. Then he curled one leg over the branch, turned to face the bird and said, "Greetings brother woodpecker. I am a lone hunter, seeking trophies to hang on my pillar."

The bird cocked its red crown sideways, showing rows of jagged tattoo-like patterns on its chest and neck. As it scrutinized the shield from its perch, its golden backfeathers bristled and its black tail flapped up and down in jittery glee.

"Yes, yes. I can see Tama Ramun and Salang on your shield. You need one more, Burak. May all serpents with venom spit on him."

"Do you know how I can find him?"

"He usually tries to seek favours from Ribai around this time, when men sharpen their machetes to clear land for sowing. Rumour has it that the river god hides himself among the crocodiles whenever he senses the visit."

The woodpecker skipped towards the shield in search of crawling insects. As its head bobbed about and between the trophies, it said, "Don't walk on the ground, for the jungle is difficult to traverse. If you follow the branches of the canopies you should be able to reach the *Batang Lupar* in five days. Keep the evening sun to your left and the morning sun to the side of the hand that has caressed an uncaring bough."

Bujang thanked the bird and strapped his belongings securely to his back. He stepped close to the edge of the bough, then bent and straightened his legs as he used his weight to sway it up and down.

At the fourth swing, he leapt into the air with arms outstretched. The branch he grabbed snapped under his weight and swung him to a lower branch. He squatted low as he landed on a thick limb that bowed, and then again his body sprung forward with arms outstretched. Above him, giant hornbills and hawks flew in great heights, and the spirit of a sacrificed pig ran upwards, bearing an important message to the gods. Like they that raced to their fate, Bujang jumped from branch to branch by using the momentum of springy boughs to help him reach ever farther.

As the day began to spread the first grey layer of night, he selected a sturdy branch and sat down with his back leaning against the straight spine of the tree. Feeling the first chill of the night, he unfolded his blanket and draped it over his shoulders. A wood owl barked, and Bujang barked back a reply.

The owl flew up to the edge of his branch, warily studying him. Its gourd-like form was covered in downy brown feathers peppered with white. The bird said, "What are you? You are too big to be an owl, and you don't perch. You let your legs hang down the side."

"I am a human," Bujang replied. "My name is Bujang Maias."

"Ah, the son of *Tok* Anjak. I have heard of you, Ape Man. I am *Tuai* Tutut, the chief of the wood owls. What are you doing here?"

"Forgive me if I have intruded into your home without permission. I am on my way to the great Lupar River. I hear that Burak goes there around this time."

"Yes, indeed he does. He leaves a trail of stench behind him after each visit. But what do you want with him? Why would the son of a peaceful ape seek the company of a monster?"

"I do not seek his favour. I wish to take his head."

A commotion of squawks and thuds of falling bodies issued from the surrounding branches. Bujang looked down and saw a few owls picking themselves up from the understory greenery.

Tuai Tutut said, "Do not worry about my kinfolk. They are only surprised that you should be daring enough to want to face Burak alone. He usually has five to seven other men with him, all of whom are uncommonly bold."

Having explained his relatives' surprising clumsiness, the bird twisted its head to the side and called out, "Bring food and call the elders. Bujang Maias shall be our guest tonight."

The chief's instruction was echoed all about them, and soon the resounding barks rose to a deafening uproar. Elder owls joined them on the branch, and younger ones brought food: raw mice and small birds, as well as palm wine that had been fermented in pitcher plants. Bujang stared at the dead animals in dismay as he tried to think of ways to decline the food without offending his host, for the feast at Semaga's house had made him wary of raw meat.

Then he had an idea and asked, "Would you like me to show you how to build a fire?"

Young owls fluttered with excitement because they had seen human campfires before, which had made them wonder what a fire was like up close. Bujang climbed down to the ground to look for a slab of stone, while the birds searched for dry branches and twigs. Wide eyes grew wider as they watched him raise smoke from the twigs with a short piece of rattan. They pressed against him when tongues of flames started licking the dry sticks. They watched with awe as he skewered the rats, and cooked these over the fire. But on tasting human cuisine, the birds decided that they didn't need fire. Fresh meat still tasted best, and their down feathers were also warm, which made the heat from the fire almost unbearable. In spite of that, both man and owls agreed that the sweet wine, made from palm nectar, was the best drink in the land.

While the males worried over the rudiments of starting a fire, the females tittered over the two heads strapped to the shield. A hero was a rare treat, and they were allowed to be less modest around ones like him. Owl-maidens began to eye him coyly, and two boldly sat on his lap. The female attention confused Bujang, and *Tuai* Tutut's act of plying him with wine only aggravated the situation. The young man tried his utmost not to show partiality to any of the females, for *Tok* Anjak had always been adamant that he only know his own kind: a seed planted in strange ground would not bear fruit but would wither and die. So he was relieved when owl musicians began to click their beaks to create a symphony in the canopy, for it gave him an opportunity to turn his attention overhead to distract himself from their feminine charms.

In the open sky, male owls danced in swooping circles to both dazzle the females and impress the guest. They dived towards each other but swung away just before collision. Some turned like spinning tops with their wings spread out. Others flew delicately, like airborne seeds caught in a breeze. Even after the females gave up and left him alone, Bujang continued to watch the dancers until he grew drowsy.

He slept fitfully that night because the air was cold. The wind rustled small leaves in sporadic gusts and made floating petals and seeds dance in swirls above the canopy. When Bujang woke up the following morning, the owls were gone, but they had left him wine and a string of rats they had attempted to cook while he slept. He called out his thanks, then placed these gifts in his basket.

The new day brought a thunderstorm that slowed his progress, but by late afternoon the sky cleared, and a warm sun and fast-dripping leaves chased off so much moisture that even before the sun had sunk low to the west, all trace of rain was gone. In the next few days, Bujang traversed the branches for as far as the light of day would allow him. He tried to seek the company of friendly animals in the evenings, but many were afraid of the heads strapped to his shield and kept their distance. Demons, however, came to crowd his dreams at night, blessing and cursing him in turn.

At the first sign of dusk on the fourth day, he chose a high branch. There he sat, staring with unseeing eyes into the horizon. Memories of pythons that had crossed his path in the past reminded him of their kindness. One had even kept him company and taught him about the manners of its own kind. There were few animals that could fight them, and he felt as though he had not learned enough about them. He wondered if he should wait a few more harvestings, or at least until he felt strong enough to face Burak.

But soon he realized that he had reached a point where he could no longer turn back. The fierce python of his dream had not just killed defenceless victims but also warriors at the zenith of their strength. Even women blessed with the strong protective spirits of weaving were not spared. Every headhunter was also aware that the taking of a trophy would grant him the powers of his victim; thus the fact that he had taken the heads of Terbai Lang, Tama Ramun and Salang had made his head a great prize to Burak. Returning to the longhouse now would only expose his people to Burak's wrath.

He lifted his face to the heavens and saw that the sun had begun to stain the sky in red gold. He imagined seeing the silhouette of the house of heaven as he wondered if there was any god who would come down on his behalf, if there was any god that would help him.

A heavy wheezing startled him out of his brooding. He climbed two branches down and parted the leaves to find an old hornbill perched unsteadily on a limb. His plumage was frayed from age, and patches of dark skin showed where turfs of feathers had fallen off. The bird looked up with greying eyes and said, "This is a good day to see you again, my son."

"*Tok* Jakun, is it you?" Bujang called out with joy.

"Yes, it is. You have become a fine young man."

"Why have you stopped visiting the herd? Father missed your company."

"It would be strange if I visited. He killed my brother, Takan."

Bujang climbed down, sat next to the bird and said with a lump in his throat, "I am sorry it happened. It was all because of me. Are you still angry?"

"I was never angry. Takan had always been trouble, and his action was against the will of the gods. The *adat*, however, requires that I take revenge on his behalf. That was why when your father walked east, I flew west and when he roamed north, I glided south. In that manner, if anyone should ask, I can rightfully say that I have looked for him everywhere but never found him."

At a loss for words, Bujang could only say, "It is good to see you again."

"Even when your spirit appears troubled?" *Tok* Jakun asked as he stared pointedly at the shield strapped to his shoulder.

Bujang unstrapped his belongings, stood up, unsheathed his sword and chopped away a branch. The canopy opened to show a wide, empty horizon filled with colours of blue, red and gold. Quietly they gazed into the shades that weavers and orchids try so tediously to imitate.

The bird broke the rainforest silence. "Today is another day for me. Each day, a new day. Yet in each new day I look forward to it being my last."

Without a word, Bujang scrambled twenty branches away and sixty feet down until he came upon a *langsat* tree heavy with bunches of ripe ochre fruits. About the tree were birds and small animals which had been attracted by the sweet scent. He grabbed stalks with thick bunches of globes, spilling white sap onto his hand and dropping overripe fruits to the ground below. His ascent was slow because he was careful not to scrape the fruits against the boughs and tear them off their stems. On seeing the *langsats*, the hornbill rocked his head from side to side with glee. They ate: *Tok* Jakun taking the marble sized globes whole, while Bujang peeled the sappy skin and swallowed the translucent, sweet, acidic flesh together with the bitter seeds.

After the meal, the hornbill stared longingly into the dark sky. "Let me bring a message from you to the warpath god," he said.

"You will fly to his house for me?"

"No, I am too weak to fly now. But my spirit will soar."

Bujang was baffled for a moment, but as the meaning of the suggestion dawned on him, he cried out, "No, you are a friend. I will not sacrifice you."

"Don't think of it as a sacrifice. Consider it your act to end the blood feud between us. In any case, if I don't die today, I will die tomorrow. Let me carry a message for you."

"I can stay with you till the end."

"If you continue to feed me as you do now, I may not pass into the spirit realm until the new harvesting. Many more will die while you wait. There is a reason why you meet me today. In the land of

Sengalang Burong, coincidences are only for the unenlightened, and I am not one of those." He chuckled and continued, "Rest assured, I have no living relatives who will avenge my death."

Bujang turned his anguished face away, for this was not a thing he could ask from a friend. The hornbill's voice rose. "I am a warrior. I will not wither under the stare of feeble spirits. I shall fly again."

The young man gazed into his face and beheld that it was neither frail nor afraid. Warrior pride had puffed up *Tok* Jakun's sparse feathers and lifted his frayed wings. The sight almost made Bujang cry, as he recalled how beautiful the hornbill had once been and saw how beautiful he was still. He pulled the sword of Keling out of its sheath and wrapped one arm over the hornbill.

Holding the blade against the old warrior's throat, he said, "Tell Sengalang Burong that I am now reaching the end of my quest. Ask him to bless me and to protect me. Plead for his mercy on my behalf, and if none is forthcoming, plead to the other gods for mercy. Goodbye, old friend."

He grasped the bird's head firmly and sliced the throat, though not severing it. Blood spurted out and splashed the white plumage of the hornbill's fluttering tail. Bujang held the convulsing bird close to his chest, where his tears became mixed with the blood that anointed *Tok* Jakun's black bosom. The Ape Man looked up and was comforted when, through a curtain of sorrow, he saw a perfect hornbill flying over the soul path. Once the spirit had disappeared into the horizon, he stood up while still cradling the body and scanned the branches for a good place to bury his friend. In the dim light, he glimpsed a large crevice in a neighbouring branch.

Tenderly he rolled the body with his blanket and placed it inside the opening before taking out the deerhorn from his basket and laying it next to the hornbill. He searched the surrounding boughs for fruits and insects, which he arrayed next to the carcass, together with some *nipah* wine. After he had covered the hole with fresh leaves stripped from drooping branches, he climbed down to the ground and returned with red clay wrapped in a large yam leaf.

He sealed his friend's grave with clay and said, "One day we shall meet again – Father, you and I – in a land where there are no taboos to separate us. That will be a good day indeed."

The spreading night pondered and the canopy marvelled as he wept and sang of the great deeds of *Tok* Jakun. The trees would never again tremble under the roar of the hornbill's wings, and branches would nevermore feel his living weight. Men would no longer hear his omen calls, for his spirit had become too enduring for a changing world.

* * *

Bujang ate the last piece of rat in his pouch. From where he sat, he could see the glimmer of a large river in the distance. He reckoned that he should reach the place by noon. After more swinging and traversing, and when he was less than a mile away from his destination, he climbed down.

His eyes were drawn to large bunches of ripe *engkala*, just a few yards from the ground: pink fruits with soft, creamy flesh that encircled drooping single stems like droplets of dew, clinging thickly onto a twig. His stomach growled. Quickly he slid down, unstrapped his belongings and leaned them against a moss-covered log before hastening away to collect the fruit. Once his arms were filled with *engkalas*, he turned back to the log. To his astonishment, he saw that his things were no longer where he had left them.

He hunched low and turned his head from side to side as he warily studied the surroundings. A few yards away stood the shield that still leaned against the log. No one was in sight in that eerily silent area – not a single bird called; not an insect chirped.

Careful not to drop the fruits, he slowly moved along the length of the log, all the while checking the ground for tracks. He came upon his basket first and placed his meal inside before hitching it to his shoulder. Then he crept forward a few yards and collected his sword. With his courage returned, he plodded towards the shield with a naked blade in his grip, while his contorted face turned left and right to exhibit his fearlessness to any hidden foe. He found the shield hooked to a horn-like branch on the trunk.

He turned around thrice as his eyes again scanned the surrounding, but he saw nothing other than the jungle and a large boulder lying in the middle of a small clearing. He shrugged and sat down cross-legged facing the rock as he leaned against the log. The creamy fruits tempted him like a feast laid before a starving man. He took a bite. A strange rumbling filled the air, and he looked up. The patches of sky above him were clear. He ate some more. Again rumblings issued, followed by a loud snort and the stench of a hundred reptiles. Bujang jumped onto his heels and bent his knees with one hand, bravely flaunting a sword, with the other hand firmly holding a fruit. A loud roar, followed by barks of laughter filled the clearing, and a strong breeze blew dead leaves into his face.

The boulder moved and slid along the ground. Bujang braced himself, for he was not sure if his sword could kill the monster. Nobody had warned him of a living rock.

Then the boulder lifted off the ground, and, as the clay and leaves fell off it in chunks, he saw that it was a giant snake with a face as large as a door and a body as wide as a tree.

Again the creature laughed. He laughed so hard, loosened scales shook moss and soil to the ground. His ancient eyes scrutinized Bujang; then they squinted, and he laughed again. With two deep breaths and a cough, the monster tamed his mirth long enough to say,

"Only pigs eat this fruit. I planted the tree here to attract pigs for my meal. "Ha-ha-ha."

With wonder, Bujang watched the snake chortle. He felt the ground move beneath his feet and saw the trees shake from the breath coming out of the reptile's mouth. More moss and earth cracked and fell off the elongated body, revealing scales that shone like mirrors and shook like dragonfly wings.

Finally the snake heaved a deep breath and brought his head close to the shield. A calmer rumble emitted from his long belly. "Ah... these are the heads of Tama Ramun and Salang. You must be Bujang Maias. I heard the birds chattering about your planned visit to *Batang Lupar*."

"Forgive me for intruding into your land, Great One, without asking for permission. I should also not have taken the food from your trap," Bujang replied.

The snake settled himself down. "There is no need to apologize. I have not laughed in many centuries. That is gift enough for me."

Cautiously Bujang asked, "Forgive me for asking, Great One. Who are you?"

The snake stared back in surprise, then he laughed. He laughed till he rolled over, adding to Bujang's discomfiture. Finally he said, "What the macaque bard told me about your first meeting with Sengalang Burong must be true. You really must have offered him *cempedak* seeds. Were you never taught the forms of the gods? I am Ribai, the river god, and I take on the form of a serpent. That is the reason why all rivers are shaped like snakes."

Ribai again laughed at Bujang's shocked face. He found the youth uncomplicated and wondered that the tempestuous warpath god had not struck him dead at their first meeting. Again he turned to study the human, until his gaze caught the terrified child-like eyes that were in contrast to the young man's warrior pose. He said, "You are here for Burak, are you not?"

"Yes, I am, Great One. I heard tales that he terrorizes the land with needless deaths."

"Who told you to go for the heads of these three men?"

Bujang replied with some hesitation, aware of the fact that he had not sought permission before the start of his expedition. "A dream prompted me to take the path of war, and a deer gave me their names. But I have not sought for omens from the gods."

Ribai smiled, contorting his reptile face into a grotesque grimace. Heroes lived within the will of the gods, but it was omens that would show the chances of a man's survival. If the omens were bad, a man could always beg the gods to be merciful and change his fate. The serpent bristled with anticipation, for the man before him had not received assurances of his own safe return. The fight between him and Burak would depend solely on his own skill.

Ribai said, "Great spirits have placed the heads of Terbai Lang, Tama Ramun and Salang into your hands. Maybe they will place the head of Burak there too. I can smell the renegade python. He will be here before nightfall. Wait for him at the bank. I will move into the river and hide myself under the water."

The god turned his face away and slithered towards the watercourse, pulling the shield along as it moved. Bujang dashed forward, grabbed for his *terabai* and broke the horn-shaped branch. He quickly picked it up, embarrassed that he had broken off a part of the deity. Ribai, however, did not seem to notice. Guiltily Bujang hid the stick in his basket and trotted after the ancient serpent.

Snaking roots gradually gave way to stilts as the ground grew wet and muddy. The low tide stretched the dark bank, which was peppered with bones and crocodiles tracks for many yards away from the jungle. The river was so wide that Bujang could only see a low line of trees in the horizon.

Ribai slithered over the mud and into the water, creating a deep trough in his wake. Bujang took off his war cap, then hid it with the rest of his belongings in the hollow of a tree, keeping only the sword by his side. He climbed up the same trunk and steadily moved between the branches to reach a mangrove tree at the edge of the bank. After choosing a limb that was only two yards away from Ribai's track, he hunkered low like an owl and waited.

The sun was midway in its descent when the sound of men cutting bamboo reached his ears. While the noise continued, five men emerged out of the jungle.

Scale-like tattoos that mimicked the patterns of a reticulated python covered the apparent leader's body. The dozen hornbill feathers sprouting from his war cap fluttered in the breeze from the fast-receding tide.

Burak eyed Ribai's track and licked his lips with a forked tongue. A youth came to stand by his side, carrying a basket that dripped maggots and tainted the fresh air with the smell of rotting flesh. In the fist of a third man was a black fowl that was struggling to flap itself free from his grip. Two other men helped the boy lower his basket, and they took out three small trophies which they placed on young yam leaves.

Soon three more men joined the party, each holding a five-foot bamboo pole in one hand. Working in pairs, one man split and frayed one end of a bamboo while another stripped tough ferns of the leaves and twisted the cord loosely between the splits to form a rough receptacle.

Bujang sweated in the heat but trembled with fear. The warriors with Burak were different from the others that he had met before. Their eyes were red-rimmed, and the scowl on each face was fierce. Their dark, rugged skin appeared like leather, and their strong arms wielded long *ilangs*. He might have to fight those men to get to

Burak's head.

The party trod down the soft bank until they reached the edge of the water, upon which they planted the *teresangs*. Rice and eggs were placed in the offering baskets, and a maggot-infested head was placed inside each. Then Burak twisted the head of the fowl back, sliced its throat and anointed the offerings with blood.

He called out over the empty waters, "Oh, great father of the river. Accept our offering here today. Give us the strength of the reptile and the speed of the serpent, so that we may ever continue to bring heads in your honour. Give us your horns of prosperity, so we may show our enemies that you bless us."

A breeze rippled the waters. Stronger it blew, until it began to whistle over the surface. The men hurried back to shore. Bujang leapt down from the branch as they neared, sinking his feet into the mud up to his shin. Eight men pulled out their swords.

Burak chuckled. "I know you. You are Bujang Maias. Finally you have come for me." He signalled his men to put away their weapons, and he raised his sword against Bujang.

One man stepped aside to pull out a jutting root and swished it about him like a whip. Four of his companions rushed to imitate him while the youth collected rocks from the bank and a seventh man broke a dried branch. Then they circled Bujang and flogged him by turn every which way he turned, until welts began to appear on his back, arms and shoulders. All the while they jeered and goaded him to strike.

Sweat dripped into Bujang's eyes. There was mud on his shoulder and mud in his hands. The more he tried to wipe his eyes, the worse his sight became. He twisted his body to avoid a blow and tumbled face down into the mud. The laughter of his tormentors was followed by a dull pain on his shoulder. The youth had thrown a rock at him. When he lifted his face to take a breath, he saw Burak standing akimbo by the side and chortling at the sport his men were playing. Bujang sprung back to a stand and swung his sword back and forth with all his might as he made a dash towards the river. The two men who stood in his way fell under his blade.

The noise behind him stopped. He turned and saw a row of dumbfounded faces returning his gaze. The wind now roared. He pulled out one *teresang* and called out, "Are you all cowards? Are you afraid of water? Come out here. You all smell so bad, you need a bath."

Bujang dug his feet deep into the mud and resolved not to move from the spot, no matter how hard they attacked. It was a good day to die, he said to himself. Even so, the hilt of his sword felt slippery, and the harder he gripped it, the more it seemed to slip out of his hand. He pressed his feet harder into the mud. Though his knees began to bend and his loins to shrink, the cold mud held him up. Then his arms came down, but he kept the sword pointing upwards and outwards so that it was soon standing like a spike between him and his enemies.

Burak gnashed his teeth, raised his sword and let out a war cry as he charged. His men unsheathed their blades and ran after their captain. The wind shrieked, and a great wall of water rolled upstream.

Then the *benak* crashed down on them.

When the tidal bore pummelled him and rolled over his head, Bujang felt a force stronger than anything he had ever experienced before. His muscles strained to pull himself out of the mud. One final heave, and his feet came free. He swam to the surface and coughed out water from his lungs and stomach. Then his feet paddled as fast as the adrenaline coursing through his body. He looked towards the bank and saw that two men had managed to get to shore before the *benak* reached them. Burak himself had been swept farther upstream, but he was fast approaching, leaving behind him a serpentine wake that turned ever darker and larger as he drew nearer.

And now something extraordinary began to take place. The sword burnt like a living fire in Bujang's hand. Suddenly his skin turned red, his feet touched the bottom of the river, and he rose over the water until the raging river's surface levelled at his waist. The long call of a male ape roared out of his throat. A second *benak* surfed up the river, crashing onto his back and breaking into a million droplets.

The indigo python reared his head and bared his rancid sharp fangs. Bujang grabbed for the neck, and the serpent coiled his body around him. Muscles, like a mighty vice, squeezed. With his free hand, Bujang punched the serpent's crown over and over until he felt Burak's hold relax. Then he tore the python loose and threw him to land. The trees snapped like twigs under the onslaught. He waded to shore. The deep water remained waist-height until he was close to the bank, where he shrunk back into his normal form.

A human Burak picked himself up from the ground. He had not heard tales of Bujang's ability to morph into a giant ape and wondered how many lives the warrior had killed to gain such powers. Laughing with glee, he unsheathed his sword. Two men, one with an angry scar across his face and the other with a twisted ankle, took their places on either side of him. Burak readied himself to kill. He wanted that power. It would make him the greatest warrior the land had ever known. It would make him a god.

Bujang scowled his contempt for the opponents as he stepped into the small clearing. Water dripped from his hair and loincloth like a torrent, and steam rose from his cooling sword. He took a deep breath and grasped the hilt with both hands. All three men raised their long *ilangs* against him, and not a single one faltered before his glare. The scarred man was the first to charge.

Bujang's iron crashed against his with a loud clang, and almost immediately it turned and swung against Burak, who was attacking from behind. He barely managed to sidestep the second blow, and soon blood began to run down his upper arm in streaks like a red palm bracelet. He drew back and stepped on a broken branch. The three men spread out and circled him. Picking up the stick with his free hand, he threw it hard at the scarred man's chest. The hit produced a loud thud, followed by a cry of pain. Bujang sprinted towards him before he could regain his breath, stabbed his belly and wrested his sword from his clenched fist. Then he dropped down on his knees and threw the blade low. A loud scream proclaimed that he had hit his mark. The second man fell on his back and rolled to his side, gripping the thigh where the blade was now embedded in the bone.

While the screams and curses of the second man filled the air, the two remaining warriors scowled into each other's faces and circled one another. Burak ordered his wounded man to be silent, but he was beyond reasoning with pain, so with an enraged shout Burak sunk his blade into the man's throat. Silence.

Bujang stood his ground when Burak turned back to face him, pulled out the sword, and charged. Their *ilangs* clashed, and instantly Burak's full weight pressed down on the crossed blades. Bujang twisted his body away, and they separated. Another ring filled the air as their irons again met. This time, the crossed blades settled hot against Bujang's right cheek. Sweat drenched him. The irons suddenly screeched as Burak pulled the handle of his sword inward and struck Bujang's throat with the hilt. The Ape Man choked and drops of spittle mixed with blood sprayed out of his mouth. He drew back a few steps and coughed to try to clear his throat, but his breath continued to whistle in agony. Burak shouted triumphantly and lunged. The jungle trembled with every single war cry, and, as he forced Bujang to retreat with every blow, his face twisted with demonic glee.

Bujang forced himself to breathe deeply and felt blood gurgling in his windpipe. Again he coughed to clear the air passage, tasting more blood. The jungle whirled around him, and Burak's face began to blur. As he evaded yet another failed blow, he shouted with his whole being and mouthed the words, "I will not die today."

His sword began to burn, and the fire was so ancient it scorched his flesh to the very bones and made him scream in pain. He arced the sword as though to fling it away but then brought it down, slicing through iron and flesh like they were nothing more than young bamboo. His vision blurred. He sensed, rather than heard, the dull thud of Burak's head as it fell onto the ground.

Bujang fell on his side, his body convulsing uncontrollably. In a haze he watched Ribai slither towards him, open his mouth and bare a pair of sharp fangs dripping with dark liquid. Was this happening, or was he delirious and dying? A violent pain pierced his throat, and the terrible burn of Ribai's potent saliva coursed into his veins.

He blacked out.

12

The buzzing of a thousand flies, like a million tiny hammers, invaded his consciousness. Bujang tried to open his eyes, but they were loath to wake. A breeze swept over him, washing away the stench that had attracted the insects, and with the wind came the warmth of the sun. Then a searing thirst engulfed him. He rubbed a dry tongue against the roof of his mouth, willing it to find even a drop of moisture that was not there. He tried to call out but could only manage a hoarse breath. Rolling on his side, he involuntarily released a silent cry as life rushed back to his stiff limbs. He could move neither his arms nor legs, and he wheezed heavily as agony spread like a sudden tide over his body. When the pain subsided, he turned his body another time. His shoulder ached, and he was forced to roll on his back.

He opened his eyes and focused on the surrounding of an overcast jungle. Stilt roots caked with greying clay showed that the tide had been low for two to three days. Five yards away lay Burak's bloated body, and a charred head rested next to it. He moved his eyeballs and searched for a campfire in his limited line of vision, but there was none. A thin cloud of ash puffed out of his mouth as he coughed. Recalling the blow that Burak had struck, he moved his left arm and touched his throat and found that scabs had formed along the line of his Adam's apple.

Slowly, he pushed himself up from the ground. As though he

were a plaster idol coming to life, clay cracked and fell off him in chunks. His legs shook as he tried to stand upright, and he struggled to stay conscious. He looked down at his stiff right hand and saw that it still gripped the sword. The tip of the blade shook as he tried to slide it back into its sheath. From that elevated vantage point, again he studied his surroundings. There was no sign of the other two corpses, but a new stream now trickled down to the large river and telltale tracks of wild dogs surrounded the area.

He half shuffled, half hobbled towards the trophy. As he neared it, he saw that the fleshy parts of the cheeks and chin had been scored away. The crown, however, was still covered with a thin layer of melted flesh and fat, though only a few strands of hair remained.

Bujang dragged himself to a large yam bush. He chose a wide heart-shaped leaf and broke it off at the stem. The stinging hairs of the plant were ineffective against his clay-covered hands. He returned to the head and wrapped the whole skull, including its loose jaw, in the leaf, then twisted the stalk tightly around the bundle to secure it.

A loud flap made him look up in time to watch a hornbill land heavily on a branch in front of him. He eyed the creature guardedly.

It said, "You have earned the strength and valour of four great warriors. You shall now walk the path they walked."

"What is that path you speak of?"

"It is the warpath, the way to glory and great heroic deeds."

"I have gained what I set out to do. I wish to return to my people."

The hornbill cocked and twisted its head to one side. Then it puffed its feathers and sank lower on the branch. "Why do you wish to go back to an inglorious life? Don't you know that with the strength you gain comes also the thirst? It was the hunger for more blood that woke you. A man with lesser desire would have died. Did you not find the scent of ripe meat tempting?"

"This is not the path of my father, *Tok* Anjak."

"Your ape-father had killed before. It was his spirit that led you to these three men. And it was his spirit that rose up against Burak. Behold, the gods have now appointed you a hunting dog in the house of heaven. Either you hunt or you die starving."

The hornbill pulled out a tail feather and dropped it to the ground. "You shall spill blood again, else the hunger will drive you insane." With a roar of wind, the bird plunged into the air and swooped upwards.

Cradling the trophy in one arm, Bujang carefully stepped over roots and broken branches to reach the feather. He picked it up and stared down unseeing at the prize, for he was too tired to think.

Then he thought of his trophies. Laboriously he approached the hollow tree where he had hidden his belongings. They lay there undisturbed, thus proving the worth of the protective powers of Tama Ramun and Salang. Bujang strapped the yam-leaf bundle below the other two heads on the shield.

Though a strong urge to lie back down on the ground swept over him, he made himself unbind the sword and loincloth around his waist. He stood for a moment and then trudged towards the river and etched new tracks on the smooth surface of the muddy bank. The water he sank into was cool and tasted full of life. Ash and mud washed away in the milk-hued tide as he massaged his sore muscles. He scrubbed the soiled red loincloth and slapped it over his shoulder. On his return to shore, he wrapped on a fresh dark cloth. Feeling revived, he slung his belongings onto his shoulder and started his trek through the jungle for home.

Young tender leaves came within his grasp, and fragrant jungle fruits grew in great bunches along his way. Bujang ate as he walked. He ate when he rested, and he ate even as the land lay covered in a blanket of darkness, yet he would not be satiated. The hunger tormented him, and his legs grew heavier with each passing day. Every step felt like a thousand, and every mile like an unattainable distance. Visions of meat drenched with blood and fat plagued his dreams.

On the fifth day, he reached a point where the jungle sloped down to alluvial land dense with low overgrown trees. A tan watercourse lay beyond, the Klauh River, a tributary to the *Batang Lupar*. Bujang took a deep breath because this was the river *Tuai* Semaga had warned him about. Crocodiles basked along the dark banks, appearing like discarded logs that had been washed to shore. He contemplated making a detour, but it would cost him many more days. His stomach growled painfully. Part of him felt too wary to cross, while the other part was desperate to be home. But he must decide soon whether to cross, while the tide was still low.

A shout some distance behind startled him. He turned and recognized a face and form he knew, though he would not have expected to see him here: Raung's dark silhouette stuck out against the jungle green.

Though fourteen men stood with him, it was four less than the number that had left the longhouse. Roughly hewn bamboo spears added despair to their sorry forms, and not a single hunting dog was in sight.

Raung barked at Bujang, "Hey, you. Have my people come to their senses and thrown you out?"

"I am one of you now, Raung." Turning his face to address the other men, Bujang continued, "Come, let us return together. Your wives and children wait."

Raung said, "Of course they wait. They wait to kill us. You have turned Upa against me with your black magic. You have turned the women in the longhouse against us with your spirit charm."

"Come home peacefully."

Raung roared with rage, "Home! Home! That was my home, my house, my people. I will return ... and I will return with your head." Having issued the threat, he charged.

Bujang reached for his sword but stopped short of unsheathing it. These men were from the longhouse that had elected him as chief. He had sworn to protect their families. It would not be right for him to spill their blood, for they were his people now. He looked down the slope. The gods had decided for him, he would cross.

With all the remaining strength he could muster, he crashed down the incline. On reaching level ground, he stumbled over jutting roots and gasped for air like a drowning man. He called out to crocodile sentries between pants, alerting them to his approach.

"Allow me to pass, brothers. Allow me to use this path. For my heart pines for home and my body yearns for the company of my fellows."

The bushes behind him whipped, and the air thundered with the shouts of his pursuers. The moment he burst out of the jungle, the ground came to life. He jumped and barely avoided a crocodile's snapping jaw. He ran, all the while concentrating on what was right in front of him, never farther ahead. Steadily he approached the river and with quaking relief, splashed into the muddy water. As his feet sunk into the soft riverbed, one part screamed for him to return to dry ground while another urged him forward. With every step he took, his belly grew tighter, for he could almost feel the sensations of teeth sinking into his thigh. When the water reached his waist, the flat surface wrinkled, and he stopped. Saurians surfaced and surrounded him. He could neither move forward, nor turn back.

An old reptile snorted behind him, "What is this? What manner of joke is this? Your markings are familiar, but why are they only on one side? Is Semaga trying to play a trick on us?"

Bujang held his breath as his mind tried to understand what the old crocodile meant. Then slowly it dawned on him; Semaga had burned a tattoo on one side of his leg. Recalling how a crocodile would scorn any display of weakness he decided not to explain, for he had no wish to learn what these reptiles would do to cowards, especially ones who had run away from gifts meant to protect them. He resumed wading onwards to the opposite bank.

The crocodiles parted to let him through, although each eyed his underwater thigh curiously, for a half amulet was a thing unseen and unheard of among their kind. They must send a messenger to Semaga, to find out what he meant by tattooing only one leg. The cries of men in pain mingled with hissing bellows by the edge of the jungle turned the reptiles' attention away from him. Once more, they submerged in the low tide.

Eleven men ran down the empty bank, snapping their heads about and pointing sharp weapons down to the ground. On realizing that no danger confronted them, their callousness returned.

Raung laughed on seeing Bujang traverse the water. He called out, "Hey, coward. Come back and fight us."

Bujang stopped and turned to face them. "I am now one of you. I shall not fight you, brother."

"You are a coward. I will never admit a coward as my brother."

"Come and return to the longhouse. I will receive you back."

"Who are you to say that we may or may not return? You are a wanderer, an abandoned child. Neither your mother nor your father wanted you. Why should we want what others have thrown out as rubbish?"

On hearing Raung's humiliating words, the men laughed and taunted him, one after the other.

"You are not a man. You are rubbish your father spit out with no regards to your mother's labour."

"I shall stretch your skin over my shield and make a pretty

tobacco pouch out of your hide."

"Your tattooed shoulders will make a fine ornament on my war-vest."

Confidence, like sweat, bled out of Bujang's body. Even the slow flowing water of the river felt like a thick woven wall pushing against him. He looked heavenward but was not pacified by the golden, red sunset. He looked down and balled his hand into a fist, but he found no strength in the dark Kayan tattoos that stared back at him. Then he felt the burning glare of a black dragon-dog eye, in the centre of his black rosette tattoo. He was no longer a boy, and if he would not be a man now, he would be nothing.

Drawing a deep breath, he looked up and faced his tormentors. "I am abandoned by my flesh father, but my foster father never left my side. He guided me to the heads of Tama Ramun, Salang and Burak. Which of you can claim to have a father who loved you more?"

Raung screeched like an angry hawk. He jumped into the river, followed by his warriors. Ruthlessly they advanced, kicking up a cloud of yellow mud while Bujang stayed his ground and waited for them. Water swirled around them. Suddenly the men's war calls turned to screams of terror as the ochre murkiness came alive with crocodiles. Tails whipped through the air and jaws jumped out like lightning, grabbing any man that tried to run back to the banks. The men's blood poured out in stark contrast to the tan flow but was soon swallowed up in the low tide.

Tears streamed down Bujang's face as he watched, for it was not an end he had wanted for them. Though no one could accuse him of spilling their blood, his soul was not comforted because he knew that he had led them into the river. He turned aside and used his shield as a float to support him as he traversed the deeper ends. On reaching the other side, he bowed to the crocodiles there and asked for permission to pass.

Staggering away as fast as he could, he fled the saurian territory. He did not stop even when it grew dark. He did not look for a safe place to spend the night, for the cries of Raung and his men followed him accusingly through the jungle. He did not stop to eat, for the grief was like acid, burning a hole in his stomach. His tired limbs cried out for relief, but it only made him run harder.

He fell. Screaming in frustration, he struggled to get up. He had not wanted them dead. He had wanted so much to see them return to their families. What would he tell the wives they left behind? What was he to tell their children?

Again he tripped and fell. This time he stayed down. Covering his face with his hands, he wept. He cried because he called them brothers and they had rejected him. He cried because he believed that he deserved to be rejected because he had led them to their death. He crushed his legs against his chest and curled like an infant. The ground soaked up his salty tears.

"U ...ha, u ...ha," an old voice called out in the dark, "Whose child is this, crying all by himself in the night? Can he still not find his way home? A father never prays in vain. A father never forgets the one whom he had been given to love."

Astonished, Bujang wiped his face and saw the form of a man so old he shone like the moon. A cooking pot twice his size was strapped to his back. The young man sat up and said, "I am Bujang Maias, son of *Tok* Anjak. Why are you here, grandfather?"

"I heard a child crying. Is he hungry? Come, help me find firewood. I will cook some rice to cheer him up."

Bujang wiped his face once more of the last tears, got up and went into the jungle carrying only his sword. He approached a thirteen-foot tree and looked up at the naked branches before knocking on the soft trunk. No spirit responded, so he arced his sword high in the air, slammed it down and flung large chunks of wood to the ground.

The cut grew wider with every stroke, and soon the tree began to creak. He pushed the trunk towards the gaping bruise, and as it fell, neighbouring branches snapped. The limbs were stripped of leaves and the trunk chopped into three-foot logs, which were split into firewood. He carried as much as his shoulders could hold back to the campsite. When he returned with a second load, the old man already had a fire going and above the flames, sitting on five rocks, was the pot that had been filled with rice and water.

Grains as white as newly hatched grubs bubbled within, and starch-rich liquid spilled over the gaping rim. The old man was cooking enough rice to feed fifty grown men, and though the arms that stirred the thick mass with a piece of wood seemed frail, the bulk moved as if it was only water that was being churned.

As Bujang trudged in and out of camp to bring firewood, his tired brain wondered where the old man got the rice grain from. He also wondered where he had found water. He sensed that the stranger was not human, but in his despondent state he did not care if he meant him the worst possible harm. He was exhausted, and he expected every single exertion to be his last.

When he returned for the fifth and final time, the old man unfolded a wide mat, placed it on the ground and sat down cross-legged upon it. He patted a spot, indicating for Bujang to sit next to him.

In a steady voice ringing with the strength of ancients, he said, "See, my son, how the rice cooks. Yet it will not cook without water. Is it the water that cooks it? Yet water will flow away without the pot. Then can we say that it is the pot that cooks it? Yet what use is water and pot without fire? So it must be the fire, then? But how can fire come to be without wood? And who will bring wood if there is no man?

"Do you ever consider the ground you trample on every day?

She is lower than you, yet large beyond measure. You treat her like a servant, although it is by her blessing that your life prospers. Without her, you will fall, without her there will be no trees and vines. Where will you find thread to clothe yourself? Or will you cover yourself with the skin of another man? Everything exists for a reason. A man is your brother, an infant is your child. Even the worth of your strength is the magnitude of another's need."

Green, standing stalks suddenly filled Bujang's vision. He was a child again, sitting in the field where his mother worked and listening to an old man who had never stepped into his longhouse.

"Life sprouts from the ground and renews hope. Every new birth renews hope. Is there a mother who looks upon her child with terror at birth? Is there a father who calls his newborn a murderer, a thief, a plunderer? No, there is hope and there is joy. Every Dayak yearns for hope just as much as he yearns for rice when he is hungry."

The old man got up and gave the pot one final stir. The fragrance of steaming hot rice pervaded the century-old air, turning it fresh and wholesome. Then the soft grains were scooped onto wide leaves and placed on Bujang's eager hands. Uncaring of the heat, he gorged on large handfuls of searing rice. The old man chuckled and gave him another helping and then another, until his frenzied eating calmed down.

Then the stranger scooped some for himself. "Every new growth renews hope, yet you have to know when hope will come, so as to have more hope. Seek it in the dark sky before the break of dawn. Seek my seven stars in the east. If my daughters are hidden from you, then seek my three stars. They cluster much like the three points on your chest. When you see their lights, prepare your fields, build your storehouse and sharpen your hoe, for it will soon be time to plant. Cleanse the land with fire and smoke to rid it of disease and hungry spirits. Then watch out for the new moon after your evening meal, for it marks the beginning of planting. Etch these words into your heart and never forget them, that they may bless you and many generations to come," he said and gave Bujang another helping of rice.

They ate until Bujang became sleepy. Feeling safe, he lay on his side and drowsily watched the old man continue eating.

"*U …ha*. Eat, my son, eat. The rice is good and sweet. Like the hand of the woman who grew it. A woman whose skin is warmed by the sun and cooled by the rain. *U …ha*. Can I, Pulang Gana, turn my face away from such a daughter? Such a beautiful daughter who loves the sun and loves the rain. Her fingers are red from the colours of dye, her dreams are sweet with visions of patterns. *U …ha*. Here is the man who will bring her seeds to gladden her heart. He cries for her people, he risks his life for their offspring. Pulang Gana shall bless the hands of his daughters. They shall be as the tender shoots of new growth to him. Their shining faces shall lead him to his happiness."

Throughout the night, Bujang drifted in and out of sleep as he listened to the lullabies the old man sang.

* * *

A feeling of contentment mingled with a sense of physical fullness charged Bujang's waking consciousness. The curtain of sleep parted as he opened his eyes to a cool and shady jungle. He stretched and yawned loudly. Then he sat up to look about him. The old man and his pot were gone, while the mat that he had lain on had turned into a pile of leaves. He thought he had dreamed of the whole meeting until his eyes fell on the travel basket which was now swollen with packets of rice. A dark pouch lay on top of the basket. He opened it and saw grains of rice covered in golden husks. Careful not to touch the seeds with his blood-tainted hands, he re-tied the bag and returned it into the basket. He was humbled because Pulang Gana, the god of rice, had come down to comfort him.

With renewed excitement, he slung the travel basket and shield onto his shoulders and set his course for home. Westward he turned, away from the warming rays of the sun. Northwesterly he ran, wherever the terrains allowed him. Up and down the land went beneath his feet. With the agility of a young ape, he grasped vines and climbed sheer walls of yellow soil as fast as he ran on level ground. His feet were light, his speed as swift as a deer; his steps on the ground were so brief he barely left a trail. Jumping across streams, he flew over logs and sunning lizards. The breeze whistled past his ears, and spirits kept out of his way. He ran till the sun was high in the sky. Then he stopped to eat. He was so hungry he ate half of the food in his basket. The rice was sweet, like the river in front of his longhouse.

When he had fortified himself with the food, again Bujang ran, his feet fluttering like dragonfly wings over ripples of water. He passed grounds that lay bare under the thick canopy, and coverings of green growing beside uprooted, towering buttresses. Brooks gurgled rainwater-clear, and streams flowed milky-hued before him. Animals skipped out of his way, terrified of the heads strapped to his shield. He ran till the sun set in the horizon. Again he stopped and had a meal, consuming all the remaining rice in his basket. He was close to home, but he did not want to surprise his people in the night, so he slept in the pitch dark with his back protected by a tree and his sword unsheathed. In the morning, when all was light, he would return to the house with war cries and show the people his trophies. Then they would know that he came to them as a hero, not as an enemy.

* * *

Minutes after he awoke the next morning, Bujang stood up and filled his bamboo bottle with water from a stream. He stretched his arms and took a deep breath. He could smell smoke and wondered if his people were preparing land for sowing. After studying the sky, which was dark with rain clouds, he hitched his belongings to his back and sprinted the remaining miles home.

On nearing the vicinity of his longhouse, Bujang cut down palm branches and stripped them of their leaves. Bunches were wrapped around his sword while thick strands were stuck into his war cap to show that he had taken heads. Then he wrapped braided leaves around his forearms and calves because he had returned from a successful expedition. He stomped his way back to the longhouse as he wielded his shield. He swung his sword in arcs and called out a succession of strong, loud and victorious shouts to chase bad omens away from the surroundings.

Children playing about the perimeter of the building ran up the ladder screaming. Teenagers stood transfixed as they stared wide-eyed at his heroic approach. Again he called. The women shouted back replies and hastened down to meet him. Soon teenage boys added their voices to the crescendo. Gongs and drums were sounded chaotically. The symphony of joy travelled down the river and reached the ears of distant houses, where all could hear that the house of Bujang Maias was no longer cursed by the gods.

Inside the longhouse, Upa silently rejoiced. Quickly she shaved her eyebrows and trimmed her hair to signal an end to her period of mourning. Then she picked up a winnowing tray and went out to meet Bujang. Proudly, he placed the bride price on her tray, and she walked the whole length of the house, followed by a procession of women, to show the people her lover's ardour. He was a headhunter, and she an accomplished weaver. By bringing home the trophies that would assure the fertility of her fields and the protection of her home, he had proven to the community that he was the perfect husband for her. Then the tray was placed in her family gallery, among offerings of food and wine. Mendakap fed the heads with betel nut and betel vine leaves. He marvelled at the beauty of their strong brows, and he felt encouraged by the fierceness of their dead eyes, reasoning that all forms of evil and sickness would not dare remain in a house guarded by such spirits.

Then the augur took his seat next to the chief and wondered at the scabs peeling off a shield-shaped form painted on the warrior's throat. He predicted that no common enemy would have the strength to cut into his chief's neck. He released a long breath as his fingers traced the stars of Orion drawn above the cusps of Bujang's belly, for he interpreted it to mean that the people would never again miss a planting season.

In front of them the women sang in turn to welcome the three spirits. They sang of the blessings that would now reside in the house, of food, health, strength and courage.

The celebration continued through the next day, and the next. One after another the women sang without ceasing for seven days and seven nights. As though to prove that the spirits of Tama Ramun, Salang and Burak were truly great, the people experienced no lack that week. The only meat they ate came from one small pig, yet each member of the twenty families had more than enough to eat. The augur took that as a great sign of the blessings of the gods, for though the source was limited, the food was abundant.

On the eighth day after Bujang's return, teenage boys went into the jungle and lugged back two banana trees that were chopped flat at the base. They strapped them to opposite pillars in front of *Akik* Baling's family room and arranged the leaves of both trees to meet in the centre of the ceiling. Women placed rice wines around the base and hung uncooked gourds and breadfruits on the branches. Onto those same limbs, Mendakap added the trophy heads. Children giggled as old folks placed two brass gongs, one larger than the other, side by side. Five women hung up woven cloth on the wall behind the gongs. Then Bujang was dragged from where he sat in the common gallery and made to sit on the bigger gong. Childish laughter teased the blushing groom, but when the sound of delicate clinking shells came out of Upa's family room, the riot hushed.

A sight more beautiful than a field of orchids growing high in the canopies appeared before him. Upa's woven skirt, which was filled with geometric designs of black lines and ivory hooks set against a red sky, enveloped her hips even as the shells sewn to its hem enhanced her every move. A long-sleeved indigo jacket covered her shoulders and breasts, and over her middle she wore a corset of rattan rings that clung tight to her waist and flared upward to her breast.

Bujang Maias's jaw dropped, and the people laughed with joy, for his astonishment was their delight. Upa shyly kept her head down as she took her seat to his left. Then Mendakap rolled out a red betel nut from a coconut shell bowl. He placed it on a block of wood, swung a machete over it and sliced out perfect halves. The crowd called out appreciatively. The couple was a perfect match, for neither was inferior to the other. The augur then threw the two halves into the air, and they dropped, one face up, the other face down.

Mendakap called out, "Today is a good day for *Tuai* Bujang and Upa's wedding. May they be blessed with fertile fields and many offspring."

The people cheered and the feasting continued with renewed vigour. Youngsters banged vigorously on brass gongs and drums, which both added to the joy of the wedding as well as prevented the sounds of bad omen from being heard above the din. Bujang and Upa stood up and walked among the people as a couple, pouring rice wine into a coconut bowl for each and everyone. The adults blessed them with promises of health, children and many good harvests to come, and the children trailed after them, hoping for sips of the sweet brew.

The noise of riotous youth soon gave way to a melodious tune performed by the women of the house. Calls demanding for a dance from Bujang rang out from among the people. The young chief laughed good-naturedly, then frowned and stomped his feet a few times. He waved open-palmed hands in the air as his legs jumped nimbly over imagined terrains and treaded lightly in mythical jungles. Turning his head to his left and right while flexing his shoulders to exhibit strength and fearlessness, the hunter searched his surroundings for danger. Wide-eyed youths watched with wonder at the tale told by his gestures.

Suddenly, amid the dance, Gamit's mother callously stormed in as a strutting rooster, stomping her feet now and then to get attention as she swung her hips and shoulders. She poured wine into a cup, made the bride drink and dragged her to the floor. Upa's eyes were bold as she looked into her husband's face. She put down the cup, turned on one bended knee and swayed her hips. Her arms strayed delicately from her side, with hands so fluid they were like the wings of a perched hornbill playing with the wind. Those same gifted hands had plucked ripening fruits from branches and planted seeds in fertile soil for her family. Her life-giving fingers wove a tale of blessings and love in the air. While the people watched, entranced, she filled a coconut shell with *tuak* and offered it to another woman, who rose to dance. One after another dancers rose, to either charm the people with their grace or to make them chortle at their comical gait.

Finally *Akik* Baling got up and danced around the banana tree, all the while waving a sword in the air. After he had cut down a few bundles of food from the branches, he handed the sword to Bujang. The young man danced thrice around the tree and cut down a trophy head each time he passed. Then the sword was passed to other members of the house, and more blessings were cut down from the branches.

The people roared with every strike as hope returned to their hearts. Some claimed that they had caught basketsful of fish just by throwing a net into the river that morning. Others said they had filled their baskets with fern and fruits before they were even a mile away from the longhouse. The old smiled contentedly, for they had not felt hunger since *Tuai* Bujang's return. Now they righteously complained that their grandchildren ate too much for their own good.

That night, *Inik* Baling took out her grandson's sleeping mat and lulled him to sleep in the common gallery. *Akik* Baling lay himself down next to the boy, too dizzy with rice wine to do much else. Taking his hand, Upa shyly led her new husband into the family room. A few youngsters called out and were smacked smartly behind their heads by the elders. Nobody teases a hero who had brought prosperity back to the house. The absence of the newlyweds, however, did not lessen their merrymaking.

13

Dusk brought little relief to the sweat-drenching heat. On the open veranda, men with bent shoulders and bowed legs sat or squatted as they cleaned and sharpened farming knives of many forms. Geramun called out when he stepped off a bamboo ladder, and those not far of hearing returned his greeting. Straddled to his back was a burden basket filled with raw pineapple to tang his broth, wild ginger to aromatize his fish and ripe bananas to sweeten his rice. Girlish giggles gushed from a gallery window as his son Gamit also climbed onto the veranda and strutted after him.

Geramun unslung his basket and placed it inside the door of the gallery; then his eyes fell on Kumat's grandfather, who was sharpening a knife. The old man's face was so close to the whetstone that the blade he was sharpening would at times appear about to brush against the tip of his nose. It was believed that one of the old man's eyes was already in the land of the dead, for often he would call a greeting to friends long gone and make children run from him screaming in fright.

Geramun told his son to take the basket to his mother. Then, from the wall next to his family door, he took down three hanging knives – a small blade, a machete and a sickle-like weeding knife that jutted at a cross-angle from the wooden handle. Sitting down in front of a whetstone on the veranda, he called for his six-year-old daughter,

Dalai, to help him pour water over the blades as he sharpened them.

Soon, Bujang came to squat next to him, and, while he worked, they talked about the land, the river and of things that needed to be fixed in the house.

Finally the young chief asked, "Have you been to the planting fields?"

"Yes. I took Gamit with me. There is not much growing there now, only weeds. We saw six deer. That is not a good omen for the rice field."

"Let me talk with the augur. Maybe we can arrange for a proper time and get everyone to go down to the field together."

Geramun's hand stopped grinding. He nodded towards Kumat's grandfather and said, "There is no lack of willing workers. But many have traded strength for wisdom in this house."

"You are right, *Apai* Gamit. But we may yet be surprised by the vitality found in our bones. Not all spirits are unfeeling."

Bujang returned to his quarters and asked Upa to collect betel nuts and *sireh*, while he shredded fresh tobacco leaves. All these items were arranged in shallow baskets and placed in the common gallery. In this way the community learned that the chief was calling for a meeting, so right after dinner that evening they all congregated in his part of the house.

After the usual greeting and an explanation as to why the meeting was called, Mendakap said, "The days have grown warmer and longer. According to the traditions of our forefathers, we should now be preparing for the planting of rice seeds."

Akik Manyi, an old man from the farthest end of the longhouse, said, "Our harvest last year was not good. It may be worse this year. *Apai* Gamit told me that he saw deer in the old planting field."

The comment elicited murmurs that were accompanied by nods or shakes of the head.

206

Inik Gamit said, "It is impossible to clear new jungle now. Most of our men are too old to go head-hunting, and our boys are too young to hunt their first wild pig. We only have Bujang and Geramun, and they only have three arms between them."

The old woman was right, the crowd conceded: clearing jungle was hard work even with twenty strong men.

Bujang half rose from his seat, lifted an arm and asked for silence, "I shall seek the omen birds and hear what they say."

Mendakap gazed wonderingly at his chief because augury was his responsibility. Yet he wondered if the spirits had given Bujang a revelation during his war expedition.

Bujang continued, "My eyes had constantly fallen on a hillock two miles upriver. My heart tells me that we should plant our seeds there. We cannot continue farming the land downriver, for the presence of deer means that it is time to let the land fallow."

Akik Kumat's voice was barely discernible as he asked, "If we used water that had been soaked with the heads you took, can we not make the land yield again?"

Bujang bent his head in thought. He replied with a question, "Is it wise to coerce land that has now been claimed by deer?"

Shoulders dropped, and a few shed tears of frustration, each either wishing that they were still young, or fantasizing of having even five men as strong as Bujang and another five as persevering as Geramun. A woman hushed a crying toddler.

Mendakap swept his gaze over the people. "*Tuai* Bujang is right. We will have no end of trouble from these animals if we continue planting there. They are messengers from the gods, warning us to give the land back to them for a season."

Inik Gamit said, "We can clear the land next to the field."

Mendakap's eyes widened and his voice rose as he said, "That is taboo. You know that."

"At least the jungle there is familiar to us and the trees are not as large as the ones on the hillock that our chief suggests."

Geramun said, "Mother, it is still work. Maybe we will not clear as much land on the hill, but at least we will be free of a curse. *Tuai* Bujang has offered to seek the call of the omen birds. Let us wait until we receive their message."

Mendakap was at a loss, for his impression of Bujang was of one who was still young in the knowledge of the customary laws. Diplomatically he said, "Well, since we will be clearing new land, I pray that you will hear the calls of the white-rumped shama, rufous piculet, black cricket and scarlet-rumped trogon on your left and in that order. May they call when you are near a sturdy stick, so that you can catch the essence of their blessings in the twig and bring these auguries home to us."

Bujang grinned, thankful for the augur's reminder. He would need to go soon, for the Pleiades had started appearing high in the eastern sky before sunrise. "As Pulang Gana said, work should have begun with the appearance of the seven stars."

Gasps of horror greeted his statement. An old woman, *Inik* Taup, said, "You must not speak like that. It is wrong to use the names of the gods so lightly."

Bujang said, "But I did meet him. He gave me seeds fresh from his fields. Let me get it from my room."

When he returned to the gallery with Upa, a small crowd had congregated outside his door. He poured the life-giving seeds into his bride's hand. The old women crowded around her and stared with wide, wondering eyes at the grains that shone like pearls encased in gold. For the remainder of that evening, the allocation of work was discussed with suppressed optimism, as the people tried to keep their voices low so as to hide their plans from mischievous demons.

The following morning while it was still dark and mist covered the ground like billows of smoke, Bujang lowered a bamboo ladder to the ground as quietly as an invading scout. Then he climbed down with only a jungle machete strapped to his side and a paddle slung over one shoulder. Just as stealthily, he unmoored a small dugout boat and sat in the stern. It sunk so low on the water surface that it appeared as though he was only floating on a leaf.

The cold current hastened his journey upriver. Startled monkeys hooted, warning him not to approach, as well as telling the herd of his presence. To either side of the river branches drooping with dew covered leaves teased the rising tide. By the time he turned towards a group of trees standing on their roots, swift morning light had cleared the mist. He berthed and tied the boat to the sturdiest branch he could reach.

A moment later, a streak of blue splashed into the river and flapped upwards. A nearby branch shook under the weight of the kingfisher as he landed grasping a slapping fish in its beak. Bujang called with a loud *Ooi, Embuas*. The bird studied him for a moment and promptly turned his back on him. His head jerked up and down as he tried to swallow the morning catch.

Another *Ooi* came from Bujang. Again the bird would not respond. The man picked up a twig and threw it at the bird. The kingfisher squawked and flapped. Then he turned to face Bujang and wailed, "You foolish man. See what you have made me do. My brothers-in-law are waiting for you in the jungle. They are waiting to bless you, and here you are, forcing me to speak to you. Do you want the sound of wailing and mourning to fill your house?"

"No, I do not want that. I thought that since you are an omen bird, I could get a blessing from you."

"My father-in-law wishes to give you the highest blessing because of your courage. Hence he has asked Ketupong to give you a blessing. I cannot bless you together with him, else our words will become a curse."

Bujang scratched his head and decided that maybe he had been too hasty when he offered to collect the augury sticks. Then he wondered which deity had asked the birds to bless him. "Is your father-in-law Pulang Gana or Sengalang Burong?" he asked the bird.

The kingfisher almost fell from his perch. "Are you trying to kill me? I will be cursed if I utter my father-in-law's name." Embuas ruffled his feathers and crouched low as though to attack. He scowled into Bujang's face but received only a question-filled gaze for his efforts.

The bird straightened his back and sank deeper on the branch in resignation. "He is not Pulang Gana." Quickly he added, "I think it best you go now. If Ketupong hears my raised voice again he will think something amiss."

Bujang searched his surroundings and decided to take a path padded with overlapping roots. He hacked through dense vegetation growing over the gentle slope until some fifty yards farther, when the foliage became thinner and the surrounding darker. On looking up, he saw that giant *kapurs* and *merantis* laced with fig vines had stretched layers upon layers of shade over the land. The ground where he stood was covered with large surface roots, dispersed saplings and little underbrush.

A bright flash of orange and black caught his eye. The white-rumped shama called, "This way, this way. Come and listen. Break a twig."

Bujang jumped into action and broke the closest sapling in half. He looked up, but the bird was gone. He panicked because he did not know where *Nendak* had wanted him to go. Next a small bird flapped down on a sapling to his left, "May you have to constantly repair the straps of your rice basket during the coming harvest."

"That is not a good thing to say."

The rufous piculet twisted his blush-red head to the side in surprise. Moss green feathers on its back puffed. "Why is it bad? That is a wonderful blessing, for it means that you will harvest more rice than your basket can carry."

Bujang thought for a while and finally pulled out the sapling *Ketupong* was perched on. The startled piculet skipped and flew to a surface root.

"Why did you do that?"

"My Chief Augur told me to break a twig when I heard your call. I thought that the tree you perch on is best."

A loud *creet creet creet* burst from a root to the left. The *Burong Malam*, a cricket, called, "It is rare to see the brave and glorious *Ketupong* made fool of by a man. Ha-ha-ha."

A flush as violent as the waves of the tidal bore spread over Bujang's face. "I am sorry, I did not mean you disrespect."

The angry piculet turned his attention to the cricket instead. "Well it is your turn to give a blessing. Quickly now, maybe he will eat you."

The stick-shaped black insect hopped higher up a vine-covered trunk. "May your back grow tired and your arm sore when you harvest your rice."

Bujang, being a little wiser, politely asked, "Why is that good?"

"It means that you will have so many rice ears to cut that you have no time to rest."

Bujang broke the nearest branch. As soon as he did that, a cackle broke out to his left. A trogon, with scarlet chest puffed and black head jiggling, struggled to control his mirth. "I must tell my beloved about you tonight. None of us believed our father-in-law when he narrated his meeting with you. She would like to hear what you did to *Ketupong*."

The cricket said, "Well *Beragai*, you best be quick with your blessing. It is a long way home, unless you intend to spend the night here."

"I have been holding back my laughter. I thought I was going to faint from the exertion while waiting for him to break your twig. But he broke a branch, ha-ha-ha."

The piculet flapped impatiently. So urged, *Beragai*, the trogon, said, "May you be forced to repair the rafters of your house because it will bent under the weight of your rice bins."

Bujang smiled on hearing the blessing, for he could see that it was a good one. He broke a branch and was rewarded with another loud cackle from *Beragai*. Then the birds flew, off while the cricket disappeared into the crevices of a root. Bujang slung the sticks over his shoulder and wound his way down to the boat. He looked about but did not see any other animal.

When he returned to the house, he told the people what he had seen and the blessings he had heard. They were amazed at his skill in storytelling and rejoiced over the augury sticks he had collected. Mendakap smiled with his lips, but his eyes were hard as they studied the people. He dared not voice his concerns, lest his words should nullify the blessings of the chief. About him, old folks with bent backs shuffled about to look for knives that had not been used for years, women strapped toddlers to their backs as they wove or repaired seed baskets and children swung sticks about carelessly, pretending that they were machetes. He looked down to the floor, for the measure of their joy was the measure of his despair. They only had two strong men to clear the land.

* * *

The next morning, while the stars still shone clear in the morning sky, Bujang walked down the length of the house and called out the names of the older boys. "Tuap, Kian, Gamit... Wake up! Why are you still asleep? It is time to clear the land. You will never get a hardworking girl to marry you if you wake later than the sun."

Old folks, who were putting together their tools in the gallery, laughed in response to his words. Some pulled back blankets while others wiped dripping wet hands over the faces of their grandsons. Soon a rowdy procession was making its way down the river and into waiting boats. Bujang clambered into *Akik* Baling's craft, and a few boys jumped in with him, rocking the boat precariously as they did so. Men who had grown too old for hard labour and boys too young to work remained in the house with the women.

Humming under his breath, Bujang led the group upstream towards the hill he chose. The shoulders of grandfathers fell as they measured the might of the jungle against their own bowed height. They saw that the trees were thick, and that it would be months before they could even start a fire. By then, the dry season would be over.

Yet Bujang climbed the slope with a wide smile as he studied the large trunks sparsely spaced between smaller trees. *Tuai* Laing had taught him how to fell a jungle with the least effort, and that hill, he decided, was perfect for the technique.

He returned to the foot of the slopes, picked a point and started marking his way upwards with his jungle knife. Geramun rallied the boys behind their chief. They chopped and pulled away the bushes, making a clear boundary mark up the incline. The chief reached the summit by midday; then he hacked his way down another side of the slope, thus forming a wide triangle with the river at its base.

They spent seven days clearing the border. Each day the women would come to collect food or materials for their kitchen. Then the new moon appeared and the people rested for one day. Work continued the following day and for the next month. Sometimes lightning would crack the sky and rain would rush down the trunks like waterfall. At other times the jungle would be so humid the workers would be drenched from head to toe. Hence a rest day that fell on days to honour the new moon, half-moon or full moon was met with great relief by everyone.

Once the clearing was done, Bujang taught the older boys how to build platforms at the bases of giant trunks with wide buttress roots, one on the side of the downward slope and the other on the side of the upward slope. Bujang said, "Gayut, you and your grandfather take the large trees around this area. Hack low for the side facing the river and high for the side facing the hill. You need not chop down the trees; only weaken the bases. Move on to the next big trunk after it is done. Ignore the smaller trees."

The instruction was repeated to the other groups, each sent out in twos. Boys not strong enough to use an axe were made to do smaller tasks and carried water for thirsty workers. For days they laboured and strained under the shade of the humid canopy.

At the end of the fifteenth day, Bujang called out from the top of the hill. His voice rolled down like thunder, making every man, woman and child look up. "Come up here to me, come to me. Logs shall roll down the hill and everything will be crushed. Come up to me."

Urgent calls swept down the hill as the same message was repeated from level to level. The people scrambled and climbed as fast as their young or old legs would let them. A few of hard hearing were dragged by neighbours and children. Soon every member was standing behind their chief and the largest tree on the summit. Bujang swung his axe against the tree and chopped out chunks the size of roosters from the wood. Nine, ten swings, followed by a great groan as the tree began to lean forward. Slowly it fell, then more urgently just before it crashed into the hillside. Trunks snapped under its onslaught and rammed into the line of trees below. A great avalanche rolled down the hill as the air filled with the sound of shattering wood. Boys shouted jubilantly, while older folks gaped in awe. The land was cleared of trees in minutes, allowing the late sun to burn down on soil that had been hidden from its view in a hundred lifetimes.

Bujang's offering of joy and triumph to the gods was a laugh that was as loud as thunder and as exuberant as a boatman's song. Then he said, "We shall leave the area alone for twenty sunsets. Prepare your tools for burning."

The people returned home with hope brimming out of their hearts. Their longhouse had experienced poor harvests for the length of time it had taken a newborn girl to reach puberty. That night, old and bent bones became young again as the men carved wooden sentries for the field. They ambitiously repaired old baskets and wove bigger rice containers for the expected rich harvest. Young boys were also sent to the loft with sturdier materials for the floors.

The women prepared seeds, all the while dreaming of collecting corn, sweet potato and tapioca from their labours in the field. As they wove tube-like seed baskets with multi-cone shaped bottoms, they talked of pounding grain in the wooden mortar till their arms would tire. Once the baskets were done, Upa gave each woman a few grains from Bujang's pouch to mix with seeds from their previous harvest.

Then, on the evening before the burning, Mendakap asked the people to congregate at the chief's *ruai* to decide on the distribution of land. Because he was their leader, Bujang's household was allocated the land closest to the river. Planting would start from the foot of the hill so that the first harvest would go to the chief's family, for it was his duty to provide food to visiting strangers as it would give him an opportunity to study their intent. The rest of the land was divided according to the needs and ability of each family. Finally the eldest and most industrious woman was assigned to plant the first seed.

The following morning, the people again swarmed about the hill as they searched for ferns and mushrooms. Along the edges of the field, bamboo shoots grew in abundance as proof of old wives' tales that this plant was the harbinger of fire and cleansing. At midday torches were lit and Bujang, with Geramun and five teenage boys, made his way up to the summit, waving the torch and calling for the people to return to the river. Once he was sure that the field was clear to burn, he led the others slowly down the slope, burning as they went. Flame and smoke crept down the side of the hill like rice starch spilling from a boiling pot. The land had dried wonderfully, and the fallen trees caught fire like tinder.

When he reached the riverbank, Bujang called, "Blow, wind, blow. Blow, wind, blow. Fan the fires. Kill all rot and disease in the land. Make this place fertile with the fat of giants."

The lazy breeze began to howl, and grazing flames turned into an inferno. The people standing at the edge of the field ran to Bujang's side, afraid of the tongues that seemed to suddenly sprout from under their feet. Like a flirtatious maiden, the wind teased the fire and dared it to show its vigour, so that by the day's end, each piece of broken wood had burned all the way to the ridged border. The community returned to the longhouse and rested the following day.

The morning after, before the sun appeared in the horizon, Bujang looked up to the sky and saw that the belt of Orion had travelled high in the east. It was time to sow the first seeds. Mendakap brought along the four augury sticks and Burak's head wrapped in a woven cloth to the hill. Kumat and Gamit collected water in bamboo tubes before they made their way up to where Mendakap had laid the sticks. They handed a bamboo tube to the augur, who poured its content onto the sticks as he said, "May the essence of the blessed omen birds imbue the bowels of the earth. May the life they give be as the sun and the rain to our rice seeds."

Then the head of Burak was washed and the water splashed generously on the ground.

"May Sengalang Burong make our harvest rich with the spirit of this trophy."

An old lady, *Inik* Tuap, picked up a straight stick and punched a hole in the ground. She dropped two seeds inside. The action was repeated four more times as everyone watched. Then the men dispersed into the surrounding jungle to collect materials for building temporary huts in their individual fields.

Bujang returned with bamboo poles, which he split and wove into *teresang* baskets that he planted in groups of two or three along the rice field boundary. Young children trailed after him as he placed wide leaf offerings of rice, betel vine, tobacco, eggs and rice wine into each vessel. At the base of each group of *teresangs*, he placed a *cempedak* seed.

Mendakap could not contain his curiosity. "Forgive me *Tuai*, if my question is improper. But why do you give such a poor thing as an offering?"

Bujang smiled sheepishly. "It is not an offering. It is the sign of a promise between a macaque monkey and me. That is why I do not place it inside the basket, lest the gods be offended by it. If he holds his part of the bargain, we will not lose any of our harvest to his kind."

The following day, crude fencing was put up along the borders to keep foraging animals out. Then high bamboo poles were erected and rattan vines, which children had strung with leaves, twigs and feathers, were stretched between the poles. Bujang tied one end of the pliable vine to a tall, swaying tree, making the whole contraption swing in the breeze together with it. Twigs and leaves cackled as they slapped against each other and feathers fluttered wildly in the wind to frighten away any bird that might be bold enough to fly over the field. Again they returned to the house.

The next morning the people woke to a clear pre-dawn sky that showed the Pleiades clustering as high as the noonday sun. They raced their boats to the fields in high spirits, formed a line starting from the foot of the hill and began planting, with the men walking in front, poking a wooden stick into the ground, and the women dropping seeds into each hole after them.

A drizzle started, cooling the earth further, and that rain continued on and off for the next few days. Soon healthy green shoots began sprouting from the ground. As the days progressed, wild grass also started growing next to the rice. Bujang watched Upa and the other women clear the land of weeds and realized that there was not much for him to do now that the sowing work was over. He decided to go hunting in the jungle, for it had been some time since his family had meat to eat.

He took a spear, a machete and a burden basket with him. After walking for two miles in the calmness of the shaded world, he paused on hearing the sound of chopping. He trotted towards the noise and found a familiar form that bore the face he longed to meet in his dreams, yet one he dreaded meeting in the flesh. In his dark loincloth and shin bracelets of palm leaves, and with one hand wielding an axe, the warrior-guardian Keling appeared like a lone hunter-gatherer. By his feet to one side lay a pile of split wood. Bujang had often thought of him since their first meeting, but now he wondered, with a little dread, why he was seeing the demigod again. He stepped forward.

Keling turned and nodded a greeting. Then, reading the question behind Bujang's furrowed brow, he said, "I am making a weaving loom for my wife, one which will be more beautiful than the last one I made her."

Shyly Bujang asked, "May I stay and watch? I have never learned how to make one. Upa, my wife, still weaves using her mother's loom."

Keling nodded and proceeded to teach Bujang what wood to use and how to carve the many parts needed for a perfect loom. The guardian left after he had all the pieces he required for his beloved. Bujang cut up the remaining hardwood timber and carved out the pieces he had committed to memory. As he shaped the wrap beam and the breast beam, he envisioned his wife wrapping threads to and fro between them, keeping them apart yet coupling them. Lizards were engraved into the wood, to protect his beloved's work. He formed laze rods to keep the threads untangled. As he sculpted the heddle and the shed stick, he wondered whether the designs she might weave would be as beautiful as the nourishing fern or as tender as yellow orchids. Then his pulse quickened as he imagined lizards, serpents and omen birds tempting her dreams with visions of heaven. He hewed a beater lovingly, making it thick enough to be strong, yet thin enough to be light. Lastly, he whittled the spool, scraping and polishing until it shone in the dim light of the night.

* * *

He did not know he had fallen asleep until he was startled out of sleep by snorts and squeals coming from the bushes. He jumped to his feet, picked up his spear and held it up, ready to throw as he approached the noise, unsure what he would find. It was only a small wild pig struggling in the grip of the thicket. He speared the animal, freed the carcass from its tangle, and packed it into his burden basket. That being done, he bundled the carved pieces of wood in a wide leaf and wended his way home.

That evening, the women thronged around Upa, admiring her new weaving loom.

Inik Baling cried out with joy. "My daughter, my dearest daughter. You have brought many blessings to this house with your gifts. Your husband is loved by the gods, for his hands are harsh to his enemies and gentle to his people. Behold the spirit of the lizard guards your thread. No evil will ruin your weaving."

Inik Tuap said, "Surely the most beautiful Kumang, the wife of the greatest warrior, will bless your dreams. How could she not want to see one of her patterns woven in this loom?"

Gamit's grandmother called above the other voices. "Weave a cloth for your husband. Weave a warm cloth for him to sleep in. May it fly him to the heavens at night, to learn the wisdom of gods. No disaster and hunger shall ever fall on this house again."

Upa's eyes shone as bright as the stars of Orion as she looked up to her husband. He smiled and left the women to their imaginings.

* * *

An emergent honeybee tree stood out dark against a star-filled sky. The songs of joy and contentment coming out of Bujang's longhouse grated the nerves of the Brahminy kite perched on its highest branch. The warpath god seethed as he again cursed Pulang Gana for feeding his hunting dog. He peered into the house of heaven and wondered if *Tok* Jakun had persuaded the god of rice to save Bujang. The memory of the sentimental hornbill that he had struck out of his sight made him snort. The sky began to darken and rumble.

Sengalang Burong turned his eyes upstream and listened. The people there spoke of the Ape Man in hushed, fearful tones. He searched downstream, and his ears caught the songs of bards who sang of Bujang's invincibility, and the words of shamans who spoke in awe of the three trophies hanging from his principal column. He hunched lower and surveyed the distant coast with far-reaching eyes. The time would soon come when greed would find its way into the rainforest. When terror no longer acted as a wall, then strange gods would travel up the river. When that day came, he would send a curse so terrible it would destroy the warrior who had dared shun his gift of glory. His field would be laid waste, and the woman who clothed him in motifs that made him appear pleasing to the other gods would be wrested from him. The curse would be so terrible that all the other warriors who now held him in awe would be punished too.

14

Bujang crossed the veranda between rows of drying rice grains. Without warning, a naked two-year-old boy grabbed his arm and lifted both legs up in the air. The chief swung the arm up and dangled his youngest son, Patas, which made the toddler chuckle with delight. In the distance, a teenage Baling jumped from an overhanging branch into the river. Hoots and cheers erupted about the bathing platform. Upa's voice, followed by a light thump on the veranda, made him look her way. His eldest daughter, eight-year-old Utih, began to scoop handfuls of rice into a squat basket as his wife lightly beat on the drying mat to loosen any precious grain stuck in between the latticework. Though the sun had sunk low in the horizon, the day remained warm.

Akik Baling dragged himself towards an access doorway with his feet. Bujang could hear him tell simple stories to five-year-old Lanai as her tiny hands bunched thin strips of bamboo skin for the fish trap he was weaving. She stuck her hand into the cone shaped mouth and giggled each time he good-naturedly scolded her. *Tuai* Bujang smiled, for it was rare to see his father-in-law in such good spirits ever since *Inik* Baling had passed away two years ago.

For the past ten years Bujang had been chief, the longhouse had prospered. Young boys who used to swarm about him like lost puppies were now men, and their families had plenty of meat and fish. Every rice store was full, and all the *bileks* had grains leftover from the previous harvest. As his reputation grew, families that had left the house during Raung's time returned, and his original twenty *bileks* were now forty-six. Wooden planks, which the men had carved out of timber sheets four years ago, shook as children chased each other up and down the common gallery. He laughed on hearing older folks reprimand the youngsters for their energy because the communal noise which had grown about him over the years was like music to him.

All at once, a loud *Oooi, oooi* bellowed from the river. Bathers, young and old, shouted for each other as they scrambled back to the house. Bujang immediately placed Patas in Upa's arms and said, "Take the children inside!"

He rushed into the gallery and unhooked his jungle knife from the door before stomping his way to the bamboo ladder leaning against his veranda and sliding down it. Close behind him were four of his most trusted warriors: Kumat, Gamit, Sebingkai and Nandin. Soon they saw what had caused the bathers' cries: coming down the river as it drifted on the tide towards the now empty bathing platform was a twenty-foot low-draft *sampan* with a man standing at the bow clutching two long sculling oars that he held close to his chest.

As he drew nearer, they saw that he was dark-skinned and that his eyebrows were unplucked. He wore a black cotton shirt and a red cotton loincloth. A piece of stained white cloth coiled atop his head, like a flattened beehive. More than half of his boat was covered with a thatched roof, and part of the side of that structure was walled with woven mats. The small face of a teenage boy peeped from behind one screen.

When he was about three yards from the platform, the man swung the oars up and laid them crosswise on the bow. Then he picked up a long pole and stuck it into the riverbed, effectively stopping the advance of the boat. He called out, "Greetings, great chief. Your name and the tales of your exploits have reached the coastal land of my home. I am a humble trader from a village in Sebuyau, a village that faces the great salt waters. In my boat are cloths, brass, silver and gold. I pray that a great warrior such as you will have use for such trinkets."

Bujang squared his shoulders and boomed, "What do you want?"

"I only wish to show the great chief, *Tuai* Bujang Maias, the wares in my boat. If either you or his people find any item that pleases them, then I will trade these in exchange for beeswax or camphor. I also exchange them for the stone found in the gall bladder of little grey monkeys or in the belly porcupines. Maybe you have horns of the rhinoceros or deer. You can also have silver if you can find the nest of swiflets that live on cave walls."

The sentries laughed. Bujang twisted his mirth into a frown as he waved the trader over. The man was all smiles, showing betel-stained teeth. He poled towards the side of the platform. As he moored the boat he called out instructions to the boy, who heaved a large clanging bundle onto the platform. Except for the dark trousers, he was also dressed like the older man.

The trader crawled onto the platform and squatted over the first bundle as he untied it. When the five men had formed a wall around him, he looked up and said, "My name is Hashim Bakri. This boy here is my eldest son, Johari." He spreads open the cloth and continued, "These are my wares. I hope you find them pleasing."

The men stared, all they could see were red light, white light and yellow light. Slowly the lights took form and became intricate round brass trays with welded stands, or silver and gold embossed boxes lined with tiny covered bowls. Hashim shook a string of silver bells that tinkled like raindrops on young bamboos. Then he picked up hair-skewers that sprouted silver flowers and shook like moth wings in the still air. He opened another bundle that the boy passed to him and placed a roll of cloth into the hands of each man by turn.

Gamit ran his hands carefully over the bright yellow cloth, Kumat marvelled at the softness of the red cloth, Sebingkai stared at a design of strange flowers and insects, and Nandin flushed as he imagined how handsome he would look in the dark blue batik with images of growling monsters. Finally the grandest fabric was placed in Bujang's hands. The red threads shone like polished brass yet were as soft as new beeswax and the gold threads twinkled like stars on a clear night. Bujang gasped.

Hashim coughed politely, "Will the hardworking people of the House of *Tuai* Bujang trade with this poor and humble Hashim."

Bujang nodded to his men then he turned back to the trader, "Very well Hashim. These men will help you bring your things up to the house. The rest of my people may want to see them."

Hashim broke into a wider grin. Johari passed five more bundles to his father, all of which were easy labour for four young warriors. The trader and his son walked behind Bujang as he led the way to his house. All about them well tended gardens thronged with vegetables, herbs and fast growing fruits. Close to the path were partially carved posts and well-crafted boats lying under the shade of layers of palm leaves. The ironwood ladder they climbed was sturdy and the timber floors of the longhouse polished. Thick column logs held up the thatched roof and the scent of fresh green palm added to the coolness of the house. Hashim congratulated himself for having found such an industrious community.

The wares were placed in Bujang's gallery, in the middle of the longhouse, and a horde began to crowd around Hashim to learn how they could own these wonderful items. He asked for thirty coil of fifteen-foot rattan for each bell. The brass trays were ten pounds of honey apiece or thirty-five pounds of beeswax. The red silk that *Tuai* Bujang was interested in would cost him two pairs of rhinoceros horn and the silver skewers were two bezoar stones each, though he would also accept one small jar of bird's nest in exchange. The plain red and yellow cotton cloths were cheap, for a yards length was only twenty coconut shells of rice. Nandine's favourite cloth of batik with monster pattern would cost him two skins of ten-foot snakes for every three yards.

The bartering continued late into the night. Food and wine were served to the visitors by the chief and sleeping mats were spread for them in his gallery. The fighting men watched them eat, and were pleased to see that they rejected nothing that was placed in front of them. That meant that Hashim was an honest man, and had not come to their house to curse them.

Early the next morning, men slung baskets on their backs, blowpipes on their shoulders and tied jungle knifes onto their waists. Some made their way to the great honeybee trees, others followed the river in search of aged trees that yield camphor and many made the long trek to caves in their quest for nests.

Bujang's swift feet led him deep into the jungle, his lone passage only hinted by the tell-tale swaying of the bushes he had passed. He climbed high in search of the long-tailed grey monkeys, and one by one the adults fell. Then he roamed the ground in search of porcupines, so that by evening, his basket began to sag with the weight of his hunt. He returned to the longhouse on the third morning. Upa gutted the animals, and with each bezoar that she found in the gallbladder or the intestine, Utih squealed with delight. Bujang collected thirty-five stones; then the meat of the animals was distributed to the community.

Again, he went out the following day. With the help of five teenage boys he piled spears, coconut shells, sticks and a sturdy cord-net into his dugout boat. They paddled upriver for a mile. Then Bujang slowed the boat and studied the banks on either side as they passed. A jumble of crushed twigs and trampled clay caught his interest. After paddling a farther two hundred yards, he moored the boat. The boys were cautioned to keep their voices down, and not to speak at all, if possible, before he padded alone into the jungle.

Sixteen yards from the bank where he saw the tracks, he found a small clearing of trampled fern and shredded saplings. Close by the edge of it was a small hole filled with brackish water. He returned to the boat and signalled for the boys to come to him. They each picked up a tool and formed a hushed line behind him.

Twenty paces from the clearing he showed the boys how to place the net on top of the animal's tracks. Ropes were slung over high, sturdy branches and then tied to the upper two edges of the net while wooden pegs were used to affix the bottom edges. Finally the whole stretch of net was covered with leaves and twigs. He instructed two of the older boys to take up positions in the shadow of the greeneries to either side of the net. Then he returned to the resting area with the remaining three boys, and they hid behind the bushes.

The day grew hotter, making lush leaves fume under the heat, but the boys stayed their ground and kept quiet. A huge beast soon lumbered into view, sniffing the air loudly. The rhinoceros smelled rank, like the mud and grime that clung to its bristly skin. The horn atop its head was as thick as a man's wrist, and below that was a second smaller horn. The boys cringed at the sight of its potent vileness.

Bujang jumped out of hiding, right behind the animal, and blocked its path back into the jungle. Brandishing the spears high above his head, he shouted loud and long. Behind the bushes, the three boys started to yell and beat on their coconut shells in a frenzy of adrenaline and anxiety. The startled animal bounded towards the river with Bujang right behind its heels. Suddenly the net jumped out like a wall, and it crashed into the mesh, tearing out the pegs that held it down and swinging the boys that still held onto the ropes.

Bujang plunged the first spear right behind its shoulder blade, between the joints of its hard skin. The beast turned and became more tangled in the net. Bujang struck another spear right into its throat. A river of red coursed down its chest and formed a puddle under its belly as it struggled to free itself from the net. Finally it stumbled and fell on its side panting.

The chief slit its throat to release any life remaining in its body. Then the boys untangled the net as best as they could before Bujang began hacking through its tough skin and cutting up the carcass into portions. Being leader of the hunt, he claimed the head and a hind leg that included the rump. The rest of the meat was shared equally among the boys.

Evening followed them home. Utih's excited voice called for him from the bathing platform, and immediately the tension of the hunt left his body. He lugged the meat and head onto the platform, cleaned them as best as he could. Then he bathed in the river. Utih poked the animal's head and asked him endless question about his adventure. The boys laughed as he told her about monkeys that talked to him and about crocodiles that wrestled with him. When he told her that he tossed the rhinoceros about until it fainted, her eyes widened to become as round as a wood owl's.

Hashim was impressed with the speed by which the men returned with their jungle goods. All around him was a spirit of good-natured competition as bachelors tried to outdo each other, and he noted that the competition was at its most earnest when four young women came out to serve food to them.

To the eldest girl, Bujang said, "Well, Sila, that is a pretty skirt you are wearing."

The teenager blushed and hurried along, for it was the first cloth she had completed on her own. Young bachelors bashfully turned their heads away as she passed.

Bujang called out to her mother, "*Indai* Sila. Has a bird offered to carry your rice basket for you?"

A middle-aged woman answered, "My baskets are small and not grand enough for a brave bird. This coming harvest, I will take out my late husband's basket. Maybe then a proud bird will think it large enough for him."

Gamit's mother called out loudly, "Eh... there will be a bird. It is impossible to hide the smell of ripe durians." Then she pointedly looked at her young neighbour. Kumat stooped low over his rice, his ears turning as red as a hornbill's casque, and Sila, who disappeared into her family room, could not be persuaded to venture out again for the rest of the evening.

After dinner, men and women brought out their produce and Hashim started exchanging with them the items they desired. He sold thirty silver bells for two-hundred-and-eighty coils of rattan, five brass trays for sixteen pounds of wild honey and seventy-six pounds of beeswax. The longhouse was rich with rice, and he managed to sell forty yards of yellow and red cotton for eight hundred coconut shells' worth. Nandine also got his three yard of batik, though he only managed to find one python over ten feet long. Twenty hair skewers went to Bujang, and Hashim made Upa stick them into her hair to form a halo around her head. The people gasped and remarked that she looked as glorious as the moon bursting boldly upon a dark land. Then Hashim opened the silk cloth and draped it over Bujang's shoulders. The people's cries rose like a sharp gust of wind, for the beast coiling across the whole length had the mouth of a crocodile, the body of a python, the tail of a fish and the claws of a hawk. What god was this and who was the woman who was strong

229

enough to weave such a spirit, they all wondered aloud.

Hashim solemnly nodded his head. "This is the image of a dragon. Strange men from across the salt waters say that they have seen the creature fly in the sky and swim in the sea."

Upa protectively took the cloth off her husband's shoulders. "Will this spirit not eat into my beloved's soul?"

Hashim lifted one end of the cloth, where the head snarled. He pointed to a fiery ball within the reach of a clawed foot and said, "See this ball here. This is the dragon's toy. It will harm no one as long as the ball is not cut away."

Upa nodded her head knowingly, for she too would place the diamond shape of lozenges around her spirit patterns to appease them.

Nandine asked, "Is this the greatest spirit in the world?"

"Oh, no, there is a greater spirit. This dragon has three claws, the greater spirit has five. Only a god-king may wear a five-claw dragon on his person," said Hashim. After answering a few more questions about dragons, he said, "I will return to my coastal home tomorrow."

Bujang raised a plucked eyebrow. "But some of us have not paid you in full. I still owe you five bezoar stones and another pair of horns."

"That is only a small matter. I will return after you have cleared your land and sown your seeds. It takes about five to six days to ride to my home in Sebuyau and sometimes more coming here, depending on the tide. I will return with silver bracelets for your shins and arms, and wide belts for your handsome waists with large buckles to cover your loins. Nothing will shrivel the men who wear them. And for the women, I will bring sunbeams and moonbeams and gentle bracelets for your wrists. I will show you chains of shining leaves and flowers that will encircle your necks and lie on your breasts like petals covering a tree laden with ripe fruits."

The land-clearing season was approaching, and Hashim knew from experience that it was not wise for him to stay longer. "All this I will bring after your taboo season. It will not do if my visit should bring a curse on your house."

Kumat asked, "How will you remember how much we owe you?"

Hashim winked and took out strips of bamboo that had been strapped together with soft twine. He unrolled the scroll. Half of its length was carved in Arabic script. He took out a small knife and started to bruise a clean surface.

"See this is your name." He pointed the script to Kumat. The young man was pleased to see a standing leech, an upright stick and a curling serpent for his name. It made him feel manly and strong.

Hashim laughed and patted him on the shoulder as the young man tried to trace the script on the palm of his hand. "You have a great name. It is strong and prosperous. No wonder you can pay for your cloth so quickly."

The people thronged around the trader like children, for they were curious to see this new image. Gods, spirits and heroes were carved into posts and amulets, but to carve a common man and to show him in symbols was new to them.

Then someone asked him to tell them again about his home at the mouth of the river, and the community listened attentively as he described the many wooden houses at the port. He also told them that ships, larger than the great house of *Tuai* Bujang Maias, sailed there. Some of these vessels brought pigs that were the size of men. And like men they were naked and were as pink as the merchant captains stripped of their robes. These sailors claimed to have come from a kingdom in the centre of the world. They worshipped many gods and were ruled by one. That god who ruled them covered his face with strings of golden beads lest any man, woman or child would accidentally behold his features and be killed by his glorious countenance.

Deep into the night Hashim spoke. He had told them the same story many times over, yet the people never tired of listening. Visions of flying pythons and men with claws of iron danced in their minds. One woman even dared asked if anyone had tried taking their heads.

Hashim bellowed, as though reminded of some terrible memory. "Yes, many a great pirate tried. Syed Kamal, whose boat was as long as the height of twenty men and as wide as four, attacked such a vessel once. Fire flew out of the Sina ship like water splashing out of a bucket. The pirate's boat burned and sank. Only two crewmen survived to tell the tale."

Early the following morning, while the horizon was still covered with only the glow of a hidden morning sun, twelve young men helped the trader carry the bartered goods to his boat. The craft sank low upon the water until it appeared as though the river itself would flood into it. Bundles of rattan were tied to the stern and trailed in the boat's wake as Hashim poled his way downstream.

That night, the seven stars appeared in the eastern horizon. Young men curbed their urges to go into the jungle to look for items to trade with Hashim as they whetted their knives for the land-clearing rite. Each dreamed of carrying a rice basket that surpassed *Tuai* Bujang's, yet none had the courage to weave a vessel of such size. They crowded around their chief every evening, as the privilege that was their fathers' had fallen on his shoulders and it was he who now taught them skills for hunting, fishing and planting. Then, when the Orion settled in the vault of the sky on the dawn of a new moon, the women went to the field to bury rice seeds in the warm soil.

By and by the men left the fields under the nurturing hands of their women. They climbed the straight trunks of honeybee trees and the sheer walls of caves. They paddled down sluggish and wild rivers in search of fragrant wood resin. Some went to open fields in search of stag and deer. They hunted rhinoceros, bears, monkeys and porcupines. Rattan vines were dragged over tree trunks to strip them of thorns. Each bragged to the other about the things he would acquire from Hashim. Some returned daily, some stayed away for five days, others a week and the most eager did not return for more than two weeks at a time. Since the fields had been cleared and planted with seeds, there were few tasks left that required the strength of men, so they were being tended mainly by the old and the women, who brought their children along with them.

One day during this time a strange sight appeared. Under the dome of a darkening sky lit by cracks of lightning, smoke rose from their ripening planting field. Bujang and three men – Ilong, Kang and Tubau – bent on their paddles so hard and fast their boat flew on the surface. They shot past the longhouse, and ahead of them were eight other boats that moved just as speedily. Overturned and broken dugouts drifted towards them on the tide like lifeless carcasses. Two miles later and a right turn at a bend, they dragged the boat to shore and stormed up a trampled bank. Rain gushed down from the sky like waterfall. Bujang tripped and looked down. Gayut, handsome and proud no longer, lay pale on the ground. Bujang cradled him, but the body was cold and lifeless. The men standing over him pulled out their swords, roared their wrath and charged down the field, and when they found no apparition or men to war against, their cries turned to desperate calls for parents, wives and children. Soon pockets of grief wailed out of scattered parts of the field.

Bujang stood up and surveyed his surroundings. He looked to his side, to the ground, to the sky, but there was no sight to comfort him. Rain pelted down like rocks, lightning whipped and thunders howled, yet nothing could shut out the noise of wailing men. There lay Geramun, alone. His sword was unsheathed and his body slashed and stabbed in many places. His daughter, Dalai, was nowhere in sight.

Bujang forced himself to move farther into the field, fearing what he would see, yet compelled to see. The two brothers, Ilong and Kang, were crying over their grandparents. The old woman's throat had been slashed and the old man's abdomen stabbed and cut open. Slowly it dawned on the chief – none of their heads were taken. Then hope returned, for he had not seen the bodies of women and girls. Maybe they had run into the jungle, he thought, but it was strange that they had not come out to meet them, for surely the cries of grief must have penetrated even the darkest recesses of the jungle.

Bujang ran to the boundary. He called and called. He tore the bushes with his bare hands, neither feeling nor caring of thorns. Could they have gone deaf and blind with terror? he wondered. Then he heard it: "*Apai.*" Father. The sound was as soft and as terrified as a trapped mouse-deer. He pushed aside the bush and found Utih, his eldest child. With her were two other girls. Twigs, rocks and golden wild berries filled their little baskets. They shivered and sobbed in their crouched poses as they stared up at him. Bujang reached for Utih, and she wrapped her arms around his neck as he lifted her. Then he urged her friends, Rami and Umang, to get up and follow him.

More people had turned up. Rami's father and Umang's uncle rushed towards them. More men ran into the jungle. They searched till night fell and found only one other boy, ten-year-old Jagat. The torrent slowed to a drizzle, and again they called, but no one answered.

The return journey was slower, as men who were still hopeful called out the names of their missing loved ones to the banks they passed. Utih, unwilling to be far from her father, squatted in front of Bujang at the stern. She stared wide eyed at a palm-leaf covered Geramun as her little fingers dug into her father's knee.

Gently Bujang said, "Ooi, little bird, thank you for showing my Utih where to hide. Tell the cricket that made her invisible that he has done me a great favour. Ooi, little fish, take us home safe. Cicadas, come visit us tonight. Sing to my child so no mischievous spirits will come into her dream."

A long-forgotten feeling of heaviness settled in Bujang's belly. Ahead, torches lit the bathing platform and many stood watching from the banks as they approached. His spirit lifted when he saw Patas and Lanai standing next to their half-brother, Baling. Gayut's grandmother wailed when she laid eyes on her grandson. As the bodies were unloaded, more lamentations rose, like the sound of violent wind rolling in a cave echoing and re-echoing. Gamit, the son of Geramun, had stayed behind in the longhouse to guard it. His face crumpled when he saw his father, and he roared with rage when he heard his sister was missing.

Woven blankets were raised in the gallery of affected families. Among twelve such partitions, the youngest was a four-year-old son, Ibi, and the eldest was a fifty-year-old grandmother, *Inik* Timbang. The loss of Gayut, Geramun and Bayoi weighed heavily on Bujang's shoulders, for he spent all his evenings in their company. The wailing song coming from *Akik* and *Inik* Ilong's gallery made him turn his face away in grief. Bujang grieved to see the sons of *Indai* Rani, *Apai* Sanggong and *Indai* Dindang try to keep the blankets up. The older folks who noticed their trouble went up to teach them how to do it properly. At the end of the house. He watched as two women cradled three young children as they kept the bodies of their grandparents company. Their mother, Linang, was missing.

The men and women came together in Bujang's *ruai*, and once he had taken his seat among them, Bujang asked, "Did any of you

235

receive a dream, or hear a warning from any of the omen spirits?"

He looked to each by turn, and they all shook their heads. Bujang shook his head too. He could not understand why this had happened. The spirits had never failed him in the past. Even when he had set out that morning, the omen had been good. There was no indication at all of anything bad about to happen.

Bujang said, "We know that Upa, Dalai and Muri are missing."

Gamit said quietly, "Sila cannot be found too."

"Have Jati and Linang returned?" Bujang asked as he looked to the husbands of both women. The men shook their heads.

Twelve dead and six missing. He could think of no one who would want to attack them in such a manner. Hoping to find more information to help him understand, he ordered that the four surviving children be brought forward, and immediately they became the centre of attention.

Bujang asked, "Utih, my child, what did you see?"

"I hear people screaming and crying. I hear Ilong's grandfather say 'kill them, kill them.' I was afraid so I hide with Rami and Umang."

The other two girls also gave the same account. They had heard enough to terrify them but had seen nothing.

Jagat, however, had been digging for roots at the boundary of his family's field. He had more to tell: "I only saw two men. There were many more shouts. Mother told me to run into the jungle. Then I heard her screaming and telling the men to let her go. Is she dead?"

Bujang said, "We did not find your mother. Do you remember what these men looked like?"

"They have hair on their faces, like monsters. Snakes coiled on their heads. They wore clothes like Johari and a skirt over their hips."

Gamit leaned forward. "These must be the men from the mouth of the river. Hashim said many men there dress like him and his son."

Kang asked, "If they came for slaves, why did they only take the women?"

"Maybe they need weavers," said *Inik* Tuap. Yes, that must be it, the people thought. A well-woven cloth is powerful and a pleasure to the gods. Wearers who used them were protected from evil and blessed with dreams of good omens. Yet it was their wives, daughters and sweethearts that were taken, so that soon the voices of incensed men rose and drowned the weeping of mourners for an angry span of time.

Bujang stared at the floor like one in a trance. His silence quietened the men, and the thronging crowd moved back a little. He looked up, eyes black with hatred. "I shall seek the gods. And I shall demand they meet me."

The chief stood up and walked out of the house in the dead of night with no light and no sword. The young were assured, but the old were terrified by his arrogance. Then, from the fringes of the jungle, the long call of an ape drifted towards them. Another call came from farther away and another still farther, until the sound disappeared in to the endless distance.

* * *

Bujang swung up a branch and howled. Spirits scattered away from him like mist slapped with the tail of a storm. He ran and jumped between latticed branches. He stopped and bellowed another anguished demand. Farther and higher he went, howling in between until he climbed a honeybee tree to the highest branch that could bear his weight. He looked up to the heavens and cried in agony, baring his tortured soul to the gods. Baring the pain for the loss of his mother's love, the death of his father and sister, and begging for the return of Upa. The surroundings were silent as the world listened.

Finally, exhausted, he squatted down and sobbed into his hands. Then the branch sagged and the tree groaned. He opened his eyes and saw hornbills perched beneath him, above him and beside him.

A bird spoke. "Son of *Tok* Anjak. You have the gift of *Tau Kayau*, the gift of a War Leader. What do you wish from the gods?"

"I ask for the great ones to show me the way. I ask for the spirit of warriors to strengthen my arms. I ask for courage to gird my loins that I may not shrivel before the face of my enemies."

"You shall not walk alone. For every hornbill you see, ten warriors shall heed your call. Three quarter will be warned by their guardian spirits not to go, but one third of that number will ignore the augury, for their rice has become bitter and their water is now tainted with tears of sorrow. They will die, but many more among your enemy will die. Ribai will become drunk with their blood."

"How do I find the thieves?"

"They copulate at the mouth of the Batang Lupar. The trader will come to your house again. When he does, do not kill him, for he has much to tell you about them."

"I have only one hundred-forty-two fighting men in my house. Where do I find more?"

"Send four men up the great river. Send them up to the reaches of the white waters. Tell them to invite men from every longhouse they pass to join your war expedition. While they go about that task, take more men into the jungle and carve war boats with heads of crocodiles. Carve your boats long, carve them strong. Before the first seven star sets in the western horizon, gird your sword, shield your heart and cover your crown. Go to the mouth of your tributary and wait for the other warriors."

"Then I am assured of victory."

The hornbill gave out a loud honk, echoed by eighty birds. "You shall bring your rice basket with you, and you shall fill it to the brim with the heads of your enemies. Every man, woman and child is at your mercy."

As one, the birds dived off each perched branch, and the air roared with the slap of their wings. Bujang stood up and breathed deeply. As he stared down, unseeing, at the top of the jungle canopy one hundred feet beneath him, the day slowly lightened.

* * *

Evening saw him back in the longhouse, smelling like a hornbill god. Young men stomped their feet and shouted war, for the torment of their souls had built in them a thirst for blood. Bujang sent out four men to invite more warriors to join him. He invited them to come before the Pleiades disappeared behind the horizon for another year.

Then he brought fifty men with him into the jungle and left the remainder to guard the house. By late afternoon, two giants were cut down and hewn to eighty-foot lengths. Adzes dug into the hard trunks and roughly scored away the cores. Then rattan vines were strapped onto the logs before they were dragged to the river. About twenty men laboured over each burden, their feet churning alluvial mud as they dragged or pushed the partly submerged logs behind boats paddled by the rest of their party.

When they reached the bathing platform of their house, sentries jumped into the water to help them drag the carved logs onto the muddy bank. Each log was then heaved onto the shoulders of thirty men. They trudged like a pair of centipedes until they reached the front of the longhouse, where they rolled the carved logs onto the ground. Sticks were planted, and a thatch roof was placed over the logs. Then two crossed frames were built under each log to hold it in place. Five days had passed since their women were taken.

They left the logs alone for the day as they made preparations to send the dead to the graveyard. Twelve graves were dug, and though they took great care, Geramun's dug-out casket had extra space beside it. Gamit knelt by the side of the gaping hole and said, "I will go to avenge you, Father. I am going to die a warrior, and I shall have a crown of warrior feathers as my reward. Dalai shall return home because of her brother. Wait for me in peace."

15

Gamit was the first sentry to hear Hashim's call. His pulse raced, and blood rushed to his head, making the side of his crown throb. He struggled to remain where he stood after he had waved both arms above his head to signal Hashim's return to the other men in the longhouse. *Tuai* Bujang came out from under the thatched roof of an almost completed war boat and stepped onto the bathing platform to call out a welcome to the trader. Three other stern-faced men took their places behind him.

Hashim threw a mooring rope, and Bujang caught it. The Malay man smiled as he felt the eager tugs pulling his craft to the platform. But as he drew closer, the odd silence of the sentries unsettled him because he knew them to be loud and boisterous. As his boat thudded against the timber of the platform, he quickly reached down and grabbed a red pouch filled with polished rocks and waxed, bead-like fruits. A pair of hands fell hard on his shoulders and dragged him onto the platform, where he stared up into the wrathful face of Bujang Maias.

Knowing only too well how dire his situation was, Hashim shook the red pouch in the air and said, "Be warned, if you harm either me or my son, I will scatter curses on your people. Each rock and seed will take one life from your house. The more beautiful the rock, the more precious to you that life will be."

Bujang brought his face down so close Hashim could taste his betel-vine breath. "You shall tell me whatever I require of you." And he dragged the trader back to the house.

Hashim twisted his face back and saw two men pull his son out of the boat. Nothing else was touched.

On reaching the chief's gallery, Hashim was thrown unceremoniously against a column, which rattled the three skulls above his head. Johari was made to sit behind him. Then a rattan vine was wrapped around the trader and his son, and they were held down in a painful vice-like grip. Johari moaned and wept. Hashim could feel every single twinge of his muscles, breath in his lungs and cramp in his belly, though his legs felt lifeless and his hand was frozen into a fist over the pouch of charms. His mind ran through everything he knew about these people. They scorned cowardice, so he could not allow his terror to show. Yet their bloodlust was aroused by defiance, hence demanding for his own release would only hasten his death.

Bujang squatted to face him. Hashim skewed his face into hurt bewilderment and asked, "Why are you doing this to me, *Tuai* Bujang? Have I taken anything from you without your permission?"

"You came here to spy on us. You sent men to kill my people. You sent men to take our wives and daughters."

"I have led no one here. When I returned to my village, many marvelled at the horns you traded to me, and I told them about the great and kind Bujang Maias, but I told them nothing about where your house is located."

"Then why did they come?"

Hashim searched his mind as his eyes moved to and fro. "When I was at the trading place at the mouth of the river, I saw two large, new ships from the King of Bruni. The people told me that soldiers had ridden up the river in skiffs to collect taxes for the king."

"Taxes, what is that?"

"It is gifts to the king to honour him for his benevolence."

Bujang looked to Mendakap and asked, "Who is this king he speaks of?"

The augur thoughtfully scratched behind his ear. "I have heard of people who pay homage to a man and give him food and sing songs to him."

"He is a trophy head?" Bujang asked.

Hashim laughed, but quickly checked himself. Pale, raging faces stared down at him, and he stammered, "He is a living man, but he has the same powers as a trophy head."

A buzz rose as the people discussed that amazing revelation. If he was a living man, why did he not plant his own food or seek it in the jungle? If he was old, surely he must have children or, at the very least, have adopted a few to care for him. Or maybe he was like one of the great chiefs of old who had such a great house that he needed slaves to work in his fields.

Hashim's quick mind ran through his options. The ships must still be at harbour, for it was customary for the officials to stay for some months to enjoy part of the king's taxes. He decided that if he offered to show them the way to the ships, they might let him and Johari go. His heart sank as he recalled that the admiral of the fleet was *Laksamana* Supan, one of the most vicious tax collectors in the Bruni navy, who was more pirate than government official and who would take whatever he fancied by force if necessary. Hashim would not be surprised if he promised women to his men for their loyalty. His blood chilled as he recalled his wife and two young daughters, but his woman was a Penan, and she would know when to run and how to hide from strangers.

Hashim said, "I can show you the way to the man who attacked your village. I know his ships."

Bujang watched his face wordlessly. The other men, however,

were not so calm. Tuap almost spit into Hashim's face as he said, "You? The curse-bearer? You will betray us to him."

"No, I will not. I swear. I will not betray you to him."

Bujang asked, "How will we know that?"

"Our women and daughters live in the jungle like animals whenever their sails appear in the horizon. My people have suffered in their hands too."

"Why do you tolerate their visits? Why do you not burn their vessels?" Mendakap asked.

"My people are fishermen and traders. We cannot bear arms against soldiers and men who can take our lives with more violence than a god."

Gamit stomped his feet and shouted into the trader's face, "You are a coward! You and your people!"

Hashim looked down. When he looked up again, his face was red and his eyes bulged. "My cowardice has kept my family alive."

Bujang again asked, "How will we know that you will help us?"

"A man can remain a coward for only the span of time it takes to find a way out of his predicament. When heaven gives him an opportunity to end his fears, he must take it, or he will lose everything he holds dear."

Bujang nodded thoughtfully over his words and said, "What can you do?"

"I am a trader. I will go to his ship with a special gift and maybe request for him to give me permission to ply my trade along this river. It will give me a chance to count his men and see where they are stationed."

"This river does not belong to him."

"*Laksamana* Supan is an arrogant man. He claims all things belong to him. He has no respect for the sweat of another man's brow or for the lives of his children."

"You speak as one familiar with his ways."

"When I was a boy, a government official demanded my sister as tax from my father."

Ilong spit tobacco juice onto the floor. "Your people are nothing more than cattle. You are like the pigs we kept under our house, like the ones we fatten and kill to fill our belly."

Hashim wept. Ilong was right. They toiled, only to have pirates burn their homes and take their belongings. They toiled some more, and officials would come and take their crops. Everything they produced – even their offspring – was wrested from their arms. No amount of begging or pleading brought relief. Yet they dared not protest too much, for the sake of those who still remained.

Bujang lowered himself onto the floor and crossed his legs. With a voice less harsh he asked, "What gift do you need to bring?"

"I still have the rhinoceros horn. I will give that to him."

"Will it please him?"

"He can easily trade it for another fancy, if he is so inclined."

Bujang turned to Mendakap, who had taken his place next to the chief. "What can we give him that will be a curse to him?"

The augur turned his head to one side, then to the other. His eyes ran over the people, the house and the open sky beyond the wide open windows. Finally he said, "Hashim, has this man ever killed a great warrior?"

"He came from a line of great men; that much I know. But I have not heard of him having fought anyone of great valour."

Bujang stood up. "Tuap, see to the boats. Your grandfather is too old to carve the crocodile head alone. Make their drafts low and we shall fly over the waters. I will go into the jungle and find a gift that will tear this Supan's soul from his body."

* * *

Bujang hacked away the vine that clung to his empty burden basket then returned his sword to the sheath and picked up his blowpipe. A pouch of darts and a small tube of poison dangled from his waist. Night was falling, yet he trudged onwards in the familiar terrain. A rotting log emitted ghostly light, and fireflies began to swarm about him like a fog, but they scattered as a gust of wind wound through the trees.

The song of a hawk owl reached his ears. "Yellow eye, grey eye glowing in the night. Yellow eye, grey eye bring me no delight."

Bujang approached the tree where the bird perched and called out a greeting. "Ooi, brother. What are you singing?"

The gourd-shaped body tilted slightly; then it said, "Aah, it is you, *Tuai* Bujang. I sing only a little song for the moon I adore. Why are you without light and shelter tonight?"

"I am out hunting for a beast with a powerful vengeful spirit."

"Alas, warriors are never satisfied with their lot. Always they look for more charms, more protection. Is not your arm more worthy than any strength you can find in the shadow of these greeneries?"

"I wish to send it out to my enemy as a curse. I need a spirit that will prove him craven when he faces my rage."

"But how will you make him accept this curse?"

"It will reach him in the form of a gift."

"What manner of man is this?"

"A warrior trader."

The owl turned its head to one side. "He sounds most courageous. You would do well to take his head."

"Should I send him the skin and skull of a bear?"

The bird fluffed its feathers and leaned back into a ball. "A sun bear eats honey and termites. I think a leopard is better because it takes blood and it can catch a racing animal. Your enemy will not be able to run from its vicious spirit."

Bujang thanked the bird and moved on his way. As the night grew deeper, his ears grew keener, and he could make out the sound of each animal as it moved. Ahead of him, branches snapped followed by a snarl, and a screech from a distressed mouse-deer. More snaps and screeches. Then silence. He bent his knees and lowered his standing blowpipe, pointing it forward. He slipped in one of the poison-tipped darts. As he approached the fronds of fern, which jerked to and fro clumsily, he tested the ground for twigs with his toes before putting his weight on the foot.

Bujang squinted. Soon he saw a dark form climbing up a tree with low branches. The sound of crushed bone accompanied the shivering of leaves from a branch ten feet from the ground. Slowly, Bujang slid the blowpipe forward on the palm of one hand and brought it to his mouth. He took aim and blew. The animal snarled and was still for a moment. Then the leaves started shivering again as it settled back to its meal. Bujang waited for ten, twenty breaths before the bushes beneath the tree began to snap.

With the spearhead of the blowpipe aimed to the ground in front of him, he sprang forward to where the clouded leopard stood retching. It was still fierce and stubbornly clung onto life as it crouched and snarled up at him. Bujang put down the blowpipe, unsheathed a small blade, grabbed the leopard's head and cut its throat with it. Then he lifted the still body and strapped the sixty-pound male cat into his burden basket before making his way towards a river. At dawn, he reached an open dry bank.

Bujang started a small fire and leaned a square bamboo frame over it. Then he pulled the carcass out of the basket and proceeded to brush the fur with a piece of rough bark. Spots of black fruits and giant scale-like circles glimmered against a tan background. The beast had the teeth and claws of a demon, and the pattern of a python painted onto its skin, proving to Bujang that there could be no better spirit to use against Supan.

He looped a rope over a sturdy branch and hung up the animal by its hind legs. Then he took out the small knife from the pocket of his sword sheath and sharpened it on a rock. The musky scent of the clouded leopard grew stronger by the moment and began to saturate the warming air. The jungle about him did not stir.

Morning had grown bright by the time Bujang finally plunged his knife under one side of the hind leg. Careful not to cut into the flesh, he dragged the blade up to the tailbone and separated the tail from the body's vertebrae. Then the knife ran down the underbelly and forelegs. He stripped off the skin by turning it inside out and cut off the vertebrae right under the skull. Carefully, he inserted a thin piece of hot iron into a hole under the skull left behind by the separated vertebrae. He twisted the iron rod slowly. Next he carefully pulled the brain out. With a branch, Bujang spread wide the licking flames and tamed them into glowing embers. He scraped the underside of the skin as clean as he could and stretched it over the frame that he had leaned over the embers.

The sun burned. Bujang chopped down a palm tree and cut it into two logs, which he laid in parallel to each other in front of the fire. Then he stripped bark from a nearby tree and covered the logs with it. Next the palm leaves were layered on frames built over his makeshift floor.

Turning yet again to the edge of the jungle, Bujang collected more bamboo and herbs. He cooked the brain and roasted the meat of the leopard over a second fire. Three days he stayed, and three days the sun burned down. Relief only came with the night. On the fourth day Bujang returned to his longhouse.

* * *

Hashim stared down at the fur with wide eyes and gaping mouth. The thunderstorm outside echoed the churning inside his belly. He assured all within hearing distance that no one, not even a king, could refuse such a gift. Mendakap then told him that he should return to the trading port the following day, but that his son, Johari, would remain in the longhouse. He turned to stare at the chief's back, but since he had arrived, Bujang had not spoken a word to anyone.

It was close to noontime when Hashim reached the mouth of the Lingga tributary. He moored his boat and waited by the bank. A roar raced through the air, soon followed by a rolling body of water. Smaller ripples of waves rushed into the headwater, making his boat buck and jerk at its mooring. Once the water settled, the trader again got into his boat and paddled out into the Batang Lupar.

On the third day, the double masts of two hulking Siam-crafted ships appeared in the horizon, their battened sails reefed and green flags flapping high. A lazy tide propelled Hashim downstream, and he took the opportunity to bathe, rest and eat. The whole time he stared into the distance, as though entranced by the bright banners of busy, small crafts moving about the large ships.

Hashim calculated that if Supan had not changed his guards' routine, there would be about eighty soldiers on watch at any given moment. And guns, reputed to spit fire as accurately as blowpipes, lined the ships' gunwales. He wondered what he should do, for Bujang had not given him any instruction but instead had only stared out to the horizon from his veranda like a man in a trance.

Canoes and sailboats passed Hashim, some moving upriver, some downriver. He watched trading boats drag timber, rattan or sago logs behind them; then his eyes caught sight of a familiar merchant boat paddled by four natives and followed by a dugout of six men. Idris was lucky, for he had found people willing to send his body and goods back to his family. Hashim wondered if his friend had died from fever or if a poison dart had pricked his face. The Ibans were a strange race, he thought, and sighed. Life was either of great or of no value to them. He had been afraid when he first learned to ply the waters with Idris and his father, but from the older man he had learned that the Ibans had their own set of rules, and as long as he followed them, they would respect him in return. He washed his hands and face then said a prayer for his friend's soul.

His heart was heavy as his gaze again returned to study the activities on the river. Trade was their lifeblood. The interior was rich with dammar resin, dragon's blood dye, birds' nests, bezoar stones, horns of stag and rhinoceros, as well as pelts of magnificent animals. Hashim's brow furrowed as the shadow of an idea began to creep into his mind. Supan and his men could only collect tax from the villages along the river, not in the foothills where jungle products were the richest. The prospect of more wealth might appeal to the admiral's greed, and telling him that a feared headhunter wished to become vassal to him would appeal to his vanity.

Hashim was familiar in dealing with arrogant and violent men. Always engage their vanity, he reminded himself. His mind made up, he laid the clouded leopard skin over the bow like a blanket and perched its snarling head on the prow. Then he stood and pushed against both oars, keeping his eyes fixed on the highest mast.

* * *

It did not take long before the skin, and his craft, were noticed. Hashim forced a wide grin on his face as a skiff approached, filled with five men in dark clothing whose brows were adorned with bright, pointed bands.

"What do you want?" an angry boy-man called out to Hashim as he pulled out a sharp, rippled *kris* stuffed to the side of his thigh-length sarong.

Hashim pointed to the pelt and grinned wider. "I have a king's gift to present to the great *Laksamana* Supan."

The sentry stepped into his boat and began to poke his spear at the bundles of cotton lying just inside the roofed portion of the boat. Then he stepped under the roof and began to throw more cloth and brassware about as he looked for anything that might resemble a weapon. A jungle knife and a small spear were thrown overboard.

When the sentry had finished and had returned to face him, Hashim pulled out two silver pins from inside a bag and asked, "Do you know a lady who likes pretty flowers?"

The young man took the pins from his hand and tucked it into his waist. Then he took up position at the bow, behind the pelt, and ordered Hashim to paddle to the larger ship. The ship itself was a daunting sight: hanging from the side were slaves, covered only in ragged bark loincloth and scrubbing the barnacle-covered hull. He would not want to be one of them. But he must not fear; his mission here was vital. Hashim slung the skin over his shoulder and climbed a mooring rope dropped down to him after urging the young sentry to stay in his boat.

Once he was over the gunwales, Hashim ran his eyes over the deck in bold, open wonder. Eight cannon lay to the portside, with their black mouths pointing at a busy port; under the mainmast were thick ropes coiling like sleeping serpents. Yet all about him, the scent of cinnamon, clove and ginger perfumed the air and filled his mind with visions of paradise. He put aside these thoughts, and his quick mind counted thirty men on watch.

Two bare-chested sailors looked him over and shoved him towards a raised platform built around the mainmast in the middle of the ship. On the platform was a man whose tall frame was covered in an Arabic robe of white linen embroidered with black silk. Even though the thick, well-tended beard softened the outline of his face, his eyes betrayed his violent strain. Hashim was knocked down to his knees on the open deck before the man on the high seat. The man leaned forward and glowered down at the trader. Coiled atop his shoulder-length black hair was a turban of the whitest shade Hashim had ever seen.

Hashim prostrated himself before Supan.

"Who are you?" the admiral barked.

"I am your humble slave, Hashim. I have come bearing a gift of friendship to you, the greatest of all men."

One of the sailors took the upraised pelt from Hashim's hands and climbed up the side of the platform. Another man, dressed in similar fashion to the admiral but with far less opulence, received the pelt and spread it at the admiral's feet.

Supan studied it dispassionately. "The skin of a cat? I have hundreds of these in my keeping."

"And if God so wills, then the great *Laksamana* will receive thousands more."

"You are dressed in rags, and you dare imply that you can do more than my men?"

"It is true, sir, I am poor and weak. I am so insubstantial you cannot even use me to bait a leopard. But the gift is not from me. It is from the headhunter Bujang Maias."

The platform creaked. Supan said scornfully, "There are many headhunters who claim to be great, yet even if a hundred of their best were to combine all their heroic deeds, it would still not surpass my exploits."

"There is no one who believes that more than I do, great *Laksamana*. But among the headhunters, Bujang Maias is greatly feared. He has heard of your skill and wisdom and considers it a privilege to submit himself as vassal to you."

A smile cracked Supan's face. "He is wise for a savage." Then, in a harsh voice, "What does he want in return?"

"Only that he may collect tax under your name and be allowed to keep one fifth of the hoard."

"One fifth? What use does a savage have for such wealth? Such as his kind should be satisfied with digging for grubs and worms in the ground. Tell him I will only let him have one tenth."

"As you wish, *Laksamana*," Hashim continued haltingly, "Bujang Maias, though a savage, has heard much of your valiant comeliness. If it would not be too much, he asked to see you on the day after the next new moon."

Supan's brow creased as he stroked his beard. "There is still much to keep me occupied here. I will grant him an audience."

"Then with your leave, I will return to Bujang Maias and pass him the wonderful news."

Supan waved him away, and again Hashim bowed, walked backward three steps and climbed down the rope he had ascended. The sentry, he found, was still in his boat but his silver, gold and silk were gone. Hashim forced a laugh and shook his head good-naturedly, relieved that he had been allowed to leave unharmed otherwise. "She must be very pretty," Hashim said, prompting a grin from the sentry.

Seconds later, a patrol boat bumped against his bow and the sentry jumped off. The trader was free to go.

* * *

Desperate to reach his son's side, Hashim travelled quickly and took only two days to return to the longhouse. Nearing the place, he saw that the bathing platform glared empty in the late sun. Hashim called out as he slowed the boat. When Ilong appeared from behind a thick bush of reeds, Hashim threw the mooring ropes to him. As he wound his way to the longhouse, he saw that the grounds were subdued. No child played around the perimeter of the house, and the sounds from the building itself were muffled. Only the roosters called.

Though wearied, Hashim hurried up the common ladder. *Tuai* Bujang sat exactly where he had last seen him five days ago. Hashim's heart jumped when he saw that Johari was not at the post.

"*Bapak*, Father," a young voice called. Relief rushed back into his face as he watched his son step out of the chief's family quarters holding Lanai's hand.

Men started to gather in the chief's gallery, some squatting, some sitting and many standing shoulder-to-shoulder. Hashim shuffled towards Bujang and knelt behind him. "Greetings, *Tuai* Bujang. Thank you for freeing my son from his bonds."

Silence.

Mendakap said, "The chief has not spoken the whole time you were away. Maybe he made an oath of silence with the spirits."

Hashim swallowed. "I have spoken with the Admiral. He accepted your gift and looks forward to meeting you. I told him that you wish to see him on the day after the rising of the new moon."

Bujang turned and looked Hashim straight in the eye. "Then we will meet him. The warriors I have invited will have gathered at the mouth of the Lingga River. Gamit, tell our men to ready themselves. Half shall remain here as sentries."

Hashim prostrated himself before Bujang. "Please, great chief. The ships are anchored along my village. There will be soldiers on land. Please spare my people. They have done you no harm."

Tuap said, "They share their meals with those men do they not? Then they should die with them."

"We do not share. We are forced to give up everything we have, even our children. Please spare my people."

Bujang turned to Mendakap and asked, "Will the other warriors agree to this?"

The augur rubbed the back of his ears thoughtfully. "It is difficult to say, for the young are hot-blooded and many are vengeful. If the people do not run and submit themselves, then a true warrior will spare their life."

Hashim was not comforted by this response; he could only hope that the warriors would be merciful to his people.

*　*　*

There was not much time to lose, and after a quick meal, Hashim again separated from his firstborn and clambered into one of the two war boats that were soon weighed down by a full-grown pig and 111 men, crammed knee-to-back in two rows. Wind and spray whipped into their faces as the men synchronized themselves into frenzied rowing. The low-draft boat skimmed over the surface of the water and, within the time span of a dove flying in a straight line from the house, they reached their destination.

As they drew near, a host of men who stood along the bank like a wall broke rank and surged into the river, helping them drag their boats to shore, to berth next to three other war boats. *Tuai* Ngon of Engkilili had brought 250 men, 40 of whom were Penans with scores to settle. Before the day ended, *Tuai* Munao of Simanggang arrived with 70 men and *Tuai* Massam of the old land, Lubok Antu, led in 370 men. By late afternoon, 15 war boats had lined the river mouth like jagged teeth, with sizes ranging from *Tuai* Massam's 150-foot vessel to the Penans' sturdy 60-foot boat. Many of the fighting men were from small villages scattered along the river, and on hearing of the intended expedition, had rallied themselves under a warring chief.

Hashim was once more the centre of attention as he explained the layout of the harbour and the positions of the ships. "The river there is about four miles across. The ships are anchored some two hundred yards from the banks of the trading place. You will see houses on stilts built over the waters along two miles of the banks. Please do not harm the people there."

Tuai Massam growled, "We will show mercy as we see fit. Continue your description of the harbour."

Hashim turned pleading eyes to Bujang but found no sympathy in the impassive face. He coughed and continued, "Supan's ship is the largest vessel in harbour. The hull is as high as two men, and it is equipped with eight fire-spitting guns. Thirty men keep watch at all times. The ship will carry goods and slaves. There is a second vessel for more cargo. I counted six guard ships, and each one can easily carry thirty to forty men."

Tuai Ngon asked, "Will we find our children in the first ship?"

Hashim's voice shook as he answered, "Some prisoners are kept under guard in a warehouse at the harbour, so maybe some of your offspring will be there."

Tuai Bujang asked, "How do we get on the ships?"

"You will have to climb ropes. There is no other way because the hulls are smooth and slippery."

The men began to discuss their options. Bamboo ladders were out of the question because it was impossible to keep one stable in a dugout.

Again Bujang asked, "Am I to go alone, or can I bring other men with me?"

"It is normal to bring men with you, but they may be made to wait in the boat."

"Why can't I bring them up with me?"

"The admiral is a careful man. He does not take risks."

Bujang studied the men carefully. He chose ten as part of his entourage – three small men, no bigger than young boys, a man with a limp, a one-eyed man, another two who had no right hand, a one-legged man and two men covered in ringworm.

A bewildered *Tuai* Munao asked, "*Tuai* Bujang. I do not understand. There are many strong young men here. Why do you pick this sorry-looking group?"

"Because they do not look brave and strong. If their looks can deceive even us, then they will certainly deceive the enemy." Bujang returned his gaze to the ten men and said, "Many may have ridiculed you in the past. Pray that you may be ridiculed once more when we reach the ships. Supan may want to see you for himself for his entertainment."

The small Penans grinned, for two among them had been chosen as the first warriors to lay their hands on the enemy.

Tuai Ngon asked, "What of the guns? Can these men throw them overboard before we start the attack?"

Hashim shook his head. "No, it is impossible. You need at least six men just to move one of those. But once you are within the range of the midmorning shadows of the ships, the guns can no longer harm you."

A large man asked, "But what of the sentries and soldiers? Where will they be?"

"Some will be in the ships. When I arrived, there were ten dugout boats patrolling the waters. Each was laden with five men. There may be more when *Tuai* Bujang visits."

Men experienced in war began to air out diverse ideas of tactics, one after another, to their respective chiefs. A despondent Hashim watched their animated faces. Then a thought dawned on him, and he sat bolt upright, for he thought he had found a way to save his people.

He coughed and caught Bujang's eye. "Excuse me, great chief.

I know that I am only small and insignificant compared to even the least of you. Maybe there is something I can do to help."

The murmur of voices rose, but Bujang raised a hand to ask for quiet.

Hashim continued, "The soldiers are familiar with my people. They think of us as harmless and cowardly. While *Tuai* Bujang visits *Laksamana* Supan, I can get my people to ply the sentries with wine. Sailors who drown in a drunken state are not unheard of among my people. At the very least, it will make them cross-eyed and slow when the fight begins."

The chiefs nodded their heads yes. The plan was plausible. *Tuai* Massam studied Hashim's face for a while. "If your people can do this for us, then we will spare them. But if they fail us, then our children and grandchildren will hear of it and take revenge on our behalf."

"They will not fail you, great chief."

The discussion of strategy continued, until all was settled. Then, as the light began to grey, the bound pig was laid before the four chiefs.

Bujang squatted next to it and tapped its shoulder. "Ooi, brother, bring a message to the warpath god Sengalang Burong. Tell him that we, his people, are about to go to war. Ask him to bless us with good omens and to reward us with victory."

Tuai Massam shook its shoulder. "Tell the great one to send his servant *Nendak* ahead of us to blind the enemy to our approach. Ask him to tell this white-rumped shama to give us a charm amulet."

Tuai Ngon said, "We will be travelling into unfamiliar waters. Ask him to bless us with the wisdom of his son-in-law *Kelabu Papau*. May the trogon lead us to red-leaf charms that will make our boats invisible to all malevolent spirits residing in the river."

Finally *Tuai* Munao said, "Ask the great god Sengalang Burong to send his son-in-law *Embuas* ahead of us into the land of the enemy. May the banded kingfisher weep for their death, for there will be no one left to mourn for them."

A spear was driven into the throat of the messenger-pig before a middle-aged warrior cut open its belly and carved out the liver, which was then placed on a banana leaf before the chiefs. They studied the ridge of the liver and agreed that it was smooth. This assured them that their penetration of enemy territory would be easy. The dark spots on the liver, however, were harder to interpret.

Tuai Massam, who had experienced numerous expeditions in the past, said, "I have only come across such a sign once before. That time we lost many men to our enemy. It may be that this is the same sign." Heads nodded silently, as the implication of the omen sank into their souls.

Tuai Ngon said, "Whom then shall we choose to lead us?"

A murmur rose among the men. All the chiefs were renowned for their courage, as three had led successful war expeditions in the past, while one, *Tuai* Bujang, was revered as the lone warrior who had taken the heads of Terbai Lang, Salang, Tama Ramun and the almost god-like Burak. The low murmurs about them grew to a roar as the men debated among themselves.

Tuai Ngon lifted his arm, and the noise faded away like a fast-receding tide. "Night is falling. Let us leave the decision to the gods," he said.

At that, groups of men scattered into the jungle to gather food for that night and for the next few days. Here and there, behind the latticed wall of trunk alcoves or root-covers, small fires were lit. Fresh-faced warriors whispered excitedly over the prospect of getting their first heads and bragged of the young maidens who waited for their return, while middle-aged men checked their shields and whetted their sharp swords with painstaking care. Many, like Bujang, stared at the moving tide and wished to be part of the swirling debris that was drifting to the mouth of the Batang Lupar.

Bujang felt deprived of all joy, for all the blessings from the land had come to him through Upa. Her nurturing hands had filled his belly with warm rice, and the same gifted hands had woven warm cloths to cover him from jungle mist. Her strong voice and stronger character had driven him to strive to be a better man, and she had also given him children who gurgled like brooks of freshwater to cool his fiery soul. He could not imagine life without his beloved.

* * *

Morning came, quiet and balmy. The chiefs again sat down together while their men squatted or stood around them.

Massam moved his eyes over the crowd as he said, "We must select a man to lead us, a man whom we will follow even to our deaths." He paused and watched their reactions before continuing, "Allow me to introduce myself first. I am *Tuai* Massam, the son of Ganding, from the land of Lubok Antu. I am the third descendent after Seragunting, the grandson of Sengalang Burong. My fathers and forefathers were all great headhunters. I myself am not without war experience. I have collected one hundred fourteen trophies in my lifetime and have led many head-hunting expeditions. I can lead you to war."

Ngon nodded his head as though to confirm Massam's claims. "I am Ngon of Engkilili. I am the son of Sempurau, the great chief of many spirits. I can only lay claim to thirty trophies, but I have inherited the spirits who had served my father. I am also able to lead if you will follow."

Bujang indicated with his hand for Munao to speak next. The middle-aged man squared his shoulders and said, "I am Munao, son of Pamunting, a chief from the world of Simanggang. I have swum in the great tidal bores since I was a naked child. I have taken fifty-six trophies with my sword, and today I carry the same sword with me. I have led two expeditions before. The spirits have blessed me, my family and my fields."

When the turn reached him, Bujang sat up straight and towered over the three chiefs as he lifted his face to the men around him. "I am Bujang Maias. My loin-father was a farmer named Apong. I was banished by my own people when I had only learnt to tie my own loincloth. An ape adopted me as his son. He was called *Tok* Anjak by the spirits of the jungle and was the chief of a herd of two hundred apes. I have only collected four heads: Terbai Lang, the curse of mothers; Salang, the trucebreaker; Tama Ramun, the hungry bear; and Burak, the black serpent. In my quest to get their heads, I was helped by spirits and gods. I have always hunted alone and am inexperienced in leading a war."

Warriors began to murmur among themselves, for there was no obvious choice, as each man had his own merit and all were known along and beyond the Batang Lupar as men of great valour. They were all strong, beautiful and prosperous. None of their children had died due to a weak soul, and every paddy seed they planted sprouted twenty ears or more. Massam carried a sword said to be handed down from Seragunting. Ngon's father was known to be a great shaman who visited the world of gods and dead princes to get charms. Munao was as reckless and as wild as a raging tide, and his war calls sent shivers up and down the great river. Bujang's exploits were sung in songs, though only the Kayans of Rajang could claim to have seen him in action, while the rest of his exploits were shrouded in legend and mystery.

Ngon peered into Bujang's face as he chanted under his breath. Then he said, "There are many things you have hidden from us *Tuai*

Bujang." The murmur of arguing words died down as he continued, "I dreamed last night that we were in a jackfruit orchard. Some of us fell from the branches and broke our necks, but some of us collected one fruit, two fruits or three fruits each. None of us will return empty-handed. You, however, collected so many fruits it became a hill, yet your basket continued to beg for more because no matter how many jackfruits you put into it, it was not full. It only stopped begging after every single fruit had been taken from its branch. The whole time, a man – no, a god as red as polished bronze – stood beside you. Please, brother, you must tell us who you really are, for if we do not know you, we may choose the wrong man and will be cursed by the warpath god."

Bujang shyly began his story, starting from his seventh year. He spoke of his ability to speak with animals and the things he had learned from them. The account of his first meeting with Sengalang Burong and his detailed description of the god was met with gaping mouths and bulging eyes. The antics of Kayu Batu and his herd of monkeys induced laughter, but their act of carrying Taring Ai through the jungle received nodded approvals. He talked of how he had taken the head of Terbai Lang and left it in the house of *Tuai* Laing. He spoke of meeting Semaga and his crocodile people, then of the deer spirit that led him to the three men. Hornbills, the princes of war, he said, had lent their spirits to him as he fought his enemy. Then, as he reached the story of his fight with Burak, his voice faltered. Ribai had been there and something else, a spirit within that both elated and terrified him at the same time. Then he spoke of Pulang Gana and the advice he gave, and he ended his story by listing out all the blessings that had been showered down upon him, until the day he had lost his beloved.

There was silence among the men when he finished. Insects called incessantly from the jungle about them, until Gamit broke the human silence. "I believe my chief. I have seen him change with my own eyes. Nineteen other men saw him change too. It happened on the day we went into the jungle to find wood for our war boats. *Tuai* Bujang chopped both ironwood trees alone, and as he did so, he became bigger and redder. We were horrified; we thought that his grief had changed him into a demon, but then when morning broke through the horizon, he had become a man again."

Massam said, "You have a great gift, *Tuai* Bujang. A gift you rightly earned. We will now vote for our war leader."

The selection did not take long, for the votes went unanimously to Bujang.

Immediately after, the men packed and loaded their boats, then rowed as one in a race against the wind. Feathers of hawk, hornbill and pheasant bent like fronds of fern in a storm, while plate-sized pendants of shell, bone and brass shone like brazen moons reflecting the face of the sun. Throughout their two-day journey, many saw a strange wake beside Bujang's boat, though none dared say a word, for a careless tongue was a curse.

* * *

The new moon appeared above, like a strand of windswept silver hair. In the shade of the jungle canopy, an empty doorway had been built within an invincible wall that separated men from warriors. Three chiefs and five experienced warriors stood to either side of the columns, while Bujang and Tuba, a man from Engkilili, stood just inside the doorway with fronds of fern in their hand.

Men who had received good omens and dreams struck their swords against the cross beam above their heads and stepped in to receive their fronds. Tuba carved a notch onto a stick for each man who passed in front of him. More than half of their party had cited bad dreams, and many among them declined to walk the path, so Bujang's spirit dropped when he saw Gamit step through the door; he had hoped that the young man would take the counsel of those who had asked to stay behind. Yet Gamit was not alone, for scores of men who had pledged their allegiance to the expedition had stripped off their warring fineries to be sent home to sons and brothers because their guardian spirits had warned them that they would not return alive.

Hashim was sent ahead in a hastily built bark canoe after he had promised to meet Bujang and his party of ten men two miles from the port the following afternoon.

16

The late afternoon breeze was hot, and the water blazed like broken pieces of the sun. As the ships loomed into view, Bujang stood up and placed his right foot on the gaping head of the carved crocodile on the bow of his war boat. Behind the regal warrior-garbed chief sat Hashim and ten men adorned in tattered palm leaves and twined bracelets. While they were yet ten yards away from the largest ship, ten skiffs filled with eight to twelve men armed with spears circled them. The frowning faces began to crack, and soon gushes of muffled laughter broke into a roar. Bujang kept his head high, though his wide shoulders bowed like an ape's in an unbothered pose.

Hashim smiled. "Greetings, brave soldiers. Chief Bujang here has an audience with the great *Laksamana* Supan."

A middle-aged man replied in the language of the trading ports, "Yes, we know. We expected a great warrior. But seeing the ragged group he leads, he must not be much of a chief."

Another bark of laughter. Then the head sentry gave them the sign to go ahead. Two boats had gone before them, bearing the hilarious news that the much-feared headhunter was nothing more than a pathetic savage with airs of grandeur. Expectant mirth greeted them when they reached the hull of the admiral's ship. To show his benevolence, Supan permitted four men to come up with Bujang, and to show his courage, he allowed Bujang his sword. The small Penan

Long hunched forward like a monkey and climbed up the rope after Bujang with fingers gripping and toes clutching. The others – one-eyed Bisong, one-legged Tunggal, and one-handed Nital – climbed with less grace and made a show of huffing and puffing and much knocking about on the hull, which drew more laughter from the onlookers.

Hashim, however, was not granted an audience. As he made a show of going towards the shore, he suddenly turned and asked the sentries if he could let the savages in the boat gawk at the second cargo ship.

"You see, they have never seen anything like this before in their life. It would bring many tales of greatness back into the jungle."

The sentries good-naturedly allowed them to paddle around the second boat. Then a rope was thrown down, and they were asked to climb up. On board, the Ibans and Penans stared wide-eyed and gaped at everything pointed out to them as they clung to Hashim like frightened children. Their antics and uncomeliness drew out every man in the ship, giving the visitors the opportunity to count a hundred sentries in the water and eighty men in the guard vessel. Two small men, Tumpan and Keramit, as well as Simpang, the limping man, requested to stay behind because they wanted to understand the Great Spirit that had allowed such ships to be built. Their request was granted.

Before climbing back into his boat, Hashim invited the soldiers to shore "once light sleeps beyond the horizon," for there was a wedding in his village that night and there would be much wine and many comely ladies.

One man hooted. "That would be a welcome change for us. I am tired of savage women. They scream and kick like animals."

Hashim forced a wider smile and a loud laugh. "Was that the screeching I heard coming from your warehouse in the harbour?"

"Aaargh. They are always screaming, at anybody and everybody. We keep them on shore because there is not enough room in the ship. Sometimes we do bring a few of the young ones on board."

"Well, then, you must come to my village. I promise you our women will treat you better."

Hashim struggled to climb down the rope, for his muscles were stiff from trying to hold back the terrifying blood-lust he felt boiling inside his belly. He would get his chance that night, he promised himself, and he was sure of it.

* * *

Bujang refrained from looking about him as he sat cross-legged on the deck below the raised platform, while above, his host watched his every move from a carved wooden seat covered with the leopard skin. Standing just behind him was an *Iman*, a religious teacher from the village, who had been forced to come on board to act as an interpreter because Supan did not trust Hashim.

Sliced venison, peeled fruits and wine were brought out in a silver tray for Supan, and a clutter of rice cakes and leaf-wrapped sago, together with an assortment of charred meat and fresh bananas and jackfruit filled the basket tray for Bujang and his men. Next to that was placed a clay jar of newly fermented wine.

Bisong made a show of peering closely at his food before eating it. Long, not to be outdone, picked a banana with his foot. Tunggal and Nital pretended to be outwardly embarrassed by the uncouth behaviour of the three by slapping or nudging them. The soldiers deduced that the savages must also have holes poked into their cheeks, because wine ran down their necks and over their chests to puddle about their seats. Supan was in good spirit and chortled merrily late into the night, lifting cup after cup of wine to salute his new friendship with the savage chief. Across the water, music and more laughter drifted towards them from the torch-speckled village.

* * *

Much later, a rooster crowed, and its call was soon echoed by others of its kind, the symphony building into a crescendo that rode the wind for miles over the dark waters. Thick grey fog lay heavy, as though a rain cloud had dropped from the sky to blanket the village and the ships. A deer barked, waking Nital, who stood up and walked to the portside gunwale. A sentry called out, and Nital pointed to his loins with the good hand, indicating that he wanted to urinate. Sprawled over a gun near where he stood was a soldier who was snoring away the wine he had siphoned from the stupid Dayaks. Nital unsheathed the soldier's knife and slit his throat, gleefully noting that it was a handsome head. He lowered a rope that was tied to the gun over the gunwales until he felt a tug. Then he yawned loudly and lumbered back to his chief. He kicked Bisong's foot, and the man hollered aloud in response, then sat up and looked about with his single eye. His shout apparently woke Long, who immediately began his early-morning monkey antics. The sentries were bored from watching the fog crawl over the water, so they turned their attention to the middle of the ship to watch the Dayaks shove and kick each other like a group of quarrelsome children.

Another deer barked close to the guard ship.

* * *

Supan woke up annoyed, as the commotion of thudding bodies and shouting men filled his cabin. A cry, like nothing he had ever heard before, made him jump out of bed and don his robe. He unsheathed his cutlass before striding across his cabin with the naked blade and, on opening the door, saw his worst nightmare unfold before him. Demons formed out of the mist, gnashing black teeth and shouting triumphant each time they cut down a soldier. He looked down and was enraged to see his clean deck covered in blood and entrails.

As he contemplated the insolence of the savages who dared attack a renowned admiral of the Sultan of Bruni's navy, the seriousness of the situation began to sink into his waking consciousness. Supan ducked back inside and locked his cabin door. His arms swung frantically about, over his face, his head and by his side, as he tramped up and down the room. He squeezed the handle of the cutlass, as though to juice out some courage from it. After all, it was a gift from the Sultan to his father, so surely it would ensure him victory. With renewed vigour born out of arrogance, Supan flung open the door and rushed into the melee.

Savages fell to his left and right as he slashed their spines and shoulders. Glee crept back into his soul as he watched the bodies writhe under his feet and felt their blood soak through his sandals. He shouted an order to the wind and, encouraged by his appearance, his men rallied about him. They formed a tight circle as they fought the headhunters. Proud feathers fell, then scattered before them as they advanced.

A large man loomed into view – Bujang Maias – the one whose presence itself was an omen of death to his enemies. In the distance, a kingfisher wept. Bujang lifted his arms like a hornbill about to take flight, and yelled. Then he plunged into the circle, hacking and chopping in sharp, low arcs. His hungry blade cut through their meat, sinew and bone. Yet even as the one before him fell, his grief-stricken soul would seek the next victim. Sweat and blood mingled with his tears for Geramun, Bayoi, Gayut, little Ibi and old *Inik* Ilong. Over and over he told himself that these men must die to lift the curse of mourning in his house. That these men must die so that his children might live, that his people might live.

As his eyes ran up and down the ship wildly, Supan clambered up to the raised platform. The board creaked, and he spun round. Bujang, with the sun behind his back, towered over him like a black beast. Supan felt his bowel melt. But his pride brought back whatever courage was left in him, and he lunged forward. Bujang sunk his sword right in between the admiral's chest, all the way up to the hilt.

"This is for my people," the Ape Man hissed into his face. Then he pulled out his *ilang*, swung it high and shouted a victory call to claim his right to the head.

* * *

Shortly afterwards, a late morning sun cleared the mist and revealed the carnage of battle. After looking about him, Bujang scrambled over the bloody gunwale and down to a war boat laden with thirty men. Each of them had either one or two trophies, and they stared with open admiration at the warleader's basket, which was straining with twenty-six heads. Bujang pointed the rowers to the warehouse by the pier. He squinted in an attempt to see as best as he could, but the people on the shore were still too far off, and he could not recognize any of them. Nausea filled his throat as he imagined Upa alive one moment but dead in the next.

They berthed at the same moment as three other war boats, and the village people thronging about the area dispersed before them like shore-broken waves. Bujang's attention turned to the women and children left behind. So many faces, there were so many faces he didn't recognize. Young girls, some so young as to be no more than twelve, either lay or sat on the ground as though in a daze. His mind watched numbly as five strange women tended their wounds with herbs and their hunger with broth. Then his eyes scanned the open ground before the entrance of the warehouse, and he found his beloved. Approaching, he saw that she was wailing over a young girl, and when he reached her side, he saw that the girl was Sila, Kumat's sweetheart. He watched the scene as though turned to stone. Then he looked about him and saw that she was not the only child dying.

Other headhunters searched the grounds, looking for children, for wives, for lovers. Kumat dropped down on his knees next to Upa. He lifted his sweetheart into his arms, but she was beyond recognizing him. Tenderly he brushed her hair with a bloodstained hand, careful not to touch the dark bruises on her face. Yet too soon, her empty eyes closed. The trophy that Kumat had triumphantly collected for her hand would now be used for her funeral.

Between wails, Upa said, "They used us. They used us and debased us with their barbaric ways." Then, sobbing as though for her own death, and covering her face out of shame, she said, "They planted their filthy seeds in us with none laying claim on the fruits."

Bujang stared at her wide-eyed, not comprehending why a man would plant his seed in his slave, for that would make any child she bore a slave too. A feeling of disgust and hate coursed through his veins and made his skin tingle and his head pound. He said, "They used you? They used all these women and children? But some of the girls are too young to have made their first skirt."

"They were like animals excreting seeds without care onto the jungle floor," Upa wailed, and she was soon so overcome with grief, she could find no words to sing a funeral song for the dead. And when the words did come, she was too shame-filled to sing them aloud, for she could not bear the thought that beautiful young Sila would be remembered for these last few days of her life.

Kumat rocked his beloved gently, as though she was a child still crying ceaselessly in his arms. Around them, the wailing of women intermixed with the voices of their heartbroken men. Some walked away from the grounds and followed a few villagers to a plot where they buried those who had died. The soldiers had thrown the bodies into the river, but the people had fished them out and gave them a burial. Fifteen dead, and that morning they added three more to the number. All were young, but their eyes of morning dew and cheeks of blushing orchids were now gone, and Dalai was one among them.

* * *

The afternoon shadows were long on the ground when Hashim found Bujang outside the warehouse. He squatted behind Bujang and cleared his throat. The chief turned and nodded. Then he got up and followed the trader into the village.

The *Iman* stood in front of a crowd of pale faces. "Welcome, *Tuai* Bujang. We wish that our meeting with you had been happier. Our heart goes out to you and to your people."

"You have more of Supan's soldiers here with you."

"Yes, many are dead. Khadijah here," he pointed to a stout woman, "had lured four men into her bed and killed them all with her husband's *kris*."

"Then their heads belong to her."

The *Iman* swallowed before stammering a reply, "Thank you, great chief." His voice grew surer as he said, "Some men are still alive. They are only boys. Please allow them to live and let them go."

A group of seven soldiers were dragged before Bujang. They were forced to kneel with their hands tied behind their backs. By now, more warriors had begun to throng into the village. Massam, Ngon and Munao had also come with their men to count the numbers of dead in the village.

Bujang turned to the chiefs. "How many men did you lose?"

Ngon replied, "Sixty-eight from my village, Munao lost twenty-one and Massam lost over eighty-two men. How many from your side?"

"I lost twenty-nine good men." Including Gamit, Bujang did not add. He turned his face back to the prisoners. "Kill them all."

The *Iman* stretched his arms towards Bujang. "No, I beg you, great chief. Please do not kill them. They are only children."

"They will grow up to become men. And they will return for my daughters. Kill them."

A warrior shouted and grabbed the hair of one of the soldiers. His war cry was echoed by six others as they too grabbed a soldier each. They cut the heads off and gave out another shout as they lifted their gruesome prizes up high for all to see. The *Iman* closed his eyes and said a prayer for the souls of the dead men. Some of the villagers covered their faces in horror, but many watched with hard faces, feeling avenged for their sufferings.

* * *

The journey home the following day was slow because they had bodies to carry. Though some men were buried next to their wives or sweethearts in the village cemetery plot, eight traders loaned their boats to transport the dead back to their villages. Sila's body was leaned against Kumat's back because there was no space to lay her, and he would not leave her behind. As the village faded away into the horizon, a gentle wave rose and moved the boats forward on its crown. Wave after wave propelled them, as though a giant hand was moving under the water and urging them onwards. Soon the people found themselves high above the river, with the wind roaring in their faces.

As the waters reached the tributary of Lingga, they slowed.

Bujang and his men bid farewell to their short-term comrades. On seeing their approach, the men who had waited for their return at the tributary got into more boats and followed their chiefs home. Another gentle wave rose and carried the people of Simanggang, Engkilili and Lubok Antu away.

Before the sun set, Bujang and his people arrived at the house. The warriors remained outside as the dead were cleaned and prepared for funeral. The sound of wailing flooded the house as every family who had lost mourned. All families that is, except for the *bilek* of Sila, the only child of Rembai. The old woman had rejoiced when she first saw her sitting daughter, but laughed when she found her dead. She had not stopped laughing since, and she would not stop laughing now. Her relatives scolded her for being improper, and her friends cried for her because they could not talk any sense to her anymore. The spirit of grief had driven her mad. The burial took two days to complete, and Mendakap seemed to have lost a large portion of his spirit, for in that short time he had grown wizened and bent.

On the third day, the warriors entered the house, shouting victory and courage into the cursed air. They stomped and waved their prizes before the people. Women came out to receive the trophies, and mourning ceased. Joy, however, did not return.

* * *

Three months the longhouse lay in an atmosphere of resignation to their sorrows; then a new crisis started to rear its head. Upa raised her voice at *Inik* Tuap, "You are wrong. It must be something else."

"No, child, I am not wrong. Maybe it is Bujang's?"

"It cannot be his. My skirt was stained when the men took me."

"You must tell him."

"Is there nothing that can take this thing away?"

"Its death will bring a curse upon our people, upon your household. You cannot risk that."

"But what should I tell him?"

Inik Tuap shook her head, not knowing what she herself would have done if she was in such a predicament.

Upa put a hand over her belly and realized that she was beginning to show. A gecko had called from the rafters as she swept around Baling's bachelor bed the previous evening. The omen that would have brought her joy had instead horrified her.

She stepped out to the gallery, and her eyes searched for her husband and found him in deep discussion with four men. Although the scent of fresh trophies filled the air, the house was quiet with sorrow. Too many had died, and too many broken families were still trying to come to terms with the horror. She knew what the men were discussing: one of the young girls who had found herself with child but who could not name the father. Mendakap suggested that they slaughter a male pig and name it as the father. At the very least it would lessen, though not take away, the curse on their community.

Upa returned to her *bilek* because she could not bring herself to listen to their discussion. It was growing late, and her husband would soon be coming to bed. Then her breath caught in her throat as she realized that she had not allowed him to touch her since they returned. Upa again rubbed her stomach as she tried to come to a decision. She could not allow herself to be a burden in his life because he was a great warrior, a man loved by the gods, a man adored by his people. She could not shame him, but she knew that she could not hide her condition for long.

The door swung open, and Upa's eyes followed the hulking form of her husband in the hearth fire-lit room.

As he lowered himself on the mat, he asked, "Is something not right?"

"My husband, we must speak."

Silence, soon followed by a long sigh, and Bujang said, "I heard what the gecko said last night."

"What did it say?"

"That Upa, the beloved of the goddess Kumang, will soon welcome a son."

Upa crushed her skirt with her fists. "I am with child. And I do not believe that it is yours."

"Is his head hanging in our gallery?"

"One child may only have one father. There were many. I do not know who the father is." A soft weeping streamed out of Upa's mouth and blended with her words. "I do not know who the father is. I have kept myself, like a cleared field to receive your seeds alone, yet now I am carrying one of another."

Bujang turned his head away then got up and walked out of the room. Upa lay down, curled herself and covered her mouth with her hand as she wept.

* * *

The night was cold, and dew soaked the ground, but Bujang did not care as he trudged into the jungle with neither knife nor spear. He had not intended to step out of the house, but he could think of nowhere else to go. His beloved's pain was unbearable, yet his own pain would not let him comfort her. She had been with other men while still married to him. He knew, he understood from the very core of his being, that it happened through no fault of hers. Yet he felt cheated.

Bujang stopped and looked about him. He was lost. He did not recall ever being in that part of the jungle before. The ground felt strange, like clay that clung to his feet, and the trees were sparse. A wind howled and whipped past him. He turned, startled, for he

276

thought he had heard a voice call his name. A light began to flicker halfway up the slope of a low hill.

He needed directions to get home, so he started climbing the hillside. Night turned to day, and back to night again. Bujang ate leaves and fruits that grew in low bushes about him. He kept climbing, but the light never grew closer. Countless days passed, but he would not turn back. He reasoned that if a god lay at the end of the journey, he would meet him, and he would ask why his heart loved and despised at the same time. The moon waxed and waned but Bujang was undeterred. Then one dark night, while the moon slept, the light came to him.

A figure began to appear, and soon he saw that it was a woman so beautiful that to behold her was ecstasy, much like the stirring of the heart when standing on a high branch and looking into an endless horizon. Golden pins sprouting droplets of gold circled her head like a halo. Twenty gold bracelets etched with the forms of flowers, leaves and birds circled each of her arms. On each leg was a thick ankle bracelet, both appearing like living serpents curled towards their own tails. Her skin was as fair as the white of eggshells, and her calves were as smooth as the underbelly of freshwater fish. Covering her hips was a beautiful skirt immortalizing a red sky split by lightning. One golden belt was wound round her waist, and another covered her breast. Her face was perfect and without blemish.

She lifted her hand, and Bujang saw that her right thumb was bleeding. He reached out but stopped short of touching her because he felt too filthy and ugly to even be in her presence. Instead he fell on his knees. "Goddess, who has done this to you? Let me destroy him."

Kumang, the wife of Keling, smiled. "If I tell you that it was your wife, will you kill her?"

Bujang stared up in surprised. How could Upa have reached this place before him? Where was she? He turned his head to look about him, but he could see her nowhere.

"I am the goddess of beauty, and I give my knowledge to those who please me. Upa has come to despise the gift." She turned her back to him and continued, "When her mother had bathed her in the river for the first time, I sent rain from my bathing pool. When she made her first cloth, I sent dew from my house in the evening and fire from my hearth during the day. I sent dreams to her at night, filling her with visions of tenderness and valour. I have given her so much, yet she will only have you as comfort."

Bujang bowed low to the ground. "Then tell me, goddess. I have her now with me, why can I not love her as before?"

"Because you are selfish. You only think of your own pain. You forget that she bore the greater pain. Those men razed her body for their own selfish lust while you raze her soul for your own selfish gain. And if the world be filled with such as you, it will become too ugly for my presence."

"Goddess, forgive me. I am a foolish man. I have been foolish since the day I was born. I have a family now and a people who love me, but I am still foolish enough to think myself alone."

"Then be wise. I am the master-dyer, and my greatest delight is thread that has been soaked in the mordant bath of suffering. The red dye will not be bound to anything less, and my husband will only wear my brightest weaving to war."

Kumang turned her head a little and smiled down at him. Then she climbed back up the slope. Bujang continued to watch her until her light disappeared. When he turned back, he saw that he could barely make out the foot of the mountain. He began his journey home from the land by the House of Heaven and took as many months going down as climbing up.

* * *

Finally, he was home again. Children who had always known him ran away from Bujang screaming. He was unkempt and filthy, for he had not stopped to bathe anywhere since he walked out of the house six months before. On reaching the bathing platform, he took off his loincloth and dived. The water was cooling and settled his troubled mind. He went up for air and dived again, holding his breath for as long as he could, making his lungs scream, which helped him forget his troubles for a time. Finally he pulled himself out and smiled dejectedly on seeing young Baling's sorrow-filled face as the young man handed him a fresh loincloth. He wrapped it over his loins and around his waist.

He patted his stepson's shoulder. "You look well, my son."

"We are all well, Father."

"You have taken care of the family while I was gone."

"Yes, Father. I used the nets as you taught me. We had plenty of fish. I also lay the traps like you said and caught a pig one time. Other days I catch quails for our meal."

"You are a good son, and a man now."

"Muri died last month. The midwife said that the incubus overcame her. We are all terrified. Ilong says he heard her spirit cackling around the vicinity of the house two nights ago."

"Is that why it is so quiet?"

"People rush into the house before sunset and only come out after sunrise."

"Come, let us go into the house."

Baling kept his head down as he followed his stepfather up the ladder.

A quiet crowd had filled the chief's gallery, sitting away from a group of five women who sat around Upa. Bujang stopped and stared, for she had grown thin, thinner than the day he first saw her, and she appeared to have aged by ten years. A pang went through his heart when his eyes fell on her bulging belly, and another pang hit him when he noticed that her usually proud shoulders were now stooped over her burden.

Mendakap said, "*Tuai*, welcome home. We are pleased to see you returned safely to us."

Bujang approached his wife, and the women made room for him. He crossed his legs and sat next to Upa, across from the augur.

Again, Mendakap continued, "We understand why you left the longhouse. And Upa understands too. She has said that she will let you divorce her, and she would also allow herself and this child to be banished from us after it is born."

Bujang looked down at his hands. He recalled how he had met Upa, and he remembered the bridal price he paid. He had experienced a bitter life because his father was forced to reject him, and at that moment it was his turn to make the same decision, to either abandon a child or to invite the wrath of the spirits. Bujang now understood why Kumang had called him a selfish man, for he truly was one.

"The child is mine," he said to the listening crowd.

The people gasped. Bujang held his breath until he felt Upa stir. She said, "But I told you, the child is not yours."

Mendakap cut in. "*Tuai*, you must understand. The child is a bastard. It will bring a curse and great sickness upon the people."

Bujang looked into her face, and she saw that her husband had returned to her. He lifted his head proudly and scanned the faces around him. "The child is mine!"

Suddenly he stood up, stomped towards his family wall, unsheathed a knife and gave a loud war shout. He stomped his way towards the trophy column and slashed down a bunch of trophies. Again he shouted and stomped. The men rallied about him, and the house shivered with their ardour.

They ran from one end of the house to the other, stomping,

shouting, crying out their victory to the air and to the heavens. *"Bujang Maias has returned. Beware all evil. The son of Tok Anjak will not be bested. Leave this place, all you accursed spirits. Leave this place before he sets his slave warriors upon you!"*

The shouts and stomps continued for three days and three nights, until the women snatched the heads from their men and started feeding the trophies with wine and betel leaves. They sang songs of their joy and their hope. *Taste how good our wine is. Stay and guard us. Smell how good our betel vine is. Stay and help us.*

On the seventh day, Upa gave birth to a boy, and Bujang named him Nuing. Bards came to the house to sing of the chief's greatness. They sang of his daughters' beauty and of his sons' valour. The songs spread from house to house, and Bujang was held in so much awe that he was left in peace for the remainder of his life. He went through the mordant bath of his soul, and Kumang used the brightest red *engkudu* dye upon his life. As she promised, his greatest shame, Nuing, grew up to be a great war leader and became the source of his greatest pride.

About the Author

Born and raised in Sarawak on the island of Borneo to an Iban mother and Melanau father, Golda Mowe has always been interested in the culture and traditions of Borneo's indigenous people. After graduating from university in Japan and enduring ten years of corporate life, the author found herself yearning for childhood evenings spent in the longhouse, sitting in a pool of lamplight, listening to her great-aunt tell tales of jungle animals or her father recount his hunting adventures. In this way she was led back to writing and is now living in Sibu, a town on the Rejang River in Sarawak, where she expends large portions of her time researching ideas for books and short stories.

Learn more about Golda and her writing at *www.gmowe.ws* and chat to her at *alpha@gmowe.ws*. For updates on *Iban Dream* and news of author events, follow Golda Mowe on Facebook at *www.facebook.com/IbanDreamByGoldaMowe*.

Iban People
and Traditions

The following photographs of Iban life in Sarawak date from the 1950s to the present day. For more images, please follow the author on Facebook at *www.facebook.com/IbanDreamByGoldaMowe.*

ABOVE On the exterior verandah of an Iban longhouse in Sarawak, the liver of a pig is being inspected to see if the omens are favourable. [Photo©Peter Mooney]

ABOVE AND BELOW An Iban warrior dance in a longhouse depicts the terrifying of the enemy before an attack. The *parang* (machete) at the dancer's waist is unsheathed as the dance develops.
[Photos©Peter Mooney]

ABOVE The author photographed with Iban heirloom lanji and sintong baskets. Short sintongs are used by women to collect ripening rice clusters. Once these baskets are full, the rice is poured into the tall lanjis, which are carried by men. The bigger the lanji basket, the stronger the man. [Photo©Rebecca anak Rabbu]

BELOW The back of a longhouse in Sarawak. The lack of an open verandah at the back prevents enemies from sneaking in, and there is a loft to store rice. [Photo©iStockphoto]

RIGHT An Iban head-
man. Each longhouse
has an elected headman.
[Photo©Peter Mooney]

BELOW A Kelabit
longhouse feast.
[Photo©Peter Mooney]

ABOVE Throwing the large and heavy net weighted all round the edges while poised on a narrow plank on an unsteady Iban longboat requires perfect balance. [Photo©Peter Mooney]

BELOW Ibans hauling a longboat upriver through rapids. [Photo©Peter Mooney]